Why the Tree Loves the Ax

Why the Tree Loves the Ax

A NOVEL

Jim Lewis

CROWN PUBLISHERS, INC. NEW YORK

Published by Crown Publishers, Inc., 201 East 50th Street, New York, New York 10022. Member of the Crown Publishing Group.

Random House, Inc. New York, Toronto, London, Sydney, Auckland
http://www.randomhouse.com/

CROWN and colophon are trademarks of Crown Publishers, Inc.

Printed in the United States of America

Design by June Bennett-Tantillo

Library of Congress Cataloging-in-Publication Data
Lewis, Jim, 1963–
    Why the tree loves the ax / by Jim Lewis
    (alk. paper)
    I. Title.
  PS3562.E9475W48   1998
  813'.54—dc21   97-16010

ISBN 0-609-60109-1

10 9 8 7 6 5 4 3 2 1

First Edition

For Jack and Juliet, and Grace
And their parents

Why the Tree Loves the Ax

Sugartown

Why don't you just begin?

I WAS TWENTY-SEVEN YEARS OLD AND I HAD LOST MY WAY. I FOUND myself driving on an unlit highway through the middle of a black summer night: it wasn't where I'd intended to be. Somewhere an hour or so back I'd missed a turnoff that I should have taken, or taken one that I should have missed, and I was hurrying through the Texas hills toward the next town, where I would stop and check my map. Ahead of me there was a great big truck, barreling through the darkness like a factory on a thousand wheels, burning its fuel and spoiling the stars. For ten miles or more I'd been following behind the thing, growing more and more impatient, until at last I decided to pass it. I remember looking down at the green glowing speedometer, and I remember the numbers, but I never did see how fast I was going: I pulled into the next lane, the road turned slightly and dropped suddenly, my car complained, the truck bellowed and vanished, and a sign that said

SUGARTOWN NEXT 3 EXITS

appeared out of the mist. There were high beams in my face, the asphalt was lit up with spotlights, road, shoulder, railing, sky. . . . It was very quiet, and for a moment I thought that I'd driven onto the set of a film. . . . Then the car left the ground and I was

3

piloting breathlessly in the blackness, with the bright asteroids pricking my feet and the wheel turning freely in my hands. I knew right away that nothing I did would do anything. Nothing at all. . . . I heard a voice on the radio, it wasn't a man's or a woman's, it just spoke: Well, well, well, it said, and as soon as it was done we all went up and over. . . .

A couple of books that had been in the backseat began flapping violently around my ears, or else a pair of angry birds had gotten in through the window and were trying to get out again; for a second I saw my face turning in the glass, wearing an expression that suggested I found it all a little frustrating, this commotion and this sudden buoyancy. So I didn't want to fly; I wasn't really driving, either. I was along for the ride. The voice on the radio said, You are going to go to heaven now. But instead of rising, the car was falling, and the difference was disturbing.

There were people standing over me, wearing costumes and waxy, blank-eyed tragedy masks; their mouths were round and red with lipstick, and they moved very slowly, swaying one way and then the other in the observance of some formality that was lost on me. A chorus: they shook their heads sternly from side to side, and I just lay there, caressing the ground with my hands. Young lady, look what you've done. This is very bad; the car won't work at all, now. There were thousands of glimmering stars, like bits of safety glass scattered in the grass, which were like stars. I said to myself, Caroline, Caroline. Oh, you really fucked up this time.

For a long time I sat cross-legged by the side of the road, listening with my skin. A trickle of cold blood was making its way down my calf, but it didn't seem to be bothering me very much; I was getting very comfortable, and really, I didn't mind sitting there. I watched a line of red and white lights along the road, flashing like a clock ticking that tells no time, and I took two or three deep breaths. An airplane went by overhead, so far above the earth that it was silent and invisible. A woman came over to me; she was wearing an iridescent pearl grey shirt, then a pale blue shirt. Is there anyone else? she asked.

I thought she was testing me, to see how selfish I'd become. I wanted her to like me, but where was I supposed to begin? There were people all over the place. Well, for example, there's the mailman, I replied.

She turned her head. Help! she said to someone else, and then she turned to me again. Was he driving?

No, no, no. I was driving.

Is he still in the car?

In the car? The idea that he was in the car seemed to be upsetting her, and I thought I could ease her mind. No, no, no, I said. He delivers mail. Where is the car?

There was a man standing by the side of a police cruiser with its lights on and its doors open. He walked over and addressed the woman: Hello, Fay, he said in a lighthearted voice. How's she doing? I wondered why he didn't just ask me; instead, he bent down so he could look in my eyes, then reached into his jacket pocket and removed a piece of cloth, which he used to wipe my forehead. By the time he was done the lights in the road had softened into blurry astral splinters. I thought he'd purposely tried to blind me so I wouldn't know where I was. It didn't seem very fair to me and I started to stand up and protest, but he put his hand on my shoulder and gently guided me down again. You just stay there, sitting on the ground, he said. Is there anyone we can call?

I said, No. I was in the hospital, and I saw a pair of twins staring at me, one boy and one girl, children. It's not your fault, I said. I don't know what I said. The nurse looked down at me in a curious, concerned way, her head bent slightly, her brow compressed. Over her shoulder I could see a long parade of infirm women shuffling up the hallway; then she shot me with something, in the same place on my upper arm where a boy I had known a long time previously used to punch me when he wanted to get my attention. A red-haired boy. What was his name? Brown-haired. —She told me I was going to be all right, and within a second or two, sure enough, I began to feel all right. That was strange. I was going to thank her, but before I could find the words a woman doctor came to me and started strumming on some sewing thread that was strung through the skin of my face, smiling nicely all the while. It was very fine cloth, I thought, but the doll was stuffed with sand, and the sand sifted, shifted, and the figure went to sleep.

When I woke I was lying in a blue hospital room, with my battered black suitcase on the floor beside my bed, and a pale pink nurse standing over me. A curtain had been pulled around us both; through it drifted light from beyond, a picture window, a television, but there was no sound. I looked up at the nurse's face; she wore an expression of perfect candor and forgiveness, as if she knew exactly what I was feeling. So I thought I could trust her, and I asked her, Did I die?

She frowned. Die? she said softly, her voice full of wonder. Not at all. She bent down, attached a blood pressure cuff around my upper arm, and began to inflate it.

Oh. That's nice, I said. My tongue was stubborn and slow.

Well, you're very lucky, she said as she slowly let the air out again, read the dial, and wrote down the results. From what I heard, that was a terrible accident you had. And here you are, pretty much all right. She tucked in a loose corner of my sheets. . . . Not without a scratch, mind you, she went on. Because you cut your forehead, and you bruised your knee, and you broke your nose just a little. But I don't know, that's almost nothing for what you went through. She spoke to me as if she'd known me since I was a little girl, and wanted me to understand that my wounds were just a few more of life's rough spots. For a while at least, she was my favorite person, and I was going to ask her to stay with me, but I was afraid she'd say no. She gave me pills for the pain and some magazines to read, and just before she left she smiled down on me and stroked my forehead. But the doctor who came to see me an hour or so later was less tender: he looked me over quickly and then told me that I was going to have to stay in the hospital for another day or two, just in case something else went wrong.

As soon as he was gone I got up from my bed and limped on over to the mirror above my sink, to stare at myself and see what I'd become; and what I saw was a woman, poor, pale, and tired, who looked the way I would have looked, if I'd been hurt. Lucky? I didn't look very lucky. My hair was still dark blond, my forehead still high, my eyes hazel, my mouth wide, but I had two black eyes, and beneath a small strip of white tape I could see that my nose was forever bent, just a tiny bit: the bone took a slight turn at its bridge, lending my face an out-of-kilter aspect. My features were a little bit battered, like a girl who's gotten around. What a landing. I turned to one side and then the other, I watched myself from the corner of my eye, and I was unnerved. My looks had never been perfect, but they were mine, after all, I was used to them, I'd counted on them, and now they were changed. I reached up to touch my cheekbone and the reflection reached up to touch hers, staring intently back at me with an expression that I didn't recognize, somewhere between shock and fascination; my own face was a rebus, and I stood there for a while trying to solve it. In time it became too much for me and I turned away, but later that afternoon I went down to the drugstore in the lobby and bought a compact, which I took out a dozen times that evening when I thought no one was around, pretending nonetheless to check my makeup, when in fact I was studying my face, like some broken Narcissus perpetually gazing into a portable pond.

My sleep that night was occupied by a dull dream of a dark highway; the next day dissolved in an endless succession of even duller dramas on the television. All afternoon the doctors and nurses trespassed on me with needles and tubes, soaked my skin with cotton pads, pricked me, tapped me, touched me with their hands, and came to me with their questions. And what's your address? the pink nurse asked gently. And how should we bill you? I didn't know, and I wished she wouldn't ask; I had no insurance, the total was more money than I would have to spare in a decade, and even the payments were equal to a month's rent and then some.

Out my darkening window that evening the streetlights came on, first some, then others and others, spattering across the city as it got ready for the night; and money was passing from one pocket to another, cars were being started, kisses granted, drinks lifted, windows opened to invite the evening in. I was a stranger there, anxious and impatient in my hospital bed, with no other soul to keep me; and I was too far away from the town to touch it. I thought everything that would ever count as my past was already behind me in time. Of course I was wrong, but how was I supposed to know that?

Two mornings later the pink nurse put me in a wheelchair and pushed me to the front door of the hospital. I signed some papers, and I was discharged.

So I found myself in Sugartown. To the rest of America, the city was just someplace south, a name found in a high school history book, because it was near a battlefield from the War with Mexico, or the birthplace of some half-forgotten Plains hero. Its reputation barely reached beyond the surrounding counties; God knows it had never reached me. I knew roughly where it was, I knew that three or four hundred thousand people lived there, but from the vantage of my own annals it was just Faraway, an equal remove from the town in California where I was raised and my ex-husband in New York City, and as distant from them both as I could be without leaving the country entirely.

I'd already been everywhere else: for three years I'd been looking for another place to live, I tried cities the way some women try lovers, but I hadn't found the right one yet. One town was too clean, and another was too big; I didn't like the weather in another, it never poured down rain; I didn't like the people in a fourth, they were all white giants, and they walked the streets with dumb looks posted on their faces, buying bland trash in tasteless stores. Still, I'd tried to fit in each place: I cut my hair and changed what I ate, I adopted accents, I tried to live by local poetry, memorizing legends and visiting famous graves. I was studying how to want things, where to want them, and who to be.

My name was Caroline Harrison, but the name didn't mean anything yet. I'd carried my days from city to city in a bucket with a hole at the bottom, and nothing had collected but a few inches of dirty water. It was just samewater, and I wasn't getting anywhere. Oh, I'd learned a few things: I knew how to make rice and beans, and I could dance to almost any music; I could work a crossword puzzle, and I knew how to smile when I said No. I could tell a lie, and keep telling it until it was true. But that wasn't anywhere near enough to grow old on.

It was the end of the century, and I was alone. All across the heavens the constellations were coming apart, all across the ground there were fences that no one could maintain. The crest of the millennium was approaching, but somehow it seemed to be a private affair; no one would talk about it, no one had my hopes; where I saw opportunity, if only for escape from disappointment, they saw nothing but a big bright party followed by another decade. But I was ambitious and I dreamed I was better: I wanted china skin and a reputation for the ages, I wanted a revolution in my kitchen, I wanted my decisions to double the world's qualities, absolutely. So I was vainglorious: I was young. I had little enough sense of myself to be vain about, and the glories I was looking for weren't small. Every night I stared out my window, waiting for the bandit to come down from the mountains, the light in the clock tower, listening for the sound of the trumpet; every day I went out with the word Sure waiting on my lips.

There was no turn: I'd kept trying, and I'd moved again. At last I'd settled in Dallas, where I went to work for the Welfare Board, signed up for a few classes at SMU, and watched everyone carefully. As far as they were concerned, I was just another white woman trying to get by in the City of Hate: they didn't know, but I was preparing myself, one more time, for some glamorous struggle. But one more time it wasn't like that: my hands became as pale and dry as the pile of papers on my desk; the students in my sections believed in original sin and drank Diet Dr Pepper with their boyfriends on weekends; I got in the habit of guessing what everyone was going to say before they said it, and I was right almost all the time; and I couldn't eat; and the land was so flat you could see a man coming with a smile on his face from miles away. After about nine months I began to feel that familiar combination of annoyance and distress, a sense that I was on the wrong side of the island, lonely and digging for laughing treasure in empty sand. I was tired of the sensation of tears running down my cheeks, so I quit my job, packed my things, and started for the Gulf of Mexico, with no one to answer to, and years to go. I was in the hills of south-central Texas when my car left the road, throwing me and my things in a ditch outside of town.

Sugartown. The isolation of the place meant a lot to me, and so did its name. My arrival there had been an accident, but I didn't really believe in accidents. So that was where I began, before anything else, O.K. I thought it might be the city known as Home-for-simple-hearts, and I decided to stay. The day after I was discharged from the hospital I rented a cheap studio apartment in a building called Four Roses, near a mall that had been converted from a train station long ago. A few days after that I went to find a job.

I put on a dress and I walked down to an employment agency in one of the office buildings in the center of town. By then my black eyes had faded to faint charcoal-colored semicircles, and I wore my hair down over my forehead to hide my stitches as best I could. I was looking for work, I went with a department-store blush and a Cadillac smile.

There was a pale man in a brown suit sitting at the reception desk: he handed me a form and asked me to fill it out before I met with a counselor, and I took it back across the carpeting and sat on a green couch that seemed to have been stuffed with sawdust. Just one sheet of paper, they weren't asking for much: they wanted to know what education I'd had, my skills, last few jobs, my references. But the printing was so neat, the lines were so straight, the pen they lent me wrote in such a boring blue. I don't have any other excuse. The questions were so slow, and my heart began to itch.

—So I perjured myself all over the page: from the top to the bottom I filled in someone else's story, sucking liar's carbon from the tip of the pencil in between inspirations. I made up an entire life, right there in that shabby little office, in that strange little city: a better and more suitable life, one I thought they wanted. I said that I went to Catholic college in Chicago and worked in an office called Acme Prosthetics on the weekends, as a volunteer at a community center—pause, my breath quickened, I was becoming euphoric and I thought about the pink nurse—as an orderly in St. Sebastian Hospital the summer after I graduated. I listed references: a fictional professor in whose class I'd flourished and a project coordinator with an unpronounceable last name. The only truth I told was my name, my age, and my new phone number, and when I was done I held the paper in my lap as if it were the family Bible.

Cold air from a vent in a corner of the ceiling ruffled the posters on the wall. I crossed my legs and listened to the fluorescent light fixtures buzzing overhead. An imposing woman in a powder blue skirt and a white blouse with a big bow at the throat came through a door across the room; she stopped for a moment to gaze out the window, then came and stood above me. All right then, come on, she said, giving me a smile that barely made it past her coral-colored lipstick. Everything about her was enormous: her bare arms ballooned from her sleeves and her hips were as wide as the trunk of an oak; only her feet were small, and as we walked back toward her cubicle I wondered how she could stand a day's worth of the pain she must have suffered from her cheap blue shoes. She lowered herself into an office chair; it seemed to sink into the carpeting. Well, you look employable, she said as she lifted her great, gaping purse off of a second chair and motioned for me to sit down beside her. We can be thankful for that. She peered over at me. But honey, I've got to ask you, before we even begin. — She gestured at my forehead. What happened?

For a moment I was startled; then I settled slowly back in my seat and gave up one more tall tale. It was the only thing I could do. Once upon a time . . . I started, pulling my hair back. The counselor gave me a *get-out* look. . . . I was the Bride of Frankenstein, I concluded.

She paused, then let loose with a high-pitched giggle and said, Shit, honey, weren't we all.

I had a little accident with my car, I said resignedly, and she nodded.

Well. Her hands were pink, her nails were crimson. She turned up the first sheet of my application, stared down at something I had written on the page below, and spoke without looking up. Well, O.K. I'm glad you came in. Most people we get in here can't do anything at all, and if they can, then no one is going to trust them to do it. So what kind of thing are you looking for?

I had already decided and I didn't hesitate. What else was there for me to do, in a world of blindness and injury? I want to work in the field of health care, I said.

The field of health care? Doesn't that sound nice. I wasn't sure if she was being sarcastic, even when she said it a second time. The field of health care. She glanced down at my application again. You have some experience here . . .

I gestured toward Illinois. I studied nursing up north, I said. I never finished, but I interned in the hospital for a year, and when I was in high school I was a candy striper.

All right, then. She pulled a few tan-colored files out of a drawer by her side and began to flip through them, shaking her head. No, she said, and then stopped just long enough to stare at a sheet of paper that puzzled her. No. There's a hospital—are you union?

I never had time to join, I replied.

No, she said. Well, then, you can go downtown and sign up, and wait three weeks for it to process through, and then I'll have something for you. Or . . . Here she tempted me. Such a sympathetic woman, I never would have guessed she was working, from whatever distance, for the devil. There's some nonunion work, she said, if you're willing to be an orderly.

I'd like to start as soon as possible.

Of course you would, she said, and dug through her files some more. There's this, Eden View. Can you work with old people? It's just cleaning up, mostly, but it's work.

I said that was fine, and she wrote out the name and address on a square of purple paper that she removed from a multicolored stack on the corner of her desk. If you can get out there this afternoon, I'll call them.

I'll go, I said. And I went, thinking nothing, just like a pebble that's been dropped down a well.

Eden View: right away I decided it was a terrible name, it was insulting and embarrassing. No one was going to believe that you could see paradise from there, just because someone else said you could. They called it a rest home, a community. They would have called rape Love-in-springtime, and slander Legend. I thank God I won't have to die in that kind of place.

It was an asylum for old people; I found it in a neighborhood of clapboard houses on the eastern edge of town, where the city began to thin out into tired and odd-shaped public parks that never received visitors, an area so homely and forgotten that as far as I ever knew, it had no name. At one in the afternoon, I arrived outside the front door.

The building was red brick, three stories high, with a white roof on top, and it was surrounded by small, neat grounds with benches placed here and there. I walked in from the midsummer heat to a shadowy, cool reception area. At the front desk a nurse was talking on the telephone, absently twisting the line around her index finger as she spoke. When I showed her my appointment slip, she took it, examined it, and wrote down a room number on the top margin, all the while listening to the voice in the receiver and occasionally saying, Yes it is. . . . Yes it is.

I was interviewed by an old man in worn blue jeans and a cowboy shirt, and the entire hour was absurd: when I first found his open door and saw him standing awkwardly beside his bare desk, he seemed so helpless and out of place that I thought he was a patient under the delusion that he could hire me. I'm sorry, I said, and started to leave again, but he took hold of my arm high up by my shoulder, welcomed me in, and said he was Personnel. He asked me to sit and I took a hard wooden schoolhouse chair next to the door. There was a moment while he searched his desk drawers for a pencil, which turned out to be on the floor by his foot; with a groan he stooped down to retrieve it, and returned pallid and trembling from the effort. He was a puppet, and he made me feel bashful for having more blood than I could use. Now, he said. All right, then. He studied my application. I see you lived in Chicago.

That's right, I said.

I've got a grandson living there. I guess he's still in school.

He looked at me hopefully, but all I could do was nod and say, How nice.

Studying, what do you call it? The electric, the wires, and the . . . He made a motion with his hands as if he was threading a needle.

Yes, I said, and looked out the doorway at a nurse who was passing by.

He was quiet for a second, and then he abruptly sat down behind his desk and began to ask me a string of questions. They were dull, but I was honest, and he must have been just who he had claimed to be, because when the hour was done, he offered me a job, and when I went down to the nurses' office to fill out some forms, the big brusque administrator just looked me up and down a few times and told me I could start on Monday of the following week.

But I want to tell you about Bonnie, because Bonnie is where everything begins: my beautiful lie, my borrowed habits, my grief, and my rebirth. When it's kingdom come and time to tally my debts, first I'll owe her a hundred thousand miles, and then I'll owe her twenty years. So this is Bonnie.

The Friday before I started at Eden View I went back to the hospital for one last visit. Just a checkup, the doctor had said on the phone. Take the stitches out. Just another two hundred dollars, I thought, but I went. When I got to the waiting room there was a woman sitting in a chair against the wall, leaning forward with one leg tucked up under her while the other swung above the floor. She was rocking back and forth and humming a little bit, and when I sat down she looked right at me, rocking still; but she stopped humming and colored slightly, and after a moment she unfolded her leg and lowered it to the floor. Sorry, she said. I always do that when I'm nervous.

That's all right; I play with my hair, I said, and to reassure her I reached up and tucked a strand behind my ear.

She had a high forehead and hazel eyes, and her hair was about the same shade of blond as mine was; she was short-nosed and round-faced, and in the chemical light of the windowless room her skin was almost blue and her lips were almost purple. It had been raining on and off all day, and a pair of glossy yellow calf-high galoshes with the top buckles undone were dangling loosely from her dangling feet. I watched and waited for one of them to drop, and I was going to say something to her about it, but just as I started to speak the door opened and an attendant came out. Ms. Harrison? she said, and handed me a brown clipboard with some forms on it. The woman on the couch said, Got mine all done, and turned them over to the attendant, who took them without speaking and disappeared through the door again.

When she was gone, the other woman said, God, I hate this. She smiled. I'm Bonnie Moore. She held out her hand from across the room and waved it a little when she realized that we'd never meet that way.

Caroline Harrison, I said.

What are you doing here?

I just, this is my last time back. I was in a car accident and they're following up on it all.

Car crash? Oh, how glamorous. Nothing like that ever happens to me. I just get women's things. This time it was an ectopic pregnancy, the egg caught up there. Here. She rested her fingers on her abdomen. So they had to go up and get it out. She frowned and played with her hair for a second. Now they want to make sure it's all gone, which they didn't tell me in the first place it might not be.

The attendant reemerged from behind the door, swiftly at first; then she hesitated, looked at me, made a gesture, and looked at Bonnie. You, she said to me, are Ms. Moore? —No. She changed her mind just before I shook my head. I'm sorry, you. She glanced at Bonnie again. You can come in now. Bonnie got up and made a here-we-go expression with her eyes, and then just as she passed through the door she turned to look at me again. We were both thinking the same thing, and knew it; it was a charming, comely moment in conspiracy against the attendant: What was that about? Did we look alike? We didn't, really. Maybe. A little, it didn't amount to very much. Funny. And then she was gone.

Another ten minutes went by before the door opened again, and the attendant stuck her head out. Harrison? she said. Will you come this way?

There was a doctor waiting in a tiny examining room; I'd

never seen him before, but I could tell right away that he enjoyed his job and was good at it. He had the air of a man who had long ago come to love everything that he could understand, and to admire everything he still found mysterious. Hi, how are you feeling? he asked as he felt in the breast pocket of his lab coat for his penlight. You can just hop up on the table. All right? He touched his cool, clean hands to my face. Look right here, he said, and held one finger up. His breath was shallow as he bent forward to stare into my eyes, moving the light from one to the other and then back again. I could feel my pupils helplessly constricting and dilating, I could hear my own blood. Good, he said. Good. Everything looks fine. . . . He backed away and nodded. They told me what happened to your car. He smiled slightly. Maybe you were blessed, he murmured, half to himself. . . . Blessed be Caroline, who will survive her tribulations. . . .

I was tempted to believe him because he was a doctor, and anyway, it was what I wanted to hear. But was he allowed to say that kind of thing? The license on his wall didn't give him permission to prophesy.

You have the number here, he said brightly. I nodded. If something goes wrong, you can call, or just come on in. But I think you're O.K.

I can go?

You can go, he agreed.

The parking lot was scattered with black puddles and the weather weighed a ton. As I walked across the asphalt I saw Bonnie standing beside a car some distance away, the lower part of her legs reflected in a mirror of water at her feet; she was unlocking the door and she didn't see me, but when it was open she hesitated as if she'd been struck by an uncanny thought, and then looked directly my way. I waved. Hey! she shouted, and motioned me toward her. Caroline, right? I'm going to guess that you don't have a car, she said when I was close enough. I can give you a ride. Where are you going? Well, wherever you're going, I can give you a ride.

Home to Old Station.

Do you have to? she said. I mean, is there something you have to do there? We could go get lunch or a drink or something, instead.

I looked at her; it would have taken a dozen doctors to get down to the source of her soreness, but I figured a companion could find it alone. Who was I to turn her down? So I went with her.

The car rolled out of the lot like a caravan leaving the last city; there was that silence at the start as we settled in. At last she said, Ha. I'm all right, it turns out. Are you all right?

As far as I can tell, I said. The doctor just told me I was— blessed, I think, was what he said.

She took her eyes off the road to look me up and down; she wanted to know if I really thought like that, and as soon as she saw that I might, she said, I'll bet he's right. But with me, it's the opposite, my insides are all tangled up. There's always something wrong in there. I'm telling you, I mean. Always always. The eggs are always either bubbling up and going everywhere, or else they aren't there at all, or else I'm cramping. I looked over at her; she was peering through her windshield as she carefully steered down the street, wearing a look of mild surprise on her face, as if she'd never gotten used to the fact that her car moved forward at such an even rate, and changed direction when she turned the wheel. She saw me looking at her and made a gesture that I didn't understand; she could tell that I hadn't understood it, but she let it lie.

In time we came to a brown building with a neon sign outside that said Ollie's Lounge. Inside there was a dark bar with a kitchen in the back and a few tables covered with plastic-coated gingham tablecloths; overhead, the grey-brown blades of a greasy ceiling fan slowly turned. Bonnie ordered a baked potato and a glass of iced tea, and then said, Um, um, and absentmindedly tapped her knife on her napkin. When she finally spoke, it was in a tone of voice that suggested that nothing mattered much, but her eyes were wide and she sat slightly forward and bent over in her seat, as if she wanted to protect herself by protecting the table.

You just moved here, yeah and I know what you're going through, I think, she said. I came down here on a bus from Oklahoma City, about six months after my mom died, that was a couple of years ago. My father was long gone, like twenty years, and there wasn't anyone else. — She reached across and drew a packet of sugar out of the holder in the middle of the table, tore off the top, and casually emptied the contents into her mouth. The truth is, though, is that I was following a man who wanted to marry me, and he got a job down here with the phone company. Then we split up and he moved away, somewhere, and I was just too lazy to go anywhere else, so. She thought for a moment about the day he moved. I don't know. That was my crash, I'm still here, this is my city.

Through the plate-glass window at the front of the bar I could see people hurrying to and fro in the sunlight, such busy fish, such a bright fishbowl. Do you like it here?

Sugartown? she replied. Sure. She nodded, I love it here, I wish I'd grown up here. It's where nice buildings go when they die. You'll love it here, too, I can tell. She said this not because she was trying to convince me, but because it was gospel, just a song she knew and believed. Have you found a job? she asked.

I'm just about to start, I told her. I'm going to be changing bedsheets at an old-age home.

Is it good? she said.

I don't know yet, I said.

I'd like to do something like that, she said. Help out. Now I'm tending bar, but I'm not going to do it for the rest of my life. It's O.K., but I'm going to get out.

She was playing with a ring of keys, twisting them in and out of her fingers, humming very softly, not a song but sheer want of better work; she was quietly levitating just an inch or so above her seat. Do you want to conquer distant lands? Do you want to bring back spices, silk cloth, and silver? Do you want to be carried in through the gates of the city on an ivory chair? Someone dropped a glass in the kitchen and swore as it shattered. She took a sip from her soda and smiled. Soon as I pay my doctor, she said.

We rose to leave and she reached into her pocket and pulled out a crumpled twenty-dollar bill; when I started to open my bag, she said, I've got this, let me, and she touched my wrist. No, come on, I said. — Just let me, she replied. So I put my money away; but as we were walking out the door I turned back for a moment and watched as the waitress put her hand over the banknote and transferred it into the pocket of her apron without looking at it.

Out in the street, Bonnie seemed to burn a little bit, like an ember in the sun. A black dog lay sleeping on the sidewalk across the street. On a passing car radio a singer was crooning, Have you seen my baby? It was a consummate moment, everything seemed to fit into one faultless composition: calm, proportionate, meaningful. Bonnie was standing beside me; and I knew at once that I wanted her there all the time. Call it love at first sight, or sudden beatitude, or just one of those things, I don't care. She drove me home and we traded phone numbers; we stood on the sidewalk and said a thousand last things quickly, as if a whole new conversation was trying to fit itself into the time we had left. Twice she took one step toward her car; twice she gave up and took the distance back. At last she laughed and said, Good-*bye*. Call me. So it was that she became the first best friend I'd had since I was in high school. I watched her taillights glowing madly as she braked at the corner, like some strange little spaceship trying to force its way into the traffic on the main road.

At nine the following Monday morning I arrived at Eden View; by nine-thirty the administrator had started me on a tour, and for the next few hours she led me up and down the hallways. In all that time I never heard a sound louder than our heels on the floor: the residents roamed noiselessly through the place, shuffling in their bare feet, creeping along behind shiny steel walkers, wheeling inch by inch, drifting in and out of the rooms, through the foyers and down the halls, while the staff moved among them, more quickly but just as quietly. The atmosphere was at once exact and inane: each thing had its place, was named and counted and put away in a closet, each resident had a file in the office and a chart in the nurses' station, and every event and activity was scheduled to the quarter hour. But none of it made any difference. I could see right away that the years had driven the old folks deeper and deeper into disorder; their lives were shaped like hourglasses, and as they neared the far end all the natural laws that had held them together were coming undone; right before my eyes, they were returning to the original chaos from which they'd fallen.

Here we have the Nutritional Counseling Office, said the administrator. In a wheelchair outside the door sat a woman so aged that she looked like a wormwood tree. Hello, Mrs. Chapman. The woman raised her eyes and opened her mouth, but she said nothing, and we walked on.

Cafeteria. Nurses' station. Supply room. Staff lounge. In the residents' recreation room we came upon a group of old men sitting around a round table playing cards, while a thin black man dressed all in yellow played aimlessly on an upright piano that sat a few feet away from the rear wall. André, snapped the administrator. Can you come here? He hit three more notes and left the rest of the song hanging. For a moment he stared at the air before his eyes, as if he were watching the music disappear; then he produced a final, silent flourish of his hands, quit his bench, and came across the room.

Yes, ma'am? he said.

This is Caroline Harrison, said the administrator.

He reached out and shook my hand; his fingers were so long that they extended to my wrist. Welcome, he said.

Caroline is our newest orderly. I'm giving her to you. Will you show her where to change and get her started?

He nodded seriously and watched her back as she passed out the door. For a full thirty seconds he waited, one hand held up to quiet me, while I wondered if he was going to be good to me. At last he smiled. Come on, then, he said, and led me from the room.

The sunlight on the windows was ancient and brittle, the hallway was dark, the air smelled of ammonia. This way, this way, said André, and he set off down the hall in the opposite direction from the administrator. Shhh, he said. — But as soon as we'd rounded the first corner, he began to prate. I've been here three years, he said. Almost four years. Every two weeks I get my paycheck and send half of it home, go down to Western Union. I'm still here, the big lady can yell at me, but I'm still here. She doesn't like anyone but the doctors—ha!—but the doctors don't like her. They have her for blood trouble, they yell at her and she goes in her room. I put my ear to the door and *booo . . . booo,* she's crying. So I know. *I* know. — And he went on, and he never let up: for the next two hours I trailed him through the place and listened to his pitch: he gossiped, he joked and flirted, he ran down the nurses and mimicked the doctors. I caught no more than half of what he had to say—somewhere along the line it came out that he was from Kingston, and his accent was so strong that every other sentence was lost to me. He didn't notice, he laughed and talked, he sang little verses of songs, he said, Right? Yes? Right? I nodded and laughed along with him, and followed him to the next station.

The end of the day came earlier than I expected. So this was twenty-seven, I thought. These are my people, so soon; a sleep of snow and ashes. I was exhausted, I had too much to remember, and I wanted so badly for my masquerade to be successful. I wondered. In the women's bathroom I changed back into my street clothes, and the face I saw in the mirror wore a determined expression. An orderly—yes—in an old-age home—yes—in Sugartown, Texas. It was a new life: I didn't know what to expect, I really didn't know. I had no idea.

As I walked out the door, I found André waiting for me. A pair of men in dirty white uniforms passed between us with furtive looks on their faces. As soon as they were out of sight, André scowled. Custodians, he said, and clicked his tongue. Don't bother with them. They have no names: they come to here, they sit around like stones, and as soon as they steal enough drugs, they leave.

I nodded. O.K., I said. Well, O.K. Good night, and thank you so much. I'll see you tomorrow. Last words, I started to leave, but he suddenly grabbed my hand, tugging it slightly to bring me closer. He bent his head, and for a second I saw the smell of his skin. Yes, but now you listen, he said. Everyone here is very nice. Except for Billy, you keep your eyes out for him.

Who's that? I asked. Billy?

This old man, a bad man, you take my advice and watch out for him.

I started to ask him more, but he shook his head; he had already warned me, and that was all he would say.

I came home and found a message from Bonnie. Caroline? she said. Hi, it's Bonnie, we met last Friday? Hi, I just wanted to say hello. I know you started work today and so, good luck and all that. I have to work tonight too—nights all this week. But look, if you have time, why don't you come and visit me? It's this place called Uncle Carl's, on Route 36. You go out past the zoo about a mile, and it's on the right. O.K.? So come out some night. O.K. Bye.

As soon as I heard her voice I wanted to see her, but I didn't have the time right away, I didn't have the energy. We left messages for each other every few days: that was all I could manage, at the start. But I grew used to hearing her recorded voice on the phone, tentative and near, telling me, yes, she'd heard the last thing I'd said. She was waiting for me, she was thinking of me.

I went to work whenever I was scheduled to go, five days a week, eight hours a shift, sometimes in the morning, sometimes in the afternoon, sometimes at night. As soon as I got home again, no matter what time it was, I'd take a shower and fall asleep right away; there was nothing else I could do, and soon my days were divided so irregularly that I could hardly tell dawn from dusk, and the only forms of consciousness I could recognize were other people's fear and my own sleep.

There was no place on earth so filled with terrified people as Eden View. It was a death row populated by the innocent, they had long since exhausted every appeal, all they had left was waiting. So they waited, some for judgment, some for extinction, some just to know what they were waiting for. The idleness made them feel as if the waiting itself was all they were ever going to experience; it was punishment by eternal apprehension, which grew until they couldn't stand it any longer, and then grew some more. Some of them screamed and some of them shook until I thought their bones would come apart; some complained to children who had long since left them and some cried without shedding any tears. It didn't help them at all. Death was coming for them in pieces, taking their hair, their teeth, their organs, their memories, leaving them dazed, fatless, and compliant. And they were wrinkled, they were filthy, they smelled strange, and they frightened me. I tried very hard to love them all, each for what each was losing, but I'd be lying if I said I always succeeded.

There was Judith, with ninety years out of her mother and a meantime spent God knows where, she crooned to gone ghosts in a language no one could understand; she had long ago stopped eating, she lived on cups of air and the mysterious syllables of her singular vernacular. Bart, a retired businessman, who had lost his entire family in a burning house and was always trying to explain how tired he was. A colonel named Farley, a quiet man in a black shirt and a bolo tie, who would go for days without doing much more than coughing and saying, Ah! now and again, releasing a little puff of being that drifted lazily up to the ceiling. Colonel, it's time to go to sleep, please. For God's sake. —Cough. Ah! Cough. All right. Please.

I was putting the Colonel to bed one night when an old man I hadn't seen before came striding down the hall. He had enormous pale pink ears, from which tufts of reddish white hair grew, and that was all the hair he had; his nose was fleshy and hooked and his eyes were nearly black. He was wearing a dapper dark blue suit and a white shirt that was yellow with age, and he was strutting along without shoes or socks. When he was close by me, he stopped and held up his foot so that I could see the dust that had blackened its thick underside. See this? he said. See this, all this dirt? This is a slovenly place. Aren't any of you working?

Look at this. — I looked. I want my money back, he said. Give me my fucking money, or I'll set the dogs on you.

I stared at him. What?

Who the fuck are you, anyway? he demanded.

I froze.

Come on, he said.

... Caroline, I said. I'm new. ... Where did you come from? Where is your room?

Ah! he said, and dismissed me with a wave of his long ivory fingers. Get out of my way. And before I could react he disappeared down around the corner, muttering something vicious, and that was how I met Billy.

The doctors believed that he was dying, and when he waved away their recommendations they told him so, softly but insistently. Still, they never said what was killing him, and in fact he was never at all weakened. He would spend hours in the rec room, banging a basketball against the wall and catching it again with one hand. The noise drove the doctors crazy and they would send orderlies to make him stop; instead, he would pick fistfights with them, and they would have to restrain him by pinning his arms behind his back while he struggled to free himself and called them all cocksuckers and cunts.

Billy had been at Eden View longer than anyone else; in fact, he'd outlasted all of the staff, and there was no one there who remembered when he'd arrived. Once I checked his file in the main office and found that he'd been admitted about twelve years earlier, but he used to insist, sometimes that he'd just arrived, and other times that he'd been there forever. In any case, he'd managed to get himself moved into the best of the residents' rooms, a large single in a corner of the third floor, with a tiny balcony from which he could look out on the whole of Sugartown, the hills behind it and the sky above. On clear evenings he would sit outside with a penknife and carve pieces of wood into fantastic shapes, a guitar, a woman, a rosebush complete with delicate buds, which he would pass off on the staff, always warning them in a low voice that the things were hexed and might kill them if they weren't careful. Later still, he would lock himself in his room, turn his desk light on, and take out a canvas bag. Inside of it there was a rolled-up piece of cloth, and inside of that there were dozens of delicate implements—they looked liked dentist's tools—which he would use to meticulously engrave on something about the size of an envelope. No one ever saw what he was working on; if someone came to his door, he would hide it in his lap and hold it there until he was left alone again.

The orderlies said that he was the Devil's servant and he was never going to die. André told me that flowers withered and turned brown when he breathed on them, that he could light a match just by looking at it, that he had wings on his back and wore his suits to cover them, that he hid bottles of codeine in his room and had pornographic magazines delivered by mail, that he kept five thousand dollars in twenty-dollar bills rolled up in a sock in his dresser drawer. I'm telling you, Eden View ran with gossip like blood runs with sugar. But I began to watch old Billy, just out of curiosity; I couldn't help myself, the rumors were an itch. I hung by his room, playing temptation and waiting to see what he would do. I made excuses to be there: I had his pills, I needed to change his sheets, I wanted to be sure his room was not too warm.

I tried to get him into one of the games that the other orderlies played with their favorites, brief rituals that meant nothing, fair questions and simple tests. Do you know what day today is?

Do I know what day today is? Of course I do. Today is the twenty-seventy-seventh of Pestember. I don't care for a second what day it is.

What day of the week.

If it isn't Sunday, I don't know. I know it isn't Sunday.

Is it Thursday?

I don't know.

It's Thursday, yeah.

Well, shit, he said in a tone of utter disgust at my dumbness. What difference does that make?

Never mind, I said brusquely, and tried to dismiss him with a blank expression. But my cheeks were hot; I was betrayed by my face and Billy noticed it right away. Caroline is angry, he said in a schoolyard singsong voice. I don't give a shit. Caroline doesn't think it's fair that I should be so mean to her, when she's trying to make nice with an old man. She wants to be all over me, like a mood. She wants to go through my pockets, she wants what I've got. And who knows? She may be right, maybe I can help her, maybe I can use her. But—he wagged a finger at me— is she smart enough? Brave enough? Confident enough? Oh, I know I'm not supposed to ask anything like that. Because you people . . . Take a look at these, he said, holding out a pair of small pale green pills in his palm. They give me these to sleep, so I'll dream, so I won't remember what they've said to me, so every day we can start all over again at the beginning. Take them, go on, try them, you'll see.

Billy, these are yours.

I don't want them, he said. I'm giving them to you. You take them.

I put them in the breast pocket of my uniform, where I found them again a few days later, dissolved into dust and crumbs that clung to my fingertips, and as I hurried to the bathroom to wash my hands I spoke under my breath to an imaginary inquiry. I don't know what they are, I said. I don't know where they came from.

One afternoon I went to invite him to a game of bingo in

the cafeteria and found him sitting cross-legged on his bed, staring down at something that was lying in his lap. For a long moment he didn't move, just watched the thing; then he sighed and lifted it before him and I saw a chrome pistol in his hands, staring steadily back at him like a snake. He turned it, brought it to his face, and peered through the chambers, and as I watched he blew forcefully into one of the holes and then checked it again. Then he reached down to the bed and began to load it from a pile of shiny brass shells, one by one by one. I stood speechless on the floor. Beautiful, he said when he was done, and I began to back out the door, but before I could get away he spoke up. Go on and tell. Go on and be a snitch, be another disappointment. It won't help you sleep one bit. — Only then did he look up at me. Because you didn't sleep last night, did you? I know. Poor little princess. You got out of bed at about two in the morning and went to sit at your kitchen table, buck naked, but you didn't care. You made tea and read magazines, and wondered what your next man is going to look like.

He was exactly right about that, and at first I thought he'd been spying on me; but he couldn't have been, my shades had been down against the streetlights, and anyway, he hadn't left Eden View in years. It was just that he'd suddenly laid me open, and he was watching my thoughts right through my forehead. I felt him where he shouldn't have been and I panicked; but in a moment I'd collected myself and concentrated on a hell I conceived for him. Can you hear me now? I thought. Just mind your own business. I turned on my heel, walked out of the room, and carefully shut his door behind me; but I never told a soul about the gun.

At last I had a free night and a little self-possession, and I took a bus out to visit Bonnie at her bar. I found her watching over an empty room; it took her a moment to recognize me. Caroline?

she said. That's you, right? She laughed with delight, and I was delighted to hear her. I'm so glad you made it, finally. No one's coming out: they're all at home with their families. Behind her the bottles stood, with their cool glass, caramel colors, and invocations of the country, each one topped by a plastic spout. Come on, keep me company. Let me make you one of those fancy drinks, I never get a chance to make them.

. We started talking and we didn't stop. We went on, the girl and I, gently and carelessly, drinking our drinks and mentioning this and that. This trip down to Padre Island, that neighbor's barking dog in the backyard. I can't sleep, said Bonnie. Or if I do, all I dream about is dogs. Does that ever happen to you? When you dream the same thing over and over again?

Only when I'm awake, I said, and she laughed before I did.

Another drink, a sound in my ears. Slowly the world was reducing to just we two, our faces, our small questions and confessions. I lied to my doctor, I said to her. I lied to him, I don't even know why. He asked me if I'd ever been hospitalized before, and I said, Yes, once, for pneumonia. Which I never was. But I didn't want him to think I was . . . inexperienced.

Of course not, said Bonnie. Because otherwise he wouldn't respect you.

Was there another drink? Some time later I stood, stretched, and looked around the room. I'll be right back, I said. The bathroom was cold, and I was quick. When I was finished I studied my face in the dark mirror under the dim blue junkie lights, my skin perfectly clear, smooth and glowing, my eyes hidden in shadows.

Do you have any brothers or sisters? asked Bonnie when I returned.

Not really, I said. I was the only baby born to my mother alive: she had one miscarriage before me, and another after, so there I was. She didn't talk about it, but there I was. — I held my hands out on the table as if I were cupping an invisible infant.

She sipped and stared at the bartop. I have some stepbrothers somewhere, she said, but I never see them. My mother's dead, and my father could be anywhere, you know, so I don't know a soul except for you. Even though I'm sort of very social. Sociable. But just to a point. I don't really know a single person, except for the people that I see in here, and I only see them here. And you. Does that make you uncomfortable?

I said, No, not at all. I was playing brave and everclear, but in fact the moment was painful; the debut of a friend was so great a moment that I could hardly stand to consider its consequences. No new lover with his hand on my naked ass could have gotten close to me so quickly.

She was embarrassed, she looked down and nodded. Looked up. Without flinching she rose from the table and went to make us each another drink, and I walked over to the jukebox, played five songs, and forgot right away what they were. We met at the table again. We were too good for anybody. —Boo! to the bosses, to the rude ones and the tattletales. I like that shirt, said Bonnie. It was loose and black. I like the buttons.

Later, she talked a little bit about mothers who ran their boys in gangs, and I answered her with a brief elegy on child brides, rooming-house whores, and after-hours abortionists. She told me a story that began with a description of a piece of one-hundred-year-old lace, and another that ended with the sentence, I had to change all the locks on my fucking doors, which cost me about two hundred dollars that I didn't have. I told her a few things I had learned about landlords, which led me to a remark on the saleswomen at makeup counters, and another on table manners. I added some thoughts on the smell of burning hair. She made a point about skin, and the nerves beneath the skin, all the while gently stroking the inside of her wrist with the index finger of her other hand.

I was married, I said, out of nowhere.

Tell me, tell me.

His name was Roy. I met him in New York, he worked for the City. So what happened. . . . I fell in love with him, and then I married him. I took his name. —I took his name. We lasted about a year.

How was it? she asked.

It was perfect until it ended, I said, and then it was a perfect tragedy. Bonnie pursed her lips and lowered her eyes, and I gave her a moment. . . . I married him, O.K., and I was faithful to him, but I couldn't stay married. I left, and when I left I didn't take anything, but that didn't make it any better. Well . . . that was long ago and far away. . . .

A middle-aged man walked through the front door of the bar, looked around at the room, and found it deserted but for the two of us. We stared at him. He hesitated for a moment, and then said, Sorry, and left again.

I changed the subject, I didn't really want to talk about New York. I have this fear of heights, I said. I've had it all my life. I get it when I'm on a balcony or near a high window, or when I'm looking down a stairwell from a few stories up. But it's not that I'm afraid I'm going to fall, or someone's going to push me. It's that I'm afraid I'm going to jump. I start to hear this voice in my head, and the voice is me. *Go on,* I say to myself. *Just go on, just jump.*

Bonnie nodded. When I was younger, she said—and then she started laughing and couldn't stop, and I laughed along with her without knowing what was funny. She began again. When I was younger, I used to fake not having orgasms.

Not having orgasms, I said.

Right. I would just stare at the ceiling, even when I was getting all ganged up inside, trying not to show it. It was a lot of work. But I didn't want some guy to know he'd made me lose control, so I'd lie there going—she made a noise like a matron trying to suppress a cough. I had this one, poor little skinny boy, who thought it was his fault and went down on me for about an hour, and never even knew how many times I busted. — She exploded with laughter, so violently that she had to wipe her chin. Oh God, she said. Oh fucking God. Who told me I was nothing but a place to put things?

I went to the jukebox again, she went behind the bar to mix us another round. When she returned, she sat the glasses down on the table and immediately lifted one of them up again. What time is it? I asked.

She pointed to a clock behind the bar that read eleven-thirty. About eleven, she said, and sighed. I'm drunk, she went on. I'm dry and I'm drunk. She interlaced her fingers and turned her palms out so that her knuckles cracked loudly. I'm dry, and I'm drunk, she said again. So this is what I'm going to do. I'm going to start paying more attention to things. I'm not going to go around in my little daze anymore. You're so much smarter than me, more thoughtful, right? You always try to know what's going on. I bet you don't get caught at things the way I do.

I'm going to finish everything I start, I insisted. You have far more self-control than I do, I can tell, you don't give up as easily. So I won't write letters that I never send; I won't put the book down on page ninety-two; I won't leave food on my plate.

When we had finished pledging our improvements, we shook hands across the murky table. It's a deal, said Bonnie. Done.

Early the next morning I was at Eden View; I was tired, my neck ached, my eyes itched. As I walked through the lobby I passed one of the janitors mopping down the floor, and the smell of the cleaning fluid got right to me and made me dizzy and irritated.

DID YOU REMEMBER TO SMILE? said a discolored sign in the staff lounge; I couldn't remember where I had left my work shoes. The fibers of my ugly yellow uniform were making fun of me. André came in and found me half-reclined on the couch. You look like you've been poisoned, he said, shaking his head with exaggerated disapproval. Come on, pretty Caroline. He handed me a Styrofoam cup: Have some coffee. If the big lady comes in, you're going to get in trouble.

I wasn't scared of the administrator, but I drank the coffee and when I was done I went on my rounds. The clocks in the hallways kept stopping and starting again, and the sun shining through the windows was sharp enough to slit my throat.

I went to the assignment board to see what test was waiting for me, and there it was: I was supposed to give Judith a bath. She was waiting in the patients' lounge. —No, she wasn't waiting, but she was there, sitting in her wheelchair with a single playing card clutched in her hand, while a few of the other residents played rummy with the remaining fifty-one cards at a table across the room. Do you want to take a bath? Do you want a bath? It's time. She looked up at me expectantly as I rolled her out the door and down the hall. In the washroom that she shared with four other residents I pushed her to the edge of the tub. Upsy daisy, I said, and helped her step slowly into the water. With her nightgown removed, she was naked; her tiny back was pale and curved away from her protruding spine like the dorsum of an ancient dolphin. A bleached, dying dolphin. She leaned back, showing her flattened breasts, her belly, her loose and balding sex . . . to be so old, in a body that had become so exhausted and discouraged, to be so brittle and unable. If I asked her and she understood me, what would she say she had been, before she became this phenomenon? What history had brought her here? Was it something like mine? The idea made me wince, and to keep from dwelling on it I began to wash her gently. Under my hands she was even smaller than she looked, I stroked her shoulders, and she began to make an unconscious rhythmic sound, a moaning, a singing that she couldn't hear herself; it was as if some siren living deep inside her were calling the dead to come get her. I lifted her arm to wash beneath it and her voice rose, her tune became more urgent, and all of a sudden it seemed to me that they were on their way: I could feel their footsteps on the floor outside: I could hear their heavy breathing. I didn't want them to find me so I quickly finished cleaning her, dried her down and hastily dressed her, and then wheeled her to her room and left her alone.

I spent the next half an hour wandering along the halls, hating myself and looking for a place to hide, but there was nowhere safe. From behind the clouded window of the Therapy Room I heard the sound of a man laughing; in the cafeteria I saw two janitors sitting together at a table, hunched over a box of glass ampules filled with amber fluid that they were carefully dividing between them. At last I came to Billy's room, and without thinking I knocked on his door.

Who's that? he demanded, and I heard three or four footsteps and the sound of a drawer being shut.

Me. Can I come in?

No answer, but more noises. Then the door jerked open. What is it?

. . . I need to strip your bedding.

He hesitated for a moment, and then said, About fucking time, and stood aside. I crossed the room and began to pull the sheets from his mattress; the bed was cold. He stood restlessly in the corner, and when I turned back to look at him he just cocked his eyebrow and shifted his weight impatiently. At length his silence became too much for me. Billy? I said while I pulled his pillowcases from his pillows.

He made a noise.

Where did you come from?

Where did I come from? he asked back, and at once his temper was in gorgeous flower. I was born about ten thousand years ago! he said.

Shhh, I said, stepping backward.

My father was a big black bear! My mother was the fucking moon! I left home when I was three years old. I left home, and I never looked back!

Don't shout, I said. Where did you go?

I went everywhere and I did everything. — Again his voice rose. I made a million dollars a hundred times! I promoted bum boxers who fell down, I hawked houses built on fault lines, I stole songs from their composers! I buried a thousand men, I betrayed a thousand women, I sold children into slavery! He paused. William Mahoney, they called me *Dollar Bill*. Except once when I captured a river and held it hostage for ransom; then they used my middle name, *Misery*. What the fuck do you want?

From the floor below came the sound of André on the piano playing Let's Get Lost. What do I want?

What do you want from me? What do you want? I see you coming around here like I'm payday. I know you want something. What is it?

I didn't know what to say. I wanted to know him, to sit at his feet and study with him. I wanted him to tell me stories and dirty jokes, I wanted to get into everything with him, I thought maybe he was my escape; but I wasn't going to confess all that. I was afraid he'd laugh at me. I don't want anything, I said.

Don't you lie to me, he said softly. You can lie to everyone else, but don't you dare lie to me.

He thought he had me trapped and bare, but I'd learned the right response when I was just a little girl; it had been taught to me along with my earliest manners. Well, I said, just as softly. If you don't already know what I want, you're never going to find out.

He hesitated. Bitch! he said, but by then I was already slip-ping away, laughing to myself, because I knew it was a compli-ment, and it meant that I was still alive.

I want to know more about this city:
where you were, what it was like.

WELL, I'LL TELL YOU: YOU CAN TALK ABOUT THIS LOVE AND THAT love: the minister loves his congregation and the banker loves his bank. Tristram loves Isolde, and Isolde loves her song. You can say that love defies prediction, but Bonnie was right: as I settled in I found myself falling in love with Sugartown, and every day I was seduced a little further. I felt as if I was an explorer who had stumbled onto the place over some uncharted mountain range, becoming the first outsider to discover that particular landscape, peopled with those shopkeepers and police, those office workers strolling through the downtown plazas, the Mex-ican lawn crews, the ranch hands who came into town on week-ends to dance and fight, the lowriders who tooled down the Strip on Saturday nights—all of whom had been living there in isola-tion, rendered characters in a shimmering society.

It was still a relatively new city; Spanish settlers had founded it centuries earlier, but it had remained an outpost until the late 1800s, when the great ranches started springing up nearby; then it became a way station for cattle on their way to market. It had grown gradually since then, left unaffected by the oil booms and busts that had staggered the growth of the rest of the state. No one had moved there without long consideration and good reason, and nothing had been built there before it was needed.

Sugartown: there were several stories to explain how it had come by its name. Some said it was because cane from Florida and Louisiana passed through on its way to California, others that it was because the water in Green River was so sweet, still others that it was a corruption of the name Saugers, he being one of the first white men to grow rich there. There were days when I walked the city all by myself, lost and gazing lustfully. I loved the place: I loved the icehouses that showed up on corner lots, where for a few dollars you could sit on a picnic bench and drink beer from dusk to dark; I loved the stadium that sat in the middle of town, a squat domed structure that was just as ugly as it could be; I loved the local stone that they used for the municipal buildings, a blue-white marble from a quarry a few hundred miles away, the handsome, rich mansion bricks made from some nearby clay, and the Spanish clichés of stucco and scalloped red roof tiles. I bought a guidebook, and I loved the stories it told, the madness of the early settlers, the wealthy, upright families, the cheating wives and cowboy murders, the hidden alleys and locked doors. I loved the years that I found written on the historical markers, telling the date when some building had gone up. I would stop and think the time all the way through: Who was then alive, who was now dead?

And my senses: the American blue sky; the smell of the trees, and the river, and the dank hallways of Four Roses; and the screeching of the birds that collected in the trees in Police Plaza. Every time I turned on the radio they were playing a song that I wanted to hear; every time I passed near a schoolyard there was the sound of boys shooting basketball. I would melt eggs spiced with jalapeños in my mouth every morning; in the evening I would sip cranberry soda at my window and think of the fields facing away from the city as they raced in their sleep down to the Rio Grande, the thousand-mile-long wind, the fine men and women cakewalking along the sidewalks, the sound of starting cars, accordion music. I used to walk to Eden View, and one night a man in an old brown panel van pulled over to the curb and asked me if I knew how to get to a famous old barbecue restaurant on the south end of town; and I was so pleased that he would mistake me for a local, and so proud to be able to give him the directions and set him on his way, that I smiled for an hour afterward. You see, I was so happy there, I was charmed, I felt safe and satisfied: I thought I was never going to leave.

Some nights Bonnie and I would just drive the streets, while she acted as my guide through the specific heights and depths of town. This coming up is Silverado, she said as we turned onto a wide and barely lit avenue, on either side of which broad lawns rose toward shadowy estates screened by tall, ancient trees. There were no sidewalks. Overhead a three-quarters moon was illuminating a layer of pale dappling clouds, so that the sky seemed to be made of faintly glowing marble. Hang on, Bonnie pulled the car to the side of the road and turned off the motor. She lowered her window and the hot sweet night wended its way in against the air conditioning. Smell that, she said. That's what heaven's going to smell like.

At the end of the avenue we went left and rolled through a neighborhood of neat little family houses; round and round we rode, past a public park softly turning to steam in the darkness, across an empty boulevard. We went over a narrow river lined with trees; on the embankment below I saw a pair of lovers kissing, the man tall and dark, the woman small and blond. Here the houses had windows with wooden shutters, and balconies were adorned with ornate wrought-iron railings.

In time we came to a bent white building. That's the oldest building in town, said Bonnie. See how the foundation's sunk at one side? It's this restaurant, now, and all the rooms inside are crooked. If you put a pen on the table, it'll roll right off. We bumped slowly over a set of railroad tracks, the road turned. An expensive blue sedan glided past us. This is all whores and drugs, said Bonnie, and has been for as long as anyone can remember. Drugs and whores. Isn't it pretty, though?

In Sugartown, the poor people lived in a neighborhood called Green River, in rows of tract houses and shotgun shacks penned in by cyclone fencing; there were Mexicans on one side of the railroad tracks, and blacks on the other. If there was a porch, it sagged, and fading color flyers from the local supermarket accumulated by the bottom stair. Outside it was inside again, familial and tough, hanging out. You could see them; they parked their pickups on their hard lawns and washed them down endlessly with rags and buckets of soapy water. At night, the orange arc lights burnished the metal and made the rest monochrome; in the morning, the dew fed the rust. Because it was summertime all the teenagers were out of school, in a world without labor. The boys would gather in circles in Bundini Park and joke at one another. The girls would watch from the bleachers, many of them holding even smaller girls on their laps; I figured they were sisters, but I wondered if they were daughters, and I'd try to imagine what it would have been like, to have been a mother so young.

If I walked back home from Eden View, I passed through Green River on my way to Old Station. I tried to take a different route every day, and once I came to a crossroads. On one corner there was an old hotel, a shabby once-blue building several stories higher than those that surrounded it, with dark windows and an unlit neon sign that read THE PIONEER. A red-and-green billboard showed a tin of chewing tobacco with a bucking stallion on the lid. Two men were leaning against the wall in the heat outside, one with a straw hat pulled down on his forehead, and the other shirtless and drinking a can of beer. They were in their early twenties and they had their eyes on me.

As I passed, the shirtless one began to sing in a high, clear voice:

> *Jole blon*
> *From Louisiana*
> *On the bayou*
> *In the moonlight*

I didn't look back, although I wanted to; I knew that if I did, I would see him standing there, with his arms open wide and a look of devotion on his face. I turned the corner like she-to-whom-all-praise-is-insufficient: I could feel my steps swaying, I could hear him following me. When I was about halfway down the block he started singing again.

> *Don't leave me*
> *Don't deceive me*
> *Stay beside me*
> *Make me happy*

What a pretty melody. What a sentiment to sing on a sunny afternoon, in this sad part of town. At last I glanced back and saw him ambling up the sidewalk with his hands in his pockets and his elbows out at his side, so that his entire being was fanned out behind him like the harlequin tail of a peacock. His voice was beautiful, and his pride was a sight, but at the last moment I thought of the word *pussy,* and I turned away.

Oh, come on, he said. Don't be like that.

But I just kept on walking.

The way from the bus stop to Eden View the following night. The weather was so hot and humid that it was impossible to tell if the sky was overcast or clear; the air was thick, the light was slow, in the privacy beneath my clothes I was perspiring. I walked down the middle of the empty street, watching the voodoo music that hung down from the canopy of trees overhead. When I reached the parking lot, I found it empty, the windows of the place were dark, no birds did sing.

In the door, then, and walking down the main hall. A few of the residents were out of their rooms, slumped over in their wheelchairs and staring down at their bare, bedsore legs, like images from old paintings of the sufferings of man. The walls were hung with grandchildren's drawings, their bright lettering laughing in the half darkness; the air smelled of weak medicine and cleaning solution, the slight sound of voices drifted out of the lounge. Someone was trying to convince someone else, softly, so softly, that there was no way to tell the words.

Judith and Bart were playing cards in the game room, or rather, they sat with a deck of cards between them and talked in low voices, thin lips to great ears. He bet her that she was an alien from outer space, and she went through the deck and named the cards, numbers and suits, to try to dissuade him; but her words came out in unearthly syllables. See, Bart said. You're a Martian, just like I said, maybe from Neptune, maybe, I don't know. They should have been put to bed an hour earlier, and I went in to gather them up. Together they rose and followed me down the hall toward their rooms— Judith's was first, and she went in without a word. Bart said, Humph, yes. Are there mountains beneath the sea? I nodded, and he made his way across the floor to his bed, moving his mouth softly.

Down the bare halls I saw darkness coming out of the rooms, a coffin-shaped stretch of shadow that reached through the door of each one. Good night, good night. Old folks in bed. Good night. There were dusky moons on the hallway ceiling and a grey penumbra down at the end, a mirage that had settled in before the door of the dining room. Good night. There was no more sound.

Billy came fully dressed out of his door, shut it softly behind him, and started down the hall into the unlit lounge. When he saw me he stopped and shouted, Hey! You there! Girl!

Billy, I whispered. Shhh. He scowled and retreated back into his room, where I found him standing stiffly beside his impeccably made bed. On his night table I saw a gold watch and an uncapped silver pen. Caroline-the-Candle! he announced. Do please sit down—he gestured to his windowsill—and we can get started. He had become very polite, but I couldn't decide whether it was because he felt polite or because he was mocking me. I went automatically to turn down his sheets. Don't, he said, and instead of lying down, he began pacing the distance from the head of the bed to the foot and back again. I took the chair by his desk. He stopped and smiled, in his unsmiling way. Out the window I could see the lights of Texas, spread like steady, pale orange stars along the floor of the valley.

So tell me, how are you? he asked.

All right, I replied.

What did you do today?

Not much.

No, goddamnit, he said, instantly glaring at me. So he had been mocking me, or else he had changed his mind. What exactly did you do today?

I ran a few errands, mostly, I said. Then I went home and read for a little while, and then I took a shower and got dressed. Talked to Bonnie on the phone.

Where did you go, on your errands? What did you read? Who is Bonnie?

I didn't want to play, but I didn't feel like fighting, so I played along: To the bank to deposit a check, I said. To the drugstore to get some soap and shampoo, to the hardware store to get lightbulbs. I read a magazine. Bonnie is my friend.

Caroline-the-Candle! he said again. And . . . Bonnie-the-Bottle. How did you meet her?

In the hospital, I said. And before he could ask: I was in the hospital because I had a car crash. That's how I wound up here, with you.

Who knows you're here? he asked.

In Sugartown? In Eden View? I don't know. No one.

No family?

No.

Children?

No.

No boyfriend?

No.

Caroline has no one but her friend Bonnie. I'd like to meet this Bonnie.

Maybe someday, I said.

Well, all right. Do you want to know what I did today?

Sure.

While you were reading magazines and doing nothing, I was out, he said. I have been roaming all over the country. I have been practicing my arts. I have had a very busy day indeed. First I went to Kentucky and I collapsed a coal mine; and don't you know, they're still trying to dig the poor men out. Then I spread my wings and flew up to Detroit, where I started a small fire, I did. And when I was sure it was burning to beat the band, I went down to San Francisco and knocked over a building or two; and then I went on my way to Kansas City, and when I got there I stopped in a church and set a priest to suffering for sex, so that he . . . well, you'll be able to read all about it in a couple of weeks.

He stopped to consider the damage he'd done. It was a lot

of work, he said. I'm tired out. So you may ask, Why do I do it? Well, I'll tell you. I like the *colors.* I like the *sound it makes.* I like the *smell.* I like what it *makes me think.* I'm the Adversary, he said, adjusting his tie and smoothing down the front of his shirt with his hands. I'm an appalling old man. He stopped and made a stage gesture of defiance. No, they cannot touch me for coining; I am the king himself. He fixed me with a delighted look. . . .

I was just sitting there listening to the old man go on about his aged dreams of revenge and mayhem; of course I didn't believe for a second that he had done all he claimed, I didn't believe in him. But he didn't care and he wasn't done. As for you, he went on, and before I could prepare myself, he was talking about me. I see you coming around, he said. I can smell you under your clothes, I can hear your heart bumping against your chest. Forty years ago I would have fucked you. I know what you want. . . .

There was mist sneaking against the window. I didn't believe him, but my skin began to freeze, my mouth was full, and I could feel my tongue search for a place to rest. I thought, forty years ago I would have let you. Billy went on: You want more of everything. More love. More fun. He was daring me to resist him, dangling feathers of fire before my face, I could feel their flames. Fame! Sex! Beauty! Billy said. I flinched and blinked. Confess, he demanded. You're greedy. For a long moment I couldn't remember how to start a sentence, I couldn't answer, and he smiled. That's good enough, he said. A glutton. Good. I can help you *rise up.* Now what can you do for me?

I was about to answer him when an alarm began to sound softly in the hallway, a high beeping noise that was meant to alert the staff without waking the residents. I got dumbly to my feet and for a moment we stood there, Billy and I, far away on our cold half-lit planet. But the summons went on, and at last I broke from his gaze.

Stay, he said, his voice at once commanding, tempting, and plaintive. We're just getting started. Don't go.

I have to go.

Don't go, he said again, and the tone of supplication was much clearer. She's dead.

I stared into his face to see what he wanted. He wanted to live forever, and failing that, he wanted me to obey him. I wanted to study him, but I had to go see what the alarm was about.

It was Judith, her heart had suddenly stopped. When I reached her room I found two nurses and Dr. Selzer, who looked up at me briefly and blindly and then went back to massaging her chest. Her flesh was as colorless, soft, and smooth as dough, and it put up no resistance to his pushing; his hands had no spark, there was no life, and his breath came more and more violently. His face began to redden, and after a few minutes had passed he stopped, abruptly started again, and stopped, dropping his hands to his sides and gasping for air. He wouldn't look at anyone, and when he spoke it was to an audience of numinous peers. All right, he said softly, and he pushed his glasses up on his nose, backed away from the bed, and walked out of the room, leaving the nurses and myself to rearrange the woman's nightgown and raise the rumpled sheets over her face.

Everything in Eden View was still. Either there was peace in the valley, or a fear so deep as to quiet all motion. I hadn't done anything wrong, but I was ashamed of myself, and I worked hard and kept my eyes lowered for the remainder of the night. Already I missed Judith, without even trying; I missed her body, I missed her tuneless and unfathomable voice, and when my shift was over I discovered that I didn't want to go home after all; I suppose I hoped that if I stayed it would be sign enough to someone that I hated Death, so I sat in the staff lounge and read a copy of the afternoon newspaper that had been left on one of the tables.

On the front page there was a picture of a young dark-skinned man, a graduation photograph from one of the local high schools. He was gazing out at the city, his eyes glazed with defiant tears. Everyone called him Domino, because he was so good at the game; and everyone was looking for him. The police said that he'd been dealing drugs, but they hadn't found a way to arrest him until he'd shot a pair of his competitors dead. They wanted him for that, so they gathered themselves together and surrounded the building where he lived; then they sneaked up the stairwell and broke through his door. He was waiting in the bedroom, and in the battle that followed he fired four bullets, hit three policemen, and then vanished down a fire escape. Below the article there was a diagram of the apartment, marked with star-shaped explosions where his shots had hit, and an arrow out the window where he'd left, wearing only sweatpants and a pair of sneakers. No one knew how he'd gotten away; the mayor was angry, and the police were embarrassed.

They believed that he was hiding somewhere in Green River, but they had no idea where. They'd sent people to bully his relatives, they'd raided bars and nightclubs, but they hadn't found him. They were going door to door; there were cruisers on every corner and helicopters constantly cutting in the hot sky; they were taking people right off the streets. There was talk of a curfew. A minister from the Baptist church called a press conference to complain, and the police chief held his own to ask for cooperation from the community.

I sat in the lounge and thought the night was all wrong; and I stretched out on the couch and slept fitfully until dawn the next day, when the administrator found me, woke me, and made me go home.

Bonnie knew a man from her bar, a regular named Adam, whom I'd met very briefly one night when I'd gone by to sit with her. He was getting married and she arranged it so that I was invited. I didn't know him very well, I didn't know his bride at all, and I didn't want to go to a wedding. A wedding! I didn't want to go. But Bonnie said, Come on, it could be fun. You don't have to meet anyone, you don't have to talk to anyone. You just need to wear some nice clothes. When was the last time you put on a nice dress and made up your face? I made a skeptical noise. She squinched her features and said, Do it for me? I don't want to go alone.

I don't have anything to wear, I said. I lost all my good clothes in the crash.

I have a dress, if you want, she insisted. I'll come over. It'll fit. It's a beautiful thing. All right?

I could think of a thousand better ways to spend a Saturday afternoon, but I knew she was relying on me to keep her company. O.K., I said.

She was right about the dress: It was an emerald green raw silk shift, a simple sleeveless thing with a scooped neck, but the whole of art was lying in it, cherubs in the shadows and chambermaids looking on. I stood before her mirror and smoothed it down my waist, and glimmers of light flushed down the front. You wear some sling-back sandals, said Bonnie, and you'll look perfect. —And here. She held out four little pills in her hand; two were small and white, one was white and larger, and one was pale blue. Take these; they'll make the whole afternoon a lot better. Water. Where do you keep the cups? She went rummaging through the shelves above my kitchen sink.

Where do they come from? I asked.

This guy came in the bar with them, traded me for a few drinks.

Do you know what they do?

I don't know exactly what they are, but he looked like he was having a good time. She turned her face away and gulped the pills down. I wanted to follow her, so I felt mine in my mouth for a second or two and then tipped my head back and let them fall into the back of my mouth; and just as I felt them pass down my throat, I saw a white flash of light. Oh, God, I thought, that was quick. But when I lowered my head again I saw Bonnie holding her camera in her hands, looking at it quizzically as the motor advanced the film.

By the time I was done with my makeup, I could feel the wedding coming on like a high, an airy burning in the hollow of my stomach, and a high coming on from the pills. The future, which until then had been a single uniform field, began to collapse into a variety of irregular shapes, like the paths through a concrete garden. My hair was sitting strangely on my head, but there wasn't much I could do about it. Bonnie took my chin in her hand and stared into my eyes. I knew exactly what she was thinking. Beautiful, she said. Green is your color.

The ceremony was in a Catholic church in a part of town that I'd never visited before; on the ride over there Bonnie sang *Froggy Went A-Courtin',* all the way through. The sun was curled up in a ball in the heavens outside the window; I could see one or two planets, hovering and ducking into the clouds. Saturn, broad daylight. On the street, people were trying very hard not to stare at us. You never checked to see what those things were?

It'll get better as it settles, said Bonnie. You know, Adam is *such* a nice man, I'm *so* happy for him. He used to come in the bar just to sit nice, and drink some, and talk. In the distance I could see hills, they were the earth's own joke. Do this, she said, taking her hands off the wheel for a moment and holding them in an attitude of prayer. I did that. We hope he stays married forever.

In the church everyone was smiling, especially the preacher, who grinned so widely and constantly that I thought his head was going to come right off and float upward toward the sky beyond the steeple. At the front, just before the pulpit, there were two stands about waist-high: on each of them there was a large, shallow pot, and in each pot there was an arrangement of flowers. Between them stood the groom, tall, handsome, strong. The preacher was at a podium a few feet back, and behind him there was an organist. Several young saints were leaning modestly against the rear wall. They were all waiting for the bride, and the bride was waiting for the music. Her name was Marie.

Bonnie and I slid into a pew near the back and sat down; she smiled at someone she recognized, and then leaned back and sighed nervously. I picked up a hymnal from the seat beside me, but I didn't open it; I just held it in my hands, caressing the dimpled cover and weaving the thin purple ribbon in and out of my fingers.

Roy and I were married in a dingy beige room at the city courthouse on a Wednesday afternoon, just behind a Cuban woman and her silent fiancé, and just ahead of two city sanitation workers who had their entire families along as witnesses. And did I believe that the flowers of paradise had descended upon us? I wasn't looking at him when he said, I do. Everything seemed just right to me, and yet not quite right, somehow. What did I know? Afterward I exhaled hugely, and spent a very innocent night with my husband, whose skin under the dusky banner of our wedlock was somehow smoother and more polished, and whose shallow respiring, as he slept, was as steady and ceremonial as a command at sea. It had been two, three, four years since I'd lain down next to him and heard him breathe, but I remembered, and I remembered how much I'd loved the sound.

The organist leaned forward and a few syrupy chords came down over the congregation; we all turned around in our seats to watch with open, expectant faces. The bride appeared at the door, a dark-skinned woman wearing a long lacy white dress and a white veil, arm in arm with her father. When I glanced back toward the altar I saw three or four other men ranged behind the groom, presenting him as one of their own. The preacher was one of them, too, but the bride was different, she was all alone, a precious and powerful little vial of perfume. When she reached the front she stopped; the music stopped and there was a hush in the room. The preacher said a few lines in a loud, hollow voice about the sacredness of the marriage bond; I didn't think he really meant what the words said, but I knew there was something he meant very deeply by saying them. The bride and groom answered by promising that they would never give up what they had right there. Then she kissed him, and the kiss was long. I thought she was going to vanish, but when they were finished she was still standing by his side. It was a miracle, right there in the church, and I wasn't the only one who noticed it; everyone was talking about how wonderful it had been, that she had been so suddenly transformed without coming apart.

Afterward there were smiling faces bobbing in the vestibule of the church, holy expressions on the angels above the door, a few flashes of a photographer's bulb on the front steps, some birds in the trees on the lawn. Bonnie checked her purse for the directions to the hall where the reception was to be held, and couldn't find them. I know where they are, she said. They're on my dresser at home. Hang on. She went over to a tall, dark man and spoke to him for a moment, and when she came back she was leading him with her hand around his wrist. This is Charlie, she said. He has the directions, so we're going to give him a ride. This is my friend Caroline.

Charlie had a smile like a handful of candy, and a low,

slightly hoarse voice. He sat in the back and hung his head over the backrest that separated us. I wanted to touch his hair, his straight black hair, just to see what it felt like. I've never been down here before, he said. Adam moved down here, to Texas. It's just like the movies, isn't it? I came down from New York—he said the city's name without blushing. —Oh, I think you have to take a right up at the intersection here, so you better get over. Do you want to just take this? He handed up the sheet of paper and as he leaned in I caught the smell of him for a moment, the heat of his clothes, skin, mouth: it went right down the front of my dress like the memory of a man's hand, and I flushed, shifted slightly, and cracked the window.

Bonnie pursed her lips and turned half around. Can you get down there, or move over, so I can see out the back?

Of course. I'm sorry, he said, and the smell went with him.

What are you doing out there? she asked, and then turned to mc and gave me a smile.

I'm just working for the government.

A spy? said Bonnie hopefully.

In the mayor's office.

At that my throat closed, and I looked at my legs so that I'd have something to see that wasn't going to show my face back. Bonnie drove innocently through a stop sign. Hm, she said. So what's the mayor's office like?

It's all right, Charlie said. Great, actually, it's disgusting. I love it, it's great.

I turned around in my seat to look at him, and he smiled at me, but his eyes were dark. I had no idea why: he was a big man and I wasn't prepared for him to start getting complicated, too. As for me, I felt doomed: my skin had become a composition of hot and cold layers, which were shifting against each other and making me red. Bonnie said, VFW, right? This must be it.

The room was large and high-ceilinged, and the floor was

swept wood scarred with a thousand heel marks. We were late and the place was already full of milling guests. High blood, each right hand holding a glass of ruby wine, a wedding. —Of course, Charlie was saying to Bonnie, and then the bridge collapsed from the weight of all those people. Don't drink anything, she said to me, and she squeezed my arm to mark the thought. Not with what I gave you. I didn't want to embarrass myself, so I sat for a while in my green dress.

A little later I saw Bonnie in a circle on the other side of the room, looking up into the faces around her, her small smile a star to wish on. Inside its vaporous halo I could vaguely see Roy, the divorced man, sitting at a desk in a government office down on Park Row, his narrow shoulders bent as he leaned over a stack of papers in front of him. He wasn't thinking about me.

Are you all right over here? Charlie asked. He was sitting back in the chair next to me, with the side of his knee very gently pressed against mine. If he was flirting with me, I was impressed; if he wasn't, I wasn't going to show a thing.

Yes, fine, I said. Then, and very deliberately, I set my face into a casual mask and tested the effect. What made you move to New York? I asked. It seemed to work well, and I was so pleased with myself that I smiled and missed his answer. I pressed on. I knew a man who worked in the mayor's office, I said. His name was Roy Harrison.

Charlie looked surprised, and at first I was afraid that I'd made some mistake—had I already told him?—and my hand trembled as I reached for a glass of wine. I only met him once or twice, but I heard a lot about him, he said, I don't know how much of it is true. Anyway, I haven't seen him in a while; I think they let him go.

Oh, he was one of my cousins, I said, realizing just a moment too late that he hadn't asked. I caught myself and smiled. What was he fired for?

I don't know. He studied my face as if he thought he were going to take me with his gaze.

What had he done? I asked. I knew there had to be another way 'round.

He shrugged and looked up. It could have been anything, he said to Bonnie, who was standing in front of us.

Are you going to come sit down? said Bonnie. It's time to eat. You two sitting over here all by yourselves, anyway, everyone's talking about it. Come on, it's time.

Around the room the guests were settling. Bonnie took me by the arm, led me over to a table and sat me down; on the white tablecloth in front of me there was a white card with my name written on it. I wanted very badly to remember what was bothering me, but I kept losing track of it: there was one loud man on my left and one dull woman on my right, and I ate cellophane food and drank two glasses of wine before Bonnie noticed my sipping and kicked me under the table, and then dipped her index finger in a glass of water and waggled it at me. There was a series of toasts, cheering and laughter. Charlie had pulled up a chair just behind me and to my right, and he was reaching over my shoulder to fill a flute with champagne. Together we watched the bride and groom dance the first dance. Have you ever been married? he asked.

I lied. No, I said. Never. Never. Bonnie was out on the floor and he had his hand on my arm, but I shook him off; I didn't want to have to maintain such a complicated balance, I felt full of food and I didn't like the song, which had changed to another song that I didn't like.

I need to go, I said. We were in a cab, Charlie and I. We were in a diner, sitting and drinking coffee. He had taken off his tie and the top button of his shirt was undone. Between us there was an old-fashioned tin bowl of sugar on the table; he opened the lid, raised up a small spoonful of the stuff, and slowly let its contents fall back. I don't know, he was saying; all of a sudden he'd become very sincere. It was an accident. She forgot her earrings by the side of my bed, and my girlfriend found them when she came home that evening. Boom. That was that.

I laughed. Oh you poor naïve man. Forgot? Like it was an accident? No woman ever does anything by accident, I told him. Unless she's crazy. Never, never does anything by accident, don't you know that yet? Didn't anyone teach you? A girl is a deliberate thing. Some time back, I couldn't remember when, I had decided that I liked him, and what he wanted from me. From my purse I drew my lipstick; I was going to be casual and reapply it at the table, but when I opened the thing I discovered that the tip was mashed, so I capped it again, excused myself, and took it to the bathroom. Harlot was the name of the color; I blew a kiss at the distant mirror. As I was sitting down at the table again, I saw a flash of green in the window, which I assumed was money, but a minute or so later turned out to be me.

Now, your man Roy was with a woman for a while, said Charlie. And she was crazy.

When was this? I asked quickly.

Maybe about two years ago.

I was in Dallas.

He looked at me curiously. I was in D.C., he replied. He didn't know anything about me; he didn't know I stole stories about my ex-husband. He looked around for the waitress.

Finish what you were saying, I insisted.

That's all there is. I think she wrecked the place they were living in. There was something else, but I can't remember what it was. . . . He glanced sideways as he tried to think of it; the entire recollection had suddenly become a problem, and it interested him deeply. As for me, I assumed that the answer was going to change the night into winter. A long moment passed while he tried to clear his mind for the missing memory to come home; I was right in there with him. — Anyway, he said abruptly, I can't remember. We were still in the diner, a beautiful bright red tow truck went by outside. After she left he got strange, he continued. There was a rumor he was drinking a lot, but I don't know if it was true.

So what happened to him?

He shrugged. I don't remember. He wasn't in my department, this is just what I heard, he said. He seemed like a nice enough guy to me. Don't look so sad.

Don't tell me what to do, I said shortly, and luckily for him he laughed. Who was she?

Who was who?

The woman.

I don't know. Someone. Ask someone. I never talked to him about it. Actually, I never really talked to him at all. He was getting bored by the subject; it was life, breath and blood to me. We're done, he said. We're going now.

On the street the warm wind was blowing, I had forgotten everything again, and I was in the mood to break faith. I wanted to make the night as complicated as I could. There were no stars, but streetlights: we were south of everyone else. My mouth was very dry. If I could only taste something, I thought, I would feel so, so much better. Later, Charlie held me with his hands grasping me by my hips, his long fingers almost meeting at the base of my spine. He kissed me violently; I kissed him like a butterfly banging against a window, and pressed my hips against his. He was solid all the way through; it was one of those perfect proportions of weight and mass that one wants to keep nearby, like a book, or a good dog. His tie and collar were undone, and the skin at his throat was stippled with tiny red shaving bumps. I left a little kiss there: Tell me another story. He smelled so wonderful, his warm skin, some soap and talcum powder, lust, liquor, and bed. Maybe maybe. Then we were in a taxi, legs entwined as we watched Sugartown turn by outside.

I stood before him as he sat on the edge of the bed in his bland hotel room, so that I wanted to jump up a ways and come down in his arms. I took his feverish head against my stomach and put my mouth on the bitter-tasting crown of his hair; and as I held him he reached up my back for the zipper on my dress and slowly tugged it down. I do think that I was with him only because I wanted to watch him take the thing off of me; nevertheless, I was sorry to see it go. It hit the floor with a slow emerald splash, but I was the only thing that got wet.

Without his suit he had no job, he was just muscle and skin and bone; I tipped him back and put my hand on the slab of his chest, he narrowed his eyes; I took his tiny nipple in my mouth, without waiting I reached down and gently weighed his balls with my fingers, and then dragged up across his bobbing erection and through his pubic hair to his belly. I bit his chest and he drew a short breath. Kiss, on the mouth, is that better? Baby? It was a trick I made up on the spot. I was having a good time.

I was on my back on the bed, his hands were around my ankles, tugging my legs apart. He leaned slowly over me and dragged his lips down my abdomen; they passed across my skin without catching on anything, until his head sank between my thighs and settled there, face to face with my wet sex. He put his hands under my ass, I reached down and touched his head as he began to kiss me, outside and then inside; his wise mouth and my glutted lips, reflecting each other's damp and shining purpose back and forth and back again, kissing until it was impossible to tell which was the original and which the double, while between them a tiny bright red bud grew, half mine and half his tongue; it was so young and tender that I wanted to weep; and then a fresh shoot burst from its tip and I began to tremble.

He was over me, his mouth glistening and swollen; there was no resistance—and with one exorbitant motion he slid inside me, gently swore, and began to fuck me. Some moments the sensation was so keen that I thought I was going to faint; some moments I could hardly feel a thing. I opened my eyes and saw his face above me, his own eyes tightly closed; just as he opened his, I shut mine again. A few seconds later he abruptly pulled out of me, and I wondered if I'd offended him. There was the soft sound of sex escaping from me as I lay there, borne up by nothing but the bed. I looked down the length of my body at him; he was kneeling between my legs, gazing up at me insistently.

Turn over, he said. Turn over.

If he'd said it again I would have refused, but he just watched me; so I rolled over as if it was a game called Sacrifice. I could smell myself on the sheets, the scent was a welcome thing, impolite. He took my calves in his hands and started to draw me back toward him, until I was up on my knees in the dark like a three-legged stool, my hands clasped behind my neck, my forehead pressed against the mattress. I breathed shallowly to calm a sudden flush of embarrassment that threatened to drive me off of the bed and out of the room; bold, big, I felt a breeze on the back of my thighs; for a moment I thought he was going to spank me, I wondered if he did that to every woman he managed to get naked beside him, I tensed and put my senses behind me. Instead, he gripped my upper thighs: then he took his finger and gently, delicately split me with it: I jerked forward involuntarily, but I didn't get far: he followed with his hips, at first hesitantly and then smoothly, and all of a sudden, there he was, really, in me all the way—and he stopped. I could hear him breathing heavily, his hand pressing gently on my back, as if he was trying to decide whether to push me down. He didn't move, so I didn't move. . . . I was following his lead . . . balanced like that, but then he left and I began to chase him, to chase myself backward, bang bang

bang. I would have done it all night, but I couldn't get away, and sooner than I expected my whole body gave up, my voice came out, and that great strong gushing thing broke all through me.

I'll tell you it's strange and it makes me wonder, how sometimes in that occult forest, when no one is looking, the ax loves the tree: and it's stranger still that the tree should love the ax.

I woke up the next day in bed with a dead man; he was just lying there on his stomach, sighing deeply, his brain shut down. Bright eleven o'clock: out the window the sun was shining, and I was young and purblind from the pall of my unfamiliar past; it was the first thing I thought about, there like some perfume I'd spilled on the bedclothes the night before. So the sleeping man wasn't my ex-husband, but he had seen him and spoken to him, and that was close enough to make me wobble on the dull point of my sad remembrance. All that time had passed and still the impression my marriage had made was deep and clear. I got up and put on my dirty dress while Charlie mumbled in his sleep. Well, he was sweet and sexy, but I never should have slept with him. And these rumors; was time, too, going to steal from me? For four years I'd had a reliable Roy fixed in my past, but the memories had become ailing leaves, and when I touched them they fell away, revealing a spray of grotesque and unfamiliar flowers. Had he grown so strangely in the intervening years? Then what was I? Another woman. He had fallen in love with another woman, I couldn't begin to imagine why. Still, I thought I knew what she looked like: she had brown shoulder-length hair and perfect skin; she wore blue jeans, men's shirts, and black bras; I couldn't see her face very clearly, but she was smiling, and she had a mean smile. Charlie didn't know what he'd done to me; he was still sleeping.

I was just about to slip out the door when he stirred and woke without taking his head from the pillow. Wait, he said sideways. I want to . . . And then he stopped, too exhausted to continue.

I went to the edge of the bed and stood above him, gazing down on his sprawled frame. I have to go to work, I said softly. A lie, but it would have been impossible for me to stay more than a minute longer.

He was trying to come up with something to say, but I couldn't help him; I hadn't been with him in his slumber. I was beginning to think he had fallen asleep again, when he spoke. Sugartown . . . he murmured. What time is it? My plane leaves at . . . Stay.

I think it's around eleven, I said. I have to be at work by twelve. I have to go. He suddenly seemed very dangerous to me and I wanted to distance myself from him as quickly as possible.

. . . I had a dream about Roy Harrison, he said with a puzzled look. Because you . . . made me dream about it.

And there I was, cornered by my curiosity all over again. Tell me.

I don't know, it was nothing. He rolled over onto his back and then slowly raised himself up until he was sitting against the headboard. You're really going to go. O.K. Will you leave me your number?

I found a sheet of hotel stationery and a pen in the desk drawer and scribbled some numbers on it, not mine; then I crossed the room to kiss him, glanced at him briefly, and started to leave. Good-bye, Caroline, he said tenderly as I was opening the door. —Oh. I turned, with the door open and the hallway behind me. But I remembered, he said. About Roy. . . .

This is your dream?

This is the real . . . I heard he had a kid with this woman, the one I was telling you about, and they were all set to get married. Then she walked out, just took the baby with her and disappeared. That was the last part of the story. I don't know. That was the end.

And I stood there for a moment, shocked and nodding stupidly, while something in me sang in pain. . . . Be gone, you devils, you've got me, you've skinned me. . . . Thank you, I said at last, and then I quickly crossed the threshold and walked away down the silent hall.

It was Sunday morning and I felt dizzy, a column of thick, turning smoke, turning through the lobby of a hotel in which I wasn't registered. Outside the revolving door the new sun was shining brightly and the walk across the front lawn was lonely, a tour through a sketchy garden suffused with air shot through with exhaust fumes from the road. By the time I reached the sidewalk any pretense of a better realm had ended. The bus stop was a half mile up the street, past the candy store, past the corporate center, past the strip mall. Already the sky was hot as a griddle. I waited on the bench with a newspaper I'd bought on the corner, tasted the yeast on my tongue, and suffered in the sun.

It was a fault of mine always to remember the past, and a twist in my vice to be most nostalgic and sentimental about those times when I'd been most unhappy, to want this season of misery or that month of boredom more sharply by far than any fond moment. God, how unhappy I was then, I'll say to myself: I wish I was there now. —And that was how it was that day. My marriage had been a mistake, I knew; nothing I had ever done had made me feel so weak; but I missed it badly. In the tree above my head a pair of birds were bickering, and it was all I could do to keep from crying in public, because it seemed to me that they didn't have anything to complain about. I hated the birds and read the paper, but the paper was just as bad.

Every article was directed at me; each was a parable that had been sent my way, and my task was to find the proper meaning and apply it to the city around me. I knew that my fate depended on discovering what was hidden within the stories, but I couldn't make sense out of any of them; I was too tired, too simple and stupid.

The police were waiting in the bus and train terminals, but they thought Domino was still in town. He had sent a letter to the newspaper written in neat letters on a sheet of school notebook paper, and they had printed a reproduction of it:

I am a master of the Game, but I didn't do this. Ask anyone. The bags were evidence that they stole from the House. They called themselves Officer Oregon, Officer Florida, and Officer Ohio. They told me to sell them, and then they tried to take more from me than I got. I told them I had enough, I didn't want to do any more, and they said Nigger you are going to die. Because my father was a black man they said that. So they framed me, but they won't ever find me. May God have mercy on you and your families.

Where was my sweet city? On the outskirts of town, a factory full of jobs had shut down; it made engine parts; the owners had disappeared. Four hundred men and women were out of work. Above the article there was a picture that showed a long, low brick building beside an empty parking lot, with a taller building rising behind it. A few men in jeans and work shirts stood outside the fence, staring at the camera with no expression at all.

And there was no nature or high thinking to console them. But what did that mean? What subtle lesson was I meant to learn? To have pity, to be angry? To quit what home I had and run? I thought it was my fault that I didn't understand.

By the time the bus came there was nothing left to read; I took my seat and stared at the floor. The backs of my thighs were raw in a kindly sort of way, and my tongue was sore and tasted of Charlie's mouth. The dress was a little bit rumpled and it no longer fit so closely, but it still had its shimmer. When a short bald man in a black silk shirt boarded the bus and sat in the seat next to mine, I was afraid he could smell the night before on me, so I pulled my hem down, shifted away from him, and turned my face to the window. A bright corner went by, and with it a revolving tableau: a car was stopped at an angle to the curb, and next to it I saw a police cruiser with its doors still open and its lights beating lazily against the noontime sun. There were two young black men facedown on the sidewalk with their arms stretched out on the pavement, while two policemen stood above them, one talking into his radio while the other was staring at something in his hand.

Old Station was crowded with Sunday shoppers, strolling in a sun so bright that I couldn't see. It was a breezy day, and the pennants that hung from the buildings were flapping loudly; a woman went by with one hand clutching her jacket closed, and another woman at my side stopped suddenly, turned around, and grabbed to get a better hold on the bag she was carrying. What had happened the night before was a secret; I wasn't going to share it with any of them, it would be a mystery to my fans and followers.

After I'd showered and changed I went out to see Bonnie at work. The place was empty and dark, and she was standing behind the bar, sipping a glass of soda water and watching a black-and-white movie on a television that was perched on the ice machine at the end of the bar. When I walked through the door, she stared at me for a moment and then put her hand up to shade her eyes. Who is that?

It's Caroline, I said.

Oh. She smiled. It's so dark in here that when you stand in the sun I can't see anything. Hello, honey. You took that guy home last night, didn't you? I saw you get into a taxi together.

I put my bag up on the bartop. We went to his hotel room, I said. I don't remember how it happened.

How was it?

It was strange, said a woman on the television. It was strange, I said. Kind of nice. I can still smell the stuff he puts in his hair.

I thought he was beautiful, said Bonnie. Was he beautiful? Do you want something to drink?

No thanks, I said. No, all right, tequila. She brought a tall glass out, set it before me, and poured a shot from the bottle. He was definitely smart about me. He was very . . .

Say when, she said as she was stopping. Is that enough?

Fine. My legs are sore. And my neck, for some reason, I have this kind of lump in my throat. She laughed, I went on. The odd part was that he knew my ex-husband in New York, and he started telling me these things about him. Bonnie was gazing at me steadily, the bottle still slightly cocked in her hand; the night before was coming back like an hour of weather. I didn't let on who he was to me.

What did he say?

He told me a lot of stories, they can't possibly all be true. That after we got divorced, he was going to marry another woman, but she left him just before the wedding. And she ran off with their baby? She had a baby, and she ran off with it? I don't know what I should do. I looked away, and without my even thinking, hot tears crept into my eyes.

She put the tequila back on the shelf and came back with a few lime slices on a napkin. What could you do? she said softly.

I shook my head; I stared at my own hands. She started to make herself a vodka and cranberry juice. That's not funny, said the woman on the television. I can't understand it, I said.

The drink Bonnie was pouring overflowed its glass, leaving a small puddle beneath. She reached along the bar for a white paper napkin and dropped it on the spill, and together we watched as a dark red stain appeared on it and swiftly spread— then slowed, and finally stopped just before it reached the edges. Maybe it isn't true, she said as she wiped the counter off and threw the napkin away. Maybe it wasn't him. Maybe he deserves it. Maybe he's lost his mind. A man will do that, I've seen it.

Maybe. The hard part is . . .

I know, she said. But listen, why don't you come over and have dinner tonight?

I'm working the night shift, I said. Tomorrow, we said in unison.

I was supposed to be supervising Mrs. Adcock's eighty-fifth birthday party that evening, but when I went down to the dining room, André was already there, standing in the bright, bright yellow light that was tumbling through the windows from the last of the setting sun. He was giggling about something as the residents filed through the door; the mirth had taken his face and made a comedy mask of it. Oh, come on in, you. Come on, come on. It's a party. Now, who all of you can guess—can guess, who can guess how old I am? That's right, he went on, although no one had answered him. I'm thirty-one years old. You can sit there, or you can sit there. We're going to sing this afternoon. You can sing, or you can just listen. That's right. He looked over at me and started laughing again. Caroline, are you going to help me keep these people in line? he said. We've got games, guess what year it is; we got races, wheelchairs against walkers. No, you go on and get some coffee or something. I've got this under control.

I smiled and blew him a kiss, and left him to his fun. The hallway was cool and shadowed, and cooler still because it was so quiet; the only noise was a faint note or two from André's piano as he touched the first few seconds of a song and then for some reason stopped again, leaving an even deeper, elliptical silence hanging. The air was dull.

I had just reached the stairwell when I spotted the administrator coming toward me down the hall; I hoped to slip through the door before she saw me, but she called my name as my hand reached the knob. Caroline! she said. Just a minute.

I waited while she made her way down the hall, pacing stolidly on her thick legs. Your employment agency called here looking for you, she said as she approached me. They want you to call them back, she said as she passed. Squeak squeak went her rubber heels on the linoleum. What a cold sound, it made my spine ache with dread.

Upstairs I found Billy lying in his bed, listening to the radio, and as soon as I came to his door he turned his eyes on me. Come in, he said. I stood a few feet inside the door frame and he rose up on his elbows to address me. You left last time. . . .

I'm sorry, I said.

Never mind. You have a job, nobody else has a job. I see it from my window. Nobody's working, he said. Everybody just walks around, looking for something to do. But there's no money to do anything, so they go back home. And the kitchen counts for more than the bedroom, but the cupboard is bare. They'll get like chickens in a barnyard when the rooster's been gone too long. You'll see. Be careful. He looked at me more closely. How are you, my darling one?

I blushed and smiled nervously; I could feel my teeth between my lips. I spent the night with someone last night, I said. This man I met at a wedding, and I went back to his hotel room.

Billy merely nodded. He told me some stories about my ex-husband; he didn't know I knew him. They worked together, and these things get around.

What things?

Rumors, gossip, speculation. News.

He fumbled in the drawer of his bedside table for a forbidden cigarette, lit it with a shaking hand, and inhaled deeply. Are they true? The paper burned, and puff, a blue-grey plume with amber edges started for the ceiling, only to break into threads and disappear as it was overcome by the cloud of dull grey smoke that he exhaled.

I don't know.

Of course they are: all stories are true. The ash went on the floor.

Then what should I do?

Well, we'll have to see about that. But you'll do something, I know you will. Because you will, because you do. I didn't raise you to be a coward: Don't ever be jealous, don't ever be scared, don't ever repent. That's what I always told you. He paused for a moment and then started down, descending toward some distant and obscure matter. . . . I remember when you were just about seven or eight years old, and that neighbor boy started picking on you. Shouting mean things when you walked by, pushing you when you were on line for the bus, teasing, bullying. Picking on you. Do you remember what I told you then?

I was going to protest that I wasn't his daughter, and whatever wonderland of generation he had entered wasn't helping at all, but I suddenly realized that I might as well let the child be me. No, I said. I've forgotten. Tell me again.

Told you to go after that little fucker and teach him a lesson. Told you, Don't you ever take anyone's shit, or don't come home if you do. Do you remember what you did?

No, I said.

You were only seven, eight years old. I swear. So you cozied up to him, and you lured him out one cold weekend for a swim in the river, and when he'd stripped down and jumped in the water you stole all his clothes and took off. — And then he started laughing, a high, staccato bark that snapped off the walls. It was about a five-mile run back home for that boy, covering up his little blue pecker with his hands the whole way. Oh my, he said. Oh my, oh my. Caroline, my flower, my one love, my girl.

I stood there mute by the side of his bed while he finished his cigarette, carefully extinguished it on the base of his lamp, and then laid the butt on his night table. He wheezed, he sighed a few times, and then he turned out the light. It was dark outside his window, and the city at night suddenly appeared on the other side of the glass. With a soft tearing noise the room separated from the present and began to push forward in time. Billy, I said. There was no answer, no sound. For a moment I thought he was dead and I felt a soft, keen whistling noise in my ears; but then his breath began again and the whistling faded. I tucked him in just to have something to do with my hands.

At length he said, Everybody's got something bad that they're good at. We'll find yours, little one. Now, go on, now. You can go. When I'm ready for you, I'll let you know. I went to pick up the butt of his cigarette, and as I reached for it I could hear him faintly snoring; he was already asleep, he was dreaming of drowned boys and December girls.

Down in the lounge Mrs. Adcock's party had ended; there was a large tin plate with half a cake still standing on the table and a few balloons floating on the ceiling in the corner of the room. Three or four of the residents had remained behind to stand at the piano and sing while André played. . . . My baby just cares for me. . . . I stood and listened, and when the song was over I applauded them all gently, just for having made it to such an astonishing age. Come on in here, André said. Come on and come over here. What do you want to hear? The residents were waiting on my request. Anything at all, he said. Anything at all, and he gestured to a fat plastic spiral-bound volume that was resting on the stand above the keys. I've got my fakebook here.

I went to the piano to see what he meant, and he showed it to me. It was a thousand songs, collected in a book; just the chords and the basic melody, but it was enough that he could play almost anything that was requested of him. Cheat sheets, he called them: they were just quick outlines, but anyone clever enough to be able to embellish them on the fly could pass for really playing. Have you ever seen one of these before? he asked.

I've been using one all my life, I said, smiling at my own little joke. But André was an honest man, and he thought I was an honest woman and meant what I said. He stood up and offered me his seat before the keyboard with a courtly gesture, saying, Please, sit and play, then.

No, no, I said. I can't.

No, he replied. Here I am hogging the thing. Go on, please, play us something.

No, really, I can't, I said. I don't know how.

We stood there, each of us avoiding a heretical place at the piano, while the old folks looked on with puzzled expressions and I felt my face begin to redden. I'm sorry, I said at last, I really can't play, and I turned and hurried out of the room.

In the bathroom off the staff lounge I started changing my clothes, but midway through I stopped and sat, I had to think. I had to frown. I could see that the whole false design of my life in Sugartown was coming apart. The agency wanted me to call: they were waiting, I was sure they'd discovered that I'd invented my résumé, they could wait a little longer. Billy was not the sordid genius I hoped he would be; he was just old and strange. The marriage I'd so deliberately left behind had shown up suddenly in the path ahead of me, changed into some monstrous form and staring. But I decided right there and then that I wasn't going to drop anything—oh, no—I was going to stay right where I was and bluff to the end.

The sky was overcast all the following day, every glass surface was sweating and all the telephone wires were hanging low. The curtains over my open window never moved. From time to time a plane from the air force base outside of town would set off a boom behind the clouds.

In the newspaper that morning I'd read that they'd found Domino at last, shot dead in the backseat of a stolen sedan parked behind a hardware store; there was a picture of the car on the front page, a quote from his mother, in her agony. My son didn't have to die, she said. When are they going to stop killing our boys?

This is a tragedy of violence begetting violence, said the mayor; but already there were rumors that the police had executed him so that he couldn't testify at a trial.

That afternoon I went for a walk, down toward Green River. Everyone I encountered on the sidewalk passed me silently, but I got the feeling that almost anything could have set them off, could have incited them to scream whatever rage they were harboring, or to stand in the intersections, challenging cars. It was eerie, and all along the way I was afraid; I kept my head down and my lips pressed together. I didn't know who I was hiding from: Domino or his mother, or Sugartown or myself, but there was something wicked around me; I could feel it crawling in the air, teasing me about my powerlessness. Caroline, it said. Try whatever you want: you can't do anything to help. I turned around and hurried home.

At six that evening I changed my clothes and set out for Bonnie's house, arriving about half an hour later with a bottle of wine in one damp hand, and my legs bare and my hair put up. Her bell wasn't working; through the window in the door I could see her sitting on the couch, a few feet in front of a television set that wasn't turned on. When I knocked, she stood up quickly, smiled, and then started across the room to let me in.

It was a small, neat place, just three rooms and a tiny kitchen, with two doorways in each, so that it was almost possible to see any spot in the place from any other. I could smell a sauce cooking; she told me that it wouldn't be done for another half an hour, so we opened the wine and pulled a pair of chairs out onto the porch to watch a wind chime sway from the corner roof beam.

O.K., I went a little crazy with the food, said Bonnie. You have to promise you'll eat it all. I nodded, but I was still thinking about the day, and my eyes must have been glassy. You look like you've been arguing with Brer Rabbit, she said.

Things are starting to go strange, I said. Maybe it's just me. But did you read about that man Domino? What happened to him?

She nodded. My neighbor came by this afternoon, a black woman from down the street. She knocked on my door and she had these T-shirts with his picture on them. Already, she had them and she was selling them. I almost bought one, but I didn't. — She looked at me and then lowered her eyes, just floating and reflecting. I should have bought one, she said.

I waited a moment. . . . And then Billy, I said. This old man at Eden View? The sky had become a deep grey green, the trees were moving sluggishly in the wind, the road was still, black and wide. All sound had slowed to a mention. My shirt was sticking to the small of my back. Every time I've seen him he's gotten just a little bit crazier, but somehow he still makes perfect sense. Now the air, too, had turned thick and green; it began to breathe humidly and heavily. Crazy, crazy.

The birds had stopped singing, the dogs had hidden themselves away. The breeze responded by whistling casually, in the hope that it might trick them all into coming out into the open again, but no one was fooled. Bonnie got up and stepped inside the house for a moment; I could hear her closing windows; while she was gone, a brand-new red sports car pulled to the curb across the street and a bleached-blond teenage girl got out. Fuck that bitch, said Bonnie from the doorway. She took her seat and raised her glass in a toast—and just then the temperature dropped about twenty degrees and the hail began, its first ice white stones falling on the shoulders of the girl as she locked her car door and ran up the walkway to the opposite house.

At first the storm was a childish ambush, and then it seemed like a party joke; the sky was a box, the lid came off and the pebbles poured down, and as they fell they made a slapstick racket, rattling against the roof and pinging on the hood of Bonnie's car and the tin mailbox at the end of her walk. Leaves tore loose from the trees and drifted down onto the road; the wind blew, the hail fell, and neither Bonnie nor I said a word, not because the storm was sacred or overwhelming, or even beautiful, but just because it was so entertaining to watch that we didn't want to miss a moment.

It stopped just as quickly as it began, leaving behind a faint hissing noise as the stones started to melt. Bonnie laughed out loud and put her glass to her lips, only to find that it was empty. She went back into the house to get the bottle. When she came out again she stood in the open door and said, O.K., it's ready, and I followed her back inside.

The food was beautiful and I told her so: there were mixed greens, and homemade bread with olives, lamb with a vinegary sauce—I've never made this before, said Bonnie, so you have to tell me if it's O.K.—new potatoes, steamed asparagus. It was the kind of meal upon which the whole world might be built, and when we were done neither of us would leave the table. I'm never going to eat again, she said. Never, never. The remains of the ice cream were melting in the container.

If you were my girlfriend, I'd keep you forever, I said. She blushed and smiled. The bottle was empty.

No, but I'm a bad woman, Bonnie said.

Bad?

I am. I'm a devil-woman, I'm never right. I should be—I get away with murder. Murder. I should be in jail. I told you about Nick? The man I came down here with? I cheated on him so often, just because I could. In a car, in a bar, in the park, after dark . . . She paused. I was a Dr. Seuss slut, she said, without so much as smiling. She lifted up a spoon and stirred the bottom of her empty dessert bowl. I mean it. It didn't seem like he cared, at all, so I did it some more. At the shore, on the floor, in our bed, in my head. He should have left me long before he finally did, she said. I was about to get it on with his best friend.

That's not the worst thing I've ever heard, I said. She paused to see if I would say more, but I made a gesture to let her know it could wait. She wanted to tell, and I wanted to listen.

Because, you know what? she went on. I don't care what I did with Nick anymore. But what else. She began to twist her fingers. I've been snitching from the till at work. Not that much, maybe twenty dollars a shift; I just ring short a few drinks and slip the money into my pocket. It's so easy, I just have to. She was leaning forward and looking intently into my face. And they're nice to me there, too. I justify it—she frowned—O.K., I don't justify it, I just take it.

I nodded and put my hands in my lap. It doesn't matter. Someday when you're rich, you can pay them back, I said.

Pay it back? she replied. Never, my God. Then what would

be the point of taking it in the first place? She was gently tapping the spoon against the side of the bowl; then all at once she dropped it, stood from the table, and said, Come here, let me show you something, and she led me into her living room.

In this here is my whole life, she said, pulling out an accordion file from the end of her only bookshelf. Carefully she untied the string that held it closed and poured a small pile of papers out onto the cushion of the couch. We sat on either side and she started to go through them. So this is my birth certificate, she said. See, Belinda Moore—but Bonnie was what I was called, she explained, because my mother changed her mind right after I was born. There was her high school diploma, her Social Security card, an award certificate for coming in second in a county swim meet. The papers on her car, a check for one million dollars, made out to cash on an Illinois bank account and signed by a stranger she'd met in a bar. A twenty-year-old letter, still in its torn envelope, from her father. And there were photographs: a fat-cheeked infant grinning into the middle distance; a little girl on a little boy's bicycle; four teenage girls before a rock face in a national park; a silver sports car; a bad dress and a long-haired date for her high school prom. There was Nick, a middle-sized, dark, and complacent-looking man, sitting back in a deck chair with a beer; Nick again, the plain mystery, with no shirt on. A silver-haired woman standing by a table in a low-ceilinged dining room. That's my mom, said Bonnie. At the bottom of the pile there was a picture of her house in Sugartown, taken from the sidewalk, and one of me in a green dress, only two days old and already a part of the past. It took only a few minutes to get through the file and when she was done she put it away again with a short sigh.

You know I've been reading a lot since I've been here: until you came with your questions there wasn't much else for me to do. I started at the beginning and I read about Antigone, who was killed by her king. I read about Iphigenia, who died to appease a wind. I read about Rome and I read about Jerusalem. Women and cities, women and history, still more secret loves that remain forever unrequited.

I don't know how much more I want to hear.

No, no, you just sit tight and listen. You started this, and you might learn something from it.

It had been a tradition, founded, so the legend went, more than a century earlier by Sugartown's first settlers, to have a community picnic once a year in Bundini Park. At first they'd held it in late September, to coincide with the end of the harvest, but as the ring of real farms was pushed farther and farther out into the surrounding counties, the celebration was moved to Labor Day and came to mean that summer was over and it was time to come home.

The morning arrived; Bonnie called me as I was watching nothing out my window, I was feeling idle and restless. Are we going to go? she asked.

I want to, I said. I want to see. It's a beautiful day, I want to walk.

I'll come over, she said, O.K. But you have to give me about an hour: I decided this morning to clean up my house, so I've been sitting here going through my things, to figure out what I want to keep.

The park lay alongside Green River, a half an hour or so from my apartment. Bonnie was supposed to be by at one; I put on a torn-up pair of jeans and a wine red vest, and I was standing by my window when she called and said she'd be late. While I waited, I sat down before my open window with a glass of iced tea and leafed through the pages of a cookbook, dreaming of dishes that I would make just to have made them. Then I got up and went to the mirror, and stared at my face, my bare throat, my bare shoulders. No Helen there, but a disobedient appeal. I was pleased and impatient, and my cheeks were flushed. When the buzzer for the outside door sounded I bolted back to the couch for my purse, grabbing for it so quickly that I knocked into the table and my glass fell over, rolled off the edge, and shattered on the floor. I looked at the mess for a second, the shards glistened with wet tea—but Bonnie rang again, and I turned away and left.

She was waiting in the vestibule, wearing a blue-and-grey-striped T-shirt and a pair of grey-tinted sunglasses that made her look as if she was grieving. In one hand she held her camera, in the other her wallet. I'm sorry I took so long, she said in a cheerful voice. I found some letters that I'd put away years ago, and I had to read them.

The ground had given up mud in a rainstorm the night before, but by the time we set out the sun was shining brightly, brightly; the sky had been starched stiff and blue, and a high breeze made the tops of the trees seem to froth as their leaves shook. There was no one in town, and I could believe, for a while, that the streets and shops had all been carefully built by a committee of serious-faced little girls, who had played there until they got bored, and then abandoned it to the birds. I mentioned it to Bonnie and she said, Crows. This man once wrote me a love letter when I was fourteen, she went on. He was thirty and I was fourteen. I just giggled and hid it from my mother. Can you believe it? Thirty. I don't know what ever happened to him. I bet he's gone to jail at least once.

You found the letter? I asked.

I found it this morning, she replied. It was beautiful, too. Wasn't *I* a little vamp.

As we crossed the ridge above Green River I looked down to the park, and I could see a thousand people spread out among whirligig rides and a faded red Ferris wheel, a shooting range, a pitching machine; long tables laid with sheets of white butcher's paper; and a bandstand by the edge of the water at the far end. That was the city shining in a field, that was what I wanted. Bonnie touched my arm and said, — Mm, and she began to walk faster, her pace staggered by the slope of the road.

Inside the gate there were rows of vendors selling balloons, bright, spinning windmill toys, T-shirts, jewelry stones set in silver, music tapes, books and pamphlets. The ground was littered with wet, torn fliers, their printing coming undone under a hundred feet, reminders of another plant closing, another housing project that was coming down, a fund for Domino's family, who were bringing a lawsuit against the city. HOMES, JOBS, said one. OUT OF OUR NEIGHBORHOODS, said another. All of the men went by with secrets, things they would never tell me, and their eyes did the opposite of shine. It was strange, because it was such a beautiful day.

As soon as we crossed over the sidewalk into the park, Bonnie slowed and picked up her head, but it was a minute or two before she spoke. Something's going to happen today, she said. I just know it. I've got my skinny jeans on. —Can you hold this for me? She handed me her wallet and I put it in my bag. Thanks. All right. So let's see what this is. And without any embarrassment she took my hand in hers and led me down toward the river, and didn't let go until we stopped. . . . This Labor Day, when we can all enjoy this beautiful weather . . . said a man from the bandstand. I think that's the mayor, whispered Bonnie. There was a crowd of people gathered in front of the stage, listening while they looked around at one another and kicked gently at the ground. I want to thank you all for coming out, and especially to thank the volunteers who are going to stay and help us clean this all up. It proves that the bonds of community can overcome any troubles. Now, I know—He stopped.

Bonnie moved. Oh, shit, she said. Did you see that?

No, what? I looked down, but all I could see was a motion traveling through the people up front, taking them and pushing them to the side as it went by, like an animal passing invisibly through some underbrush.

Someone threw some water on him, a soda or something. The speaker had turned so that he faced the side of the stage; a woman in a navy blue dress had stepped out from somewhere to hand him some napkins, and together they were examining his shirtfront. What do you think he's going to do? Bonnie asked. . . . Don't know. The woman on the stage looked out over the crowd, with her hands frozen in their position. Her eyes were a pair of perfect circles, beneath which her red mouth was another, as if she was trying to make numbers out of them, and the number she needed was zero. Somewhere a church bell was ringing, spreading its condoling sound from one edge of the sky to the other. Sorry, it said. Sorry. The man brushed his shirt a few times with the napkins, stopped, and looked down. Then he turned his head up and stared out at the hills above and behind the park, listening to the empty, silent town as it tried to talk to him. All of a sudden three policemen emerged from the crowd surrounding a shirtless man in handcuffs; he was bleeding from his forehead, there was blood in his eyes, and he sweated and spat. He stumbled when they pushed him, and when he got to his feet to protest one of the policemen jabbed him in his ribs with a billy club, and he went down again. A few of the men in the crowd yelled at them as the procession went by, but the policemen closed ranks and kept walking him, stony-faced, toward their car on the edge of the green. Bonnie said, I want to watch this. But there wasn't anything to watch: the police car drove away, with its lights flashing but its siren quiet. The man on the stage turned and walked slowly off, his speech unfinished, and that was all. After a little while they started playing music over the loud-speakers, and people began to drift away. Later, a Tejano band with a girl singer took the stage, played five or six songs to almost no one, and left again.

We wandered back to the food stands, where Bonnie bought a big plastic cup of beer. The wind had stopped, the air was still and smelled of honeysuckle and the sex of trees. The sun went behind a sudden cloud, flattening the green of the ground and drawing the silk from the blue of Bonnie's shirt. Are you all right? she said.

Fine. I'm just watching. She studied my face, then put her thumb to the corner of my mouth and wiped away some lipstick that had smudged. I was embarrassed, and when she was done I put my own hand up and rubbed the spot myself. Once again I was convinced that the flaws in my demeanor would never dis-appear and never be forgiven, and I felt myself tense with an apology. It passed just as quickly, in a cool breath of I-don't-care. Here, Bonnie said, and she stepped back, raised her camera, and motioned me over to a picnic bench. She moved. . . . Here we go. And she snapped my picture as the sun came out again, so that somewhere to this day, on some slip of stuff, shiny paper, I'm still standing, smiling and squinting in Bundini Park.

A tall man with long blond hair and a drooping mustache was watching from a few yards away, and when Bonnie lowered her camera again he came up to her. He had a dirty sunburn under his untucked and unbuttoned shirt, and he was holding a plate of rice and beans; he leaned in and said something to Bon-nie that I couldn't hear, tipping his food until it almost spilled. She stepped back from him and smiled. Well, are you going to buy me a brand-new car, and keep some gas in the tank? she teased him. But he didn't think it was funny at all. Are you going to suck my dick? he answered, smiling meanly, his mouth smutty and his eyes glistening with drunk tears. I wanted to say something, I didn't know what. But Bonnie just frowned, took my arm, and walked me wordlessly toward the edge of the green.

At the jewelry tables, I bought a thin silver chain, which I lost sometime later that night. We got dinner at a barbecue stand and took it over to a picnic table; I ate and Bonnie picked at some green beans, and then stared away from her food. Oh, well, I can't eat this, she said. She got slowly to her feet, smoothed her shirt with the palms of her hands, and took her plate over to a trash barrel. Up in the sky over her shoulder a kite cut sharply down on the end of its line and suddenly met the ground, just as I stood up to join her.

Dark was starting on its way. Up on the ridge I could see a string of lights burning in the dusk along the route of a winding street. The music over the loudspeakers had become harsh; it crackled and boomed across the emptying field. A crowd was drifting slowly out of the exit at the corner of the park; they had been leaving that way for a while and the street was scattered with groups of boys, ranged down the middle of the road, oblivious to a city bus that was trying to make its way up. The driver honked, but no one paid him any mind. A few people had stopped and turned to watch the others as they wandered out through the gates.

We were standing on the corner. Where's everyone going? Bonnie said. I didn't know. Where's everyone going? she asked a woman who was sitting on the hood of a car, holding a boy child in her lap.

Downtown, I guess, the woman said.

Are you going downtown? Bonnie asked a man carrying a six-pack of empty bottles. He stared over her shoulder at a point on a front lawn about thirty feet behind her, where there was nothing at all. Excuse me? she said. Is there something happening downtown? Still silent, still standing, he reached up, took his cap off, ran his hands through his hair, and then pulled his cap down again. I don't know, he said at last. And then it was night.

Bonnie patted the pockets of her jeans. Hang on, she said. Can you get me some money out of my wallet? I want to get something to drink.

She went into a grocery store while I waited outside; and on the crowd all came, dozen by dozen. I remember feeling as if each of them were taking a piece of me as they passed, so that I was a little bit less by the time she returned, but I knew a little bit more; later I realized that that minute was the very beginning of my ceasing to be, and knowing more than I wanted to, but at the time I felt only the most elusive sense of loss, and a trembling in my legs, my nerves, vertigo. Bonnie came out of the store carrying a plastic bottle of iced tea.

On the other side of a highway bridge I saw a series of shattered shopfronts; through the remains of one plate-glass window I saw a length of heavy rusted chain lying in the wreckage of a display of women's shoes, behind which sat the shadows of an untouched store. I don't know why, but I began thinking about Roy as we walked, thinking about Roy and the rumors about him, thinking about Billy and dead Judith, about Bonnie's empty bar, about Roy and his experiences beyond my reach. It all began to make me angry. I thought rash things, a hundred in a row, and when I was done I petitioned myself for insight and courage. On. By then there was a great crowd of us in the road, and I felt as if I were getting bigger. The moon was slung ass-low and aspirin-white above the horizon. Bonnie briefly touched my arm.

As we neared the point where the street veered left and headed toward the courthouse, I could see a newsstand, a green wooden shed long since shuttered for the night; on its roof I saw four men sitting, their legs swinging nervously back and forth as they stared at the people passing below them. I heard a great noise; it seemed to draw the oxygen out of the atmosphere, and the street felt very stuffy, like the inside of a school auditorium during a dance. One of the men on the newsstand looked down at me and said, You should go on home. His voice was very soft and calm, but it had a kind of high, quavering tone that allowed it to sing through the surrounding noise.

I turned my back on him; I put my hair up. Is this it? Whatever it is, this is it, I said to myself. Around the corner the crowd had taken up the width of the street and most of the sidewalk; it gave the impression of one form, worthy of its own name, like a body of water, rising here, opening here, turning here, but always returning back to its original state. I stood up on my toes to get a better look: it went on into the horizon, diminishing into an uncountable, mottled mass.

I saw men from the factory, with hurt, angry faces; high school boys in team-colored T-shirts, their bodies thick from the playing fields; a group of black women, calling back and forth to one another in their teasing, singsong voices; bare-chested leathermen holding hands; a coalition of drunks and drug users, with flushed faces and unfocused eyes; a circle of angry whores in high heels and miniskirts; five rockers with their fists clenched; shop stewards from the Odd Fellows' local; a complete Mexican family, down to a boy of about ten, who was still clutching a balloon from the picnic; a few thieves, a few beggars; a motorcycle gang in sleeveless denim jackets, with their ladies behind them; men out of the public housing projects, whose shoulders were ball joints, whose arms were chains, and whose hands were weights; longhairs tiptoeing on cowboy boots; three small red-haired women in a row . . . Johnnys . . . boy kings . . . my best friend.

They were so pretty that I kept falling in love; my heart began to swell until it was huge and hurt me, and I wanted some way to relieve the pressure and end the pain. It took us about ten minutes to make our way through, and when we came to the front of the crowd we found a gap of about a hundred yards of empty asphalt. — Shit God! said Bonnie. On the other side I saw a dim black line of policemen holding plastic shields, another line behind them, and farthest away a row on mounts, the beautiful horses dancing back and forth and swaying their heads. All around me these people kept pushing; they made a noise like birds flocking, a whirring, a conversation conducted with wings. Someone nearby was wearing a heavy perfume and the heat had set it free; I could smell it mixing like sugar with the bitter air. There was sweat under my breasts, for a second I worried that it would show on my vest and I tugged gently at my bra.

The floodlights came on, the video cameras started rolling on the whole gaudy show. Go on home now. It echoed off the empty office buildings.

According to the reports, all that anyone would admit to seeing was the arm that threw the bottle. It belonged to a young boy, and it was pale, bare, and brave; it waved, and the bottle—it was blue—rose up in a wide pillowy curve across the face of an office building . . . and for some time, maybe five minutes, it simply stayed there, posted against the concrete like a glassy memo pinned up on the night. . . .

It vanished in the darkness and a moment later shattered; off in the distance the dark line of policemen broke for a moment, and then healed, bigger than it was before. At once there were scores of people behind me, and still more ranged along my right; every few seconds another man would bolt out into the empty road, throw a bottle, crouch on the asphalt for a moment to watch it fly, and then dash back into the crowd again; a string of fireworks exploded in the middle of the street, twenty yards from anyone, and a policewoman raised her hand and pointed up to a rooftop where a teenage boy was standing against the night; two more policemen ducked into the doorway of the building and pulled at the door, but it was locked and they were taunted.

A fountain of hot white sparks had begun in my chest, and there was nothing left of my heart. The only sound my throat could make was the letter *g*. A storefront window broke, but I was looking down, and what I saw was an assembly of anonymous legs, torn shoes, and a single green beer bottle standing miraculously untouched and upright amidst it all. I turned to show it to Bonnie, but before I could say a word, Leviathan raised her fluked tail high out of the water, paused for a moment, and brought it down with all the vengeance in her enormous, chambered heart.

I would have expected the sound to change as the motion did, but instead my faculties shifted and split, heading gradually off into different directions; there was no variation in the noise: still the cheering, still the loud treble of a police megaphone giving instruction—I couldn't hear a word—still a steady shattering rain of bottles falling, but the crowd was breaking up and moving from below, and Bonnie and I began to slide helplessly down toward the turn in the road where there had once been a line of policemen and now were only a half dozen or so. The rest of them were among us: horses, horses, lights and billy clubs, and in the sky above, a huge repeating noise, the air was shearing. A few feet away from me there was a brawny, round-faced man bending over an open canvas bag with a few baseball bats protruding from it. He looked right up at me, grinned like a big jack-o'-lantern, and held one out. Game day, he said. Come on, miss, get one of these. You might need it.

Take it. Go on, whispered Bonnie in my ear, and I took it from him and held it in my hand, weighing it for a moment. Wait, she said, and she hurriedly brought her camera up and took my picture. Down the block I could see the top of a street lamp swaying gracefully back and forth, its bulb burning faithfully at the upper notch of its delicate arc; there was no one near it, it just waved from up above. We came to a car, there was a man inside staring through the windshield, as stiff and expressionless as a minor character in a Roman statue. So ride: who drafted you into this? The car rocked from side to side as two men, a woman, and a boy climbed onto the hood; they were going up and over, but before they could scramble off the other side, the wheels jumped forward a foot or two: the crowd split apart: the car vanished: I found myself in an empty circle, bisected by the ridge of the curb, which had long since ceased to mean anything. I reached out for Bonnie's hand, but she wasn't there; in a panic, I turned around and around, holding the bat on my shoulder and trying to spot her in the crowd; she was gone; I turned again, and at last I saw her, buried in a roiling mass of bodies, looking at me with her hands up at her sides in a gesture of surrender, her eyes widened to white circles as she was carried away, laughing at the look on my face. She reached down and a moment later the flash on her camera exploded in a burst of perfectly white illuminating mist, like some practical joke that light felt like playing; all it said was, Got you! and when it was gone, she had disappeared.

A gang of silent boys ran past me, followed by a woman pushing an empty blue-and-white baby stroller before her. Bonnie come back. I saw two policemen holding a man down in the gutter. His shirt was pulled up to his shoulders and one of his legs was bent; for a moment I thought that he was actually lying gently recumbent on the ground, while they tried to get him up—he was lounging, waiting, smoking a cigarette; it seemed to be giving off enormous soft clouds of lazy smoke, which slowly drifted sideways across the street. They started hitting him with their clubs, but still he didn't move at all, and they were getting very frustrated by it. Bonnie come back. Someone pushed me forward and I almost fell. —Hey! Hey! Now the policemen had the reclining man in handcuffs, and one of them was holding him in place with a foot pressed hard against the back of his neck, while the other was kicking him, the kicking cop with his florid face and belt full of instruments and straps waving and jingling. Very merry and mean, as the toe of his boot sank into the man's side. I was right next to them, then, a young woman standing by with a piece of boy's equipment propped up pointlessly beside her. A smear of black blood appeared on the man's chin. I thought it was all absolutely unfair: they must have been so lost to break his body like that.

And all at once I saw a sense sewn into the scene around me, like the humble saying on a sampler. Unsex yourself and mend the night, it said. Give mercy only to those who have given mercy, give friendship to our friends, give destruction to the violent. I read it once more to be sure, and then I took the baseball bat in both my hands, raised it awkwardly to my shoulder, and fixed my eyes on the back of the kicking cop's head. I was a star.

I was in a movie: I could see myself aiming for an orb that appeared from a great height, enlarging in one extended swift motion that stretched painfully; see myself, but I was someone else, watching something fall a long way; and when the fat end of the wood struck against the base of the policeman's skull it made a sharp, hollow sound, like a cardboard tube hitting the side of a kitchen counter. I wondered for a second if the bat was a toy, because it couldn't have been the officer's head that made that sound. Anyway, he had disappeared. In one sweet move I had skipped sideways about a hundred feet, the movie was over and my hands were empty. One last time I looked around for Bonnie, but she wasn't there, I was facing away down the street, and in the confusion that followed, so different from the confusion that had preceded, I began to glow painfully with the light of a thousand candles, and I ran, with the noise diminishing behind me, until all I could hear was the sound of my own hurt breath.

I was proud, the moon was my mentor, but I was frightened and freighted with the weight of what I'd done. By the time I stopped running I had reached the south end of town, it was close to midnight, and my insides had dissolved. I was so exhausted that I saw glittering strips of tinsel hanging from the trees as I passed, and ghostly dogs in the bushes, and trying not to see them took all my thinking. But I was afraid to go home; there would be men in black windbreakers sitting on the edge of my bed, standing quietly in the closet, crouching on the fire escape, waiting patiently for me to open the door. Are you Caroline Harrison? they would ask as they came toward me, their hands reaching for their pockets. You are *so* stupid. Will you come with us? We've already taken everything you're ever going to have. So I walked until I reached the interstate, and there I sat at the edge of a field and watched the stars spin hellishly in the moonless sky, and glowing satellites, and the gliding lights of an airplane.

I don't know if I slept, but if I did I dreamed of the heavens at night, and woke on a dark planet that envied its own sky. By the time I was ready to start back into town it was about five in the morning and the city was taking on its first pale tones. There were forms in the air; a plenum. I was standing still, while around me time built Sugartown out of ancient shades. An age passed and the first few roads appeared, then a neighborhood gradually materialized out of the gloom, with fences and houses, stores, a bus stop, each element forming, wavering, fading, and finally settling into place. In time parked cars appeared at the curbs, a stoplight, and at last a brightly lit diner rose up out of absolutely nowhere and announced the day by saying OPEN. I decided to stop in for a cup of coffee, I crossed some line, and when I pushed at the door, the forward wave of time broke. I heard a soft rush of receding wash in my ears, but otherwise it was still.

The woman at the register inside watched me carefully as the door closed behind me. You shouldn't be out at this hour, dear, she said as I passed. Don't you know what's happening? They've all gone crazy, all the blacks, and the trash with them. I just don't understand how they can do those things. Animals wouldn't do those things. Isn't that so? I floated past her into the dining room, like Mary Magdalene passing the biggest bitch in the Bible. They should all be locked up, she went on. If they wanted to work, they could work, just like me and my husband do, instead of dealing drugs and what all. — Sit down anywhere you like, she called to my back. The place was empty.

I took a booth at the end of the room and picked up the menu as the cook opened the swinging door to the kitchen and hung his head out. I could see his thick arm at his side, his fist wrapped around a butcher knife. Outside, an old felt green station wagon went slowly by, with a man alone in the front seat. Otherwise there was a grey street, a little wind. I ordered a cup of coffee, drank it quickly, and left.

It took me about half an hour to walk to Eden View, and along the way I practiced lying about the night before. I was home all night, I said under my breath, I was watching television alone, I wrote a postcard to a friend, I was asleep before the moon went down. It was past seven when I reached the front door;

through the glass I could see an orange-haired nurse sitting behind the main desk, drinking coffee from a blue mug and reading something on the desk in front of her. When I came in she looked up and said, You're not here this morning, are you?

I said, No. But I think I left my address book in the nurses' lounge. Without so much as a nod, she turned back to the papers on her desk; I hesitated and then walked past her and up the emergency stairs. Billy's floor was dim, and I could hear my own footsteps echoing in the hall. Outside his room I watched him through the window, lying face up on his bed like some plucked and presented fruit, with his eyes open as always, though there was nothing for him to see but the ceiling. I called to him. Billy. He didn't hear me; he was listening to the sound of his blood slowing, and the rustling of his sleeping nerves. I knocked sharply on the glass—and he started, looked up at the wall across the room, felt the bedcovers with his hands. Who's that? he said loudly. Billy, I whispered, and he jerked his head around and stared at the door. I'm sorry, it's Caroline.

What? He reached over to his night table, his fingertips trembling as he felt for the switch on his lamp.

Don't turn on the light, I said. Someone will see.

Who is that?

It's me. Billy. It's Caroline. Can I come in?

Is that Caroline?

It's me.

What time is it?

It's very late, I said. It's early in the morning. Out his window the branches of a tree were moving subtly in the dawn breeze; in the far distance I could hear the occasional low humming of a truck passing on the freeway; up above Eden View the stars were fading. Let me in, I insisted. Slowly, still half-asleep, he swung his legs off the bed, stood, and came toward me without stopping to dress, but he turned back for a moment to pull the covers up, and when he did I saw a brief flash of his griseous ass shining in the dawn light. Again he made his way across the floor until he was standing on the other side of the door, his flesh as opalescent as the skin of a fish, his dark member hidden in the shadow of his body.

Who is that? He tensed his expression while he prepared to weigh every good thing and bad thing. Caroline? He opened the door and I stepped in.

Billy, I whispered; I was so excited that my breath trembled.

Yes, my love?

There was a big fight after the picnic last night. Everybody went downtown and there was a kind of riot. Did you hear anything? There was a riot, I was there and I saw everything. All the people. Listen to me, I hit a policeman with a baseball bat. I think I broke his head right open, and I'm going to have to leave town.

He sighed and tsked. What can I do?

I don't know, don't be mad.

Mad? He smiled a little, and I could see the full black veins throbbing thickly beneath the skin of his throat. Oh, no. Oh, no. Why should I be mad? Just tell me what it was like, he said. No, wait a moment. Come in here, inside, all the way. I stood a few feet farther into his room, and he ambled back and sat on the side of his bed, the mattress barely bending under his weight. Go on. What was it like? He began to swing his bare dangling legs, like a child excited to distraction.

Oh, I said. It—

Never mind, he interrupted me with a smile and scratched his skinny old chest. I know what it was like. He looked over to the window. What day is today?

The day after Labor Day, I said. I think I'm going to have to leave here.

Yes, you are, he said. Where are you going?

I don't know. But I wanted to come and see you before I went.

Hm, he grunted quietly. Just wait. He began to nod slowly, as if he was counting off an argument inside. . . .

Almost a minute passed that way, and I had just resolved to make my good-bye when suddenly he brightened. You're going to New York City, he said. Of course you are, you've got some business there. And I'm going to give you something, and you're going to carry it to someone upstate for me. Wait, wait, wait. It's in my closet. He rose from the edge of his bed and padded naked across the room. Light! Light! he said into the open door of his dark closet, one white hand grasping at the black air; when he brought it down again light burst from above the door, falling down past his shoulders and illuminating a tiny space crammed with clothes and boxes. Wait a second. . . . A hardcover book fell from an overhead shelf and hit his shoulder; he cursed and dug around some more. Here we go, he said at last, and he turned back into the room, holding something in his hands. It was a plain white shoe box, and he carried it carefully over to his dresser and placed it on the surface. From the top drawer he produced the stub of a pencil; he licked the end and began to write carefully on the lid, his head bent as his hands scratched away. Then he taped the whole thing shut and handed it to me. It was heavy, I shook it, but nothing moved inside. Yes, there we go, he said. I'm going to send you to him.

I stood unmoving by his bed. Send me to who? I asked, but still I held the shoe box.

O.K., he said. No. Do this for me. And all your problems will be solved. He stopped and looked over at me as if he was going to secure the reign of madness in the countryside with my help. You don't look inside; if you do, they'll know. You just guard it carefully and take it to that address. Give it to whoever you find there. It's the most important thing in the world, and there'll be a prize waiting for you at the other end. He smiled shapelessly, took hold of my arm, and guided me to the door, where he fixed me with his hanging eyes. Do it, or I'm going to get you. So there's a good girl.

What is it? I asked. He hadn't convinced me yet, and I wanted to hear him talk some more.

Just a present, just some things, he said. Ha! Just some things from me. Now you go on. Good-bye, said Billy. That's all.

With that he crossed the room and climbed back into his bed, leaving me for the last time. It was midmorning, and I was sinking to the bottom of a swimming pool, while above me on the daylit deck the figures of the already-saved shimmered and stared, as they waited patiently for me either to surface or die. I didn't know if Billy's shoe box was a float or a stone, but I held on to it tightly.

It wasn't until I'd reached a streetlight a few blocks from Eden View that I stopped to read the address. He'd pressed the pencil so forcefully that the surface was smeared with graphite; there was no addressee, and I didn't recognize the name of the town. I tucked the thing under my arm and began walking again.

I'd intended to follow the long route home, away from Green River, away from the center of town, but I took a wrong turn between a bank and a high-rise, where the streets had unexpected elbows and the buildings blocked the view, and when I emerged from an alley I found myself facing the block I'd been on the night before, but from the side that had been occupied by the police. I stared down the street, with its shattered glass and charred smell. Show over, stage empty.

The night had ended in looting. Down the side of storefronts I could see broken windows, trash barrels lying on their sides, a parking meter that had been pulled from its posthole and thrown through the windshield of a car, where it lay with its unconscious head on the front seat. I saw dozens of brightly colored boxes in the gutter, the tattered empty shells of toys and appliances that had been ripped from their packaging. At my feet I saw an open bag of soda crackers, its contents forming a grey paste on the ground. There were no lights up along the heights of the buildings. A policeman appeared at my side.

This street is closed, miss, he said. He was an older man, bald beneath his blue cap, his weight weighed even further down by the tools on his leather belt—a pad, a radio, a black leather sap, his gun.

Oh, I'm sorry, I said politely. What's going on?

There was a disturbance here last night. You've got to go around.

What happened? I shifted Billy's shoe box to my other hand.

He looked at me carefully. Never mind, he said. Read the paper.

How can I get to Old Station?

You've got to take this street here—he gestured left—till you get to River Road, take that down just about a mile and you can cut back in. You shouldn't be out anyway. Where are you coming from? He reached for a black leather-bound pad of paper and began to remove the pen that was clipped to its side.

Work. Eden View, I said. I work the night shift at an old-age home on the east side. I'm very tired.

You better get home, he said. Take another route. He rocked back on his heels, and then he reached out his hand and took hold of my upper arm. Right down that way.

I'm going, I said, and walked away in the direction he had pointed out, and didn't look back.

The sun was shining, the day was hot, a sluggish breeze was westering over the town. There were policemen stationed at every other corner along the way; under the doorway eaves of a corner grocery, a pair stood holding cups of coffee. They glanced at me briefly from beneath their blue caps, and I pretended not to notice.

As I came up to the top of the ridge between downtown and Green River I smelled burning wood, and for a moment I thought, How nice. Then I looked down and saw the broken roofs; they were casting up fat gobbets of black smoke, and there was a pale grey nauseous pall of exhaled ash in the air, while here and there great flames flickered within the gloom. They were all burning down, the houses, slowly it seemed, and with stately confidence and evil cheer. There they go: photographs, clothes hung in closets, beds with their familiar sheets, attics full of old toys, slowly pulling away from this life and vanishing, through a hole in physical law, into emptiness.

Sugartown Sugartown Sugartown Sugartown. Years ago some families had come and settled the place, full families; they thought the river was as beautiful as they were themselves. It was a wonder, there had never been any music to equal it, and they established themselves in the palm of the land as it sloped down to the water. It wasn't anywhere at all, then, so they invented the place whole over the course of time. They didn't know what it would be when they were done, but they went on anyway, raising roofs and cooking meals, rolling in bed on Sunday morning. It wasn't so much work that they wanted as a new way of reckoning time, but time had come up so quickly behind them that it snatched away their senses. They were burning their own things, in a last act of ecstatic self-violence. Don't tell me it wasn't shocking.

It was still early when I arrived at Four Roses, and the lobby was still empty and quiet. Still scared, still moved, I pressed the bell to my own apartment and waited for someone else's voice, but there was no sound from the speaker. Down the street an empty train rattled by on empty tracks. The elevator was waiting for me in the front hall.

I hesitated outside my room and listened for the rustling of guns being drawn or the hiss of a waiting gas canister; I must have stood there for ten minutes or more. The door was being deliberately dumb; my room was faintly calling. So I slipped the key in the lock and slowly turned the knob, my mouth open, my hands shaking, my hips twisted so that I could run if I needed to. But when the door swung open there was no movement inside, and when I softly said hello no one answered. I crept in and shut the door behind me, and quickly crossed the room to my window so that I could check the fire escape. There was no one there, I checked it again, and then I pulled the shades, put Billy's box on my dresser, and sat on my bed. The glass that had broken the day before was still lying in dull tea-colored fragments on the floor; it wasn't me who had dropped it, it was some other girl, who wasn't in trouble, but I didn't have the energy to envy her. I felt dirty, but more tired than dirty, so I stripped and slid under the sheets, and though I thought I might never be able to fall asleep again, I slept.

I awoke past noon, dry-mouthed and dream-weary; I'd had a nightmare in which I was meeting Bonnie's relatives for the first time, and it was important that I make a good impression, but every time I tried to talk I ended up saying something obscene, and they kept turning away. There was a memory on my lips. What was it? . . . I still had her wallet, it was in my bag. I showered and dressed in a hurry and called her house with my hair still wet, but the line just rang until her answering machine picked up. Bonnie? I said when the tone went off. Hello? I hesitated, and then I hung up.

On the street outside a van was pulled over and a man was

standing by the back, filling a sidewalk vending machine with bundles of newspapers. When he was gone I went over and bought one. The headline read RAMPAGE DOWNTOWN and the story covered the front page and two pages inside, but there was no explanation in any of it. There were numbers: the size of the crowd, the squads of policemen, the property damage, the arrested, the area hospitals, the square blocks. There was a map, and a photograph of four men running up a side street. But who knew what anyone was thinking at the time?

For the entire length of the bus ride to Bonnie's house, I was the sole passenger. The driver pulled up to every stop, but there was never anyone waiting, and soon even he vanished from behind the wheel, until there was only me, sitting forward in my seat, watching out the window as the dead-calm town turned by. In time I reached the corner of her block, I stepped down to the street, and the bus rode noisily away. I ran to her front door.

Breathless, I rang her bell, but it was still broken; I knocked on her window and got no answer, so I went around to the back, stopping along the way to peek into the kitchen through the curtains. The room was vacant and perfectly clean, every dish put away, a blue glass vase of flowers on the table, a pair of photographs taped to the refrigerator door. I knew that she left a key underneath a brick that bordered her back garden, and while I went looking for it I wondered where she was and what she was doing. She had just gone out for a moment . . . she had met someone . . . she was in jail, I would go down and bail her out. The brick was a brick, and hadn't moved; underneath it lay the key, browned brass in the brown dirt. When I got the door open I heard the phone ringing, and for a moment I thought it was me, still calling from the phone booth. It wasn't me: it rang four times and then the answering machine went off; but whoever had called was willing to wait a little longer, and there was no message.

Still the bell left the whole room faintly, silently vibrating.

I shut the door behind me and stood just inside, feeling the furniture and the things on her table quivering expectantly in the soundless dimensions of her living room. Home, but the wrong mistress had entered. I walked across the room without touching anything and sat down on the couch; I could smell smoke in the air, dragging back the minutes. I waited, and I waited, and I waited.

The burning went on all that day; I watched it on Bonnie's television, drinking her wine from a water glass and listening as the reporters read their strange poetry. The firemen couldn't keep up, the flames were spreading up out of Green River, jumping from block to block, over alleyways and across streets, until they reached the edge of the neighborhood and began to threaten the houses on the hill.

There was a reporter standing on a sidewalk; on the street behind her a rooming house was in flames, shedding chunks of kindling that fell to the front lawn. Then we were all in a helicopter, riding in a diagonal over Green River. The city below looked flat and modeled, and the smoke rose above the tree line, as if it were trying to catch the attention of God. I saw men standing on the roofs of their houses, watering them with garden hoses. A kennel had gone down and then up in a spray of sparks and flaring; the animals were screaming as they burned in their cages, and everyone was crying. Boys with handguns were shooting out the streetlights that lined Bundini Park, waiting for the sun to go down in darkness. The avenues were strewn with debris from overturned trash cans, things pulled from burning houses, goods from looted stores. Everywhere people were standing wherever they wanted to, just off the curb in the road, on bare lawns, behind parked cars. A man appeared and said something about the dead and injured, three dead, four dead, eighteen injured. Stop it, I said to the television. Just stop it.

But he went on: This is just . . . he said, and paused to listen to a voice that only he could hear. O.K., he said. This is just in. We have one police officer. . . . We're told now that Sergeant Jack Frank is in the hospital with a head injury that he received in the midst of last night's violence. They put up a photograph: it was him, just a man, but his ebbing from the world was my flowing into it, and he was glaring at me as he said good-bye. Right away everything went fake. —Police are asking anyone with information about the assault on Officer Frank to call the City South Precinct, said the man on the television. I raised my hand up to hide my features for a moment; my hand was small and it looked like it was made out of plastic. I was dizzy, and I got up from the couch, ran to the bathroom, and splashed water on my pale face. The figure in the glass was the only thing in the universe that was me, and I was suddenly overcome with a loneliness so draining that my knees almost gave way. Who loved me? Who would take me in? In the next room the television was still talking. Talk talk talk, and they were never going to stop. I knew I was guilty, but I didn't think I'd done wrong. Besides, they had my tears already. Did they really want my blood, too? O.K., I said out loud. You just keep talking.

In a bag by the side of the sink I found a mess of Bonnie's makeup, and I borrowed some of it and hurriedly painted my face, reading the name of each unfamiliar color from the bottom of each container before I applied it. When I was done a more confident countenance had appeared, clear-eyed, smooth skinned, defined and transformed. They were just colors from a little glass jar, but I stood there for a very long time and studied the uncanny likening effect of her palette on my expression— because I was staring, at last, at Bonnie and me, and I felt much better.

And still the man on the television wasn't done; on and on and on he went. I couldn't imagine where he'd found the energy to keep going with such bland intensity, when I was hardly strong enough to listen to him, but he was lost in a ritual; the words wormed and wobbled up and down, lay flat and then stood like waves.

The police have just reported another civilian casualty, this time unidentified. The victim is a woman in her mid-twenties, five feet five inches tall, with medium-length blond hair. She was wearing blue jeans and a blue-and-grey-striped T-shirt. According to reports, she was crushed to death when a scaffolding collapsed under the weight of the rioters. Anyone who might be able to identify her is asked to call or stop by the medical examiner's office at Redburn County General.

Before he was finished I felt a black bullet shiver up vertically through my body, it came out my mouth as the words, Oh Bonnie. The television was blank. I was standing up, I was standing out in her backyard, staring up through the boughs of her post oak. Her house was an empty shell, there was no one home. I went inside again and stood in the door frame of her kitchen: I went to the telephone and picked up the receiver, but there was no one to call. The clock on her stove said two.

Someone wants to know how patient I am, I said to myself. This is a test. So if I wait long enough, without conceding that she's dead, then she won't be dead. I thought I should have something to drink, and I went to her refrigerator and took out a pitcher of iced tea, but my hands shook so badly that I had to put it down on the table. I thought it was a bad sign, so I went into the living room, where I stood in the center of the floor and looked around me, trying to find something to think about. I sat on the edge of her couch and immediately rose again; but the things in the room were already beginning to settle, taking on a composure that suggested they'd never be touched again. There was a tape in her stereo and I pushed the play button, but it was already at the end and it clicked itself off again immediately. That was too much for me, so I walked into her bedroom.

Enclosed within her walls there was an entire life, wanting only one spark of animation to put it into play; instead, I thought, all the warm work she'd done to create herself was going to be lost. Back in the living room I found my bag; in the bottom was her wallet, and inside that I found her driver's license: Bonnie Moore, it said, and she was five foot five. She looked like nothing, she looked like me with her makeup on. I threw the thing on her bed and turned, and found myself face-to-face with my own reflection in the mirror on the door of her closet. I could tell by my expression that I'd given up. I'd acknowledged that she was gone, so she was gone, and I craved her presence so that I could tell her how much I missed her.

At four-thirty I took her wallet and drove her car down to the hospital. I kept my eyes on the road the entire way: each white dash on the blacktop shot a bolt of electricity up through my arms as I watched it pass under the car, but I knew that if I raised my eyes I would see terrible things. Bonnie Bonnie Bonnie, I said to myself. Bonnie Bonnie Bonnie. Sweat ran into my eyes and streamed out again, tears on my cheeks, salt on my lips. Bonnie Bonnie Bonnie, I wanted to say her name as often as I could, to prove and keep proving that it was real.

I wondered what would have happened if I hadn't lost her the night before; she would have been with me at that moment, watching the television wide-eyed while the city we lived in shook itself to pieces, instead of dead, impossible and alone in the bottom of a hospital. I wanted to go back in time, but the car kept going forward. I hoped she didn't hurt; I wondered if she hated me. Had I felt differently, I might have seen more when I walked into the hospital, but all I saw was a bedlam. I might have been more self-possessed, but when I went to the reception desk all I could think to say was, I'm here for the dead woman.

The clerk made a phone call, and soon there was a policewoman. I said, My friend is missing.

You were with her last night? asked the policewoman, taking a pad of paper from her belt.

I was with her in the afternoon, until dinner, I replied. Then I left. Immediately I felt as if I'd betrayed Bonnie by abandoning her in a lie, and I hesitated. I'm sorry, I said under my breath.

The policewoman thought I was apologizing for my grief. Take your time, she said.

I left early. She hasn't been home since.

The policewoman nodded and wrote down what I said. Then she led me to an elevator; the elevator went down. At the bottom there was a coroner, who took me by the arm and led me into a brightly lit office. You're a relative of the deceased? he asked as we stood by a desk covered with stacks of manila folders.

I shook my head.

He studied me for a moment. What's your relationship?

Best friend, I said, but I didn't know if that was close enough. Were they going to send me away? I should have said I was her sister.

O.K. Do you think you can do this? the coroner asked. I was dazed, I nodded, and he put his hand on my shoulder and guided me down the hall.

He took me into a small, shabby room in the basement of the building, where they'd set up a few chairs, a table, and a stand with a television set on it. The coroner turned on the television and a black-and-white image opened on the screen, wavered, and then stabilized so I could see.

She was lying on her back with her arms at her sides. She looked very pale and indifferent, and I could tell by what little remained of her expression that dying had disappointed her. I watched her for a while: nothing changed; the vessel lay broken. I could have watched it forever, it was the most interesting thing I had ever seen, I didn't want to leave. At last the coroner said, Do you recognize her?

Yes, I said.

He said, Can you tell me her name?

For a second I just stared. Through the window I could see the policewoman waiting in the hallway outside. I turned back to the television monitor and saw Bonnie, still lying on her back, with her eyes closed. How cold was she now? I was holding her wallet in one hand and my own purse in the other. What was she thinking? She was dreaming she was me. — And all at once I conceived how to save her, and save myself: the inspiration struck so suddenly that I almost laughed out loud, it was really the strangest moment of my life: I saw all at once that my life was over and I gasped like a newborn, I gaped at the bright world, all made up of first causes. The coroner didn't notice; he bent his head devoutly and murmured something comforting.

I don't know where I found the words. Her name is Caroline Harrison, I said, and without pausing I handed the coroner my purse. This is hers.

He flinched slightly, and when he took it he held it out a foot or so from his body, as if he was afraid it was going to jump at him. Do you know where we can get hold of her next of kin?

She doesn't have any, I said. I'm it.

Then they led me out of the room again. The policewoman disappeared down the hall, and the doctor took me aside to confide in me. I'm sorry, he whispered. The police would like to talk to you some more. When I hesitated he said, Not right now, of course, but as soon as possible. He held out a card. They'd like you to call that number, tomorrow would be fine.

At the front desk an administrator handed me some forms to sign, and I signed them all Bonnie Moore. Someone else handed me back a plastic bag that held a few dollars, some change, and a lipstick. That's all there was, and they let me go. I stopped on my way to the door, turned back to face them with a pained expression. . . . They gave me the name of a funeral home, they had it waiting for me, and I called from a pay phone on the street to make the arrangements.

For two days I sat in her apartment, hardly moving and unwilling to believe anything. The telephone never rang; I wouldn't have answered it if it had. I didn't eat, and I slept on the couch with a throw for a blanket. Her mail collected in her mailbox. Throughout I spent my time trying to figure out what had gone wrong, but the chain of argument that I made dangled down and disappeared into a dark well. A city I loved had murdered a woman I loved, and I knew I was going to have to leave. I had to leave, but it didn't matter where I went; sooner or later, the Policeman was going to die, and when he died, his ghost was going to find me by seeking out my shaking, and wring my neck. Wring my neck, because I was the worst woman in the world. I was the worst woman in the world, but I was lucky. Lucky to have a double like Bonnie, just another small blonde; I was lucky that the picture on my driver's license was a few years old and not very good, the image was blurry and overexposed; I was lucky that I was wearing her makeup and colored like her; I was lucky that she was damaged just beyond whatever being a photograph could capture. I was lucky, but I was never going to be innocent, and I cried.

On the second night, moonless, starless, humid, and still, I began to disappear. I snuck into my own apartment and looked over what I had one last time. I opened my drawers and I went through my closets, but as I pulled out the things I owned, I realized that I wasn't going to be able to take any of it with me: I wanted them to be able to strip-search me and find nothing that said Caroline. I stood in the doorway and I said good-bye, to my bath towels and my unpaid bills, my cassette tapes and my near-empty address book. I just left it all behind: when I closed the door behind me I had nothing in my hands but a pair of shoes and Billy's box, which I carried all the way back to Bonnie's.

On the third day I drove her car down to an innocent-looking funeral home, a converted wooden house within a row of circumspect law offices and doctors in private practice. In the heat of the day the neighborhood was coming undone, each bond wetting and loosening. The lobby was cool and carpeted, and smelled of lilac and must. I signed a form and collected a canister, and simply walked out the door, cradling the container in the crook of my arm as if it were an infant. Her ashes sat in the front seat beside me; later, they sat on the counter by her refrigerator like some leftover offering to the god of house-keeping.

The sun rose the next morning and I started going through her apartment, looking for things I would want to keep: her album with her birth certificate and photographs, a few pieces of jewelry, all the papers from her desk drawer, her wallet and its cards. I packed a suitcase with her clothes, and took a small tulip-shaped bottle that held her best perfume, and her yellow-smelling soap.

By early afternoon I had finished. The sun was at its highest point; there were no shadows; the house was trapped in a cell of burning bright light. I went through each room one more time, just to be sure, and in Bonnie's bedroom I got down on my hands and knees and peered under her bed. In the dark there, pushed back against the wall, I found a file box, and I pulled it out and opened the top; it was filled almost to the brim with photographs. Oh, God, hello, I said, and turned quickly to be sure no one was watching at the window. No, but Bonnie's ghost was there; I couldn't tell whether she approved. Is this all right? I asked. There was no answer, so I started looking.

Of the pictures in the box, I knew why she had hidden some; some might just as well have been in her album; and I couldn't understand why she had saved some of them at all. There were snapshots of family and friends, schoolmates, old lovers, neighbors, coworkers. There were pictures of house fronts and yards, empty rooms, unmade beds, dinner tables piled high with food, of traffic on highways, of cities seen from a distance, rows of flowers, an airplane on a tarmac, the hallway of a hotel, a row of tollbooths at the end of a bridge. I saw lines of cocaine lying in a nest of aluminum foil, rusted cutlery, full ashtrays, clothes strewn on the floor, windows streaked with dirt. I saw a pair of tomatoes ripening on a sunny windowsill, a match burning in a man's fingers in an otherwise twilit bedroom, a floor of white linoleum flecked with brown and gold, a row of poplar trees made blurry by an unsteady hand. There were several dozen photographs of Nick; in many he was naked, in some he was smiling, in one he was hard; and at least as many of Bonnie herself, from every year of her life, with as many of her expressions as a camera could capture. In a manila envelope there was a portfolio of pornographic pictures, Bonnie posed spread-legged on a rug, or seen from behind as she crouched on her hands and knees; and one subportfolio in which her wrists and ankles were tied to the posts of a brass four-poster bed. In each of them I thought she was beautiful, and I wished I'd known about them, I wished she were there beside me: we had so much more to talk about. There was one picture of me, taken from behind while I sat on her porch and waited, against a background of green air, for the hail to come down.

So far as I could tell, she'd saved every photograph she had ever taken, and stored them all beneath the bed she slept in, so that nothing she'd seen would ever be forgotten. When I had finished going through them, the floor around my legs was scattered with pictures, and for a while I just sat there, sifting them through my hands and watching as one or another came up—a moment of polygonal light, another, another, an encyclopedia, an archive, never to be opened again. They were all strange and esoteric, and so specific that they might as well have smelled like her; they meant only and exactly what they meant to her; they were the turnout of her fullness, and I did the very best I could to memorize them. I tried to imagine that they were mine: my homes and rooms, my boyfriends, my own body stranded naked on a rumpled bed. I stared and I became lost in an eerie delirium of vision, a border fantasy, my being Bonnie. . . . After a while I began to believe that I could hear her voice; she was right by me, but her words were indistinct, bright music, a joke. For an instant we became identical; we separated, wavered, we were the same again, raised together on a spume of transparent time.

The period burst and she was gone. I waited and waited, trying desperately to beckon her back; she was hanging just beyond my reach, but there was no return. I could hear the faint tick tick of the alarm clock on her night table, and the twittering of my nerves. In time my thighs began to ache from sitting cross-legged on the floor. Out her window the sun suddenly darkened and then became splendid again as a small occluding cloud passed before it, and in that brief moment of shadow the summer ended and autumn began. At last I got to my feet, heartbroken and hollow, and stumbled into the kitchen carrying the box; and there I began to burn the pictures in the bottom of the sink. All that history, all that time, gone to smoke in a slaughter. It took an hour to get through them all, and when I was finished the ceiling overhead was black with soot, and I wondered why my hands weren't bloody. I washed the ashes down the drain, packed her car with the things I wanted to keep, took one last look at the house, and left.

Billy was right: I was going to carry his box to New York. The sun was halfway down, its pale yellow rays reflecting off of the water and then losing themselves in the soft scrim of dust and smoke that hung down from the sky. I was having trouble breathing, the air was like a sodden weight in my lungs; it would come in, but it lingered like deadweight before it left again. Before I got onto the highway I stopped at the bottom of Bundini Park; I left the engine running and I ran over to a flower bed, where I secretly buried the white cinders of Bonnie's remains. Over her grave I said, The Lord is my shepherd, I shall not want. Forgive us our trespasses, deliver us from evil, world without end. Amen.

I got back in the car and found the on-ramp for the interstate, but in a second I couldn't see for water-blindness; I turned on the windshield wipers just as I passed the city limits, but the rain was falling up from the floorboards. Still, I knew that in a few hours the place would be entirely behind me, and while it might take forever before it had dwindled down to nothing, I could already feel it contracting, very quietly, as it watched me leave—suffer, climb, and burn, you perfect city on the edge of the river.

New York

What were you thinking about as you left town?

WELL, I WASN'T THINKING, I COULDN'T THINK. AND IT WASN'T much like leaving at all, it was like being shot out of a cannon: the wind made me blind and the noise in my ears was the voice of a disappointed God. I waited to land in the desert somewhere, with nothing but my first name and a rag to wrap myself in. I would walk until I was old, and my hair was thin and my breasts were shriveled; I would lie to everyone I met, and run from whatever I saw in the sky; I would beg for water and eat with my hands. The Policeman's people would be looking for me; they were going to put me in prison forever, where I'd be forgotten. All I'd be able to see from behind the bars on my window would be a small corner of the sky, even as the world ended on the ground.

Billy's package was in the backseat of the car, and from time to time I'd be so overcome by the need to see what was in it that I'd want to pull the car over to the shoulder and open it up; and more than once I considered throwing it out of the window. But I needed something to carry while I went, or I would have become a cloud. I was carrying Billy's shoe box, whatever it held—his gun, a pound of morphine, a human heart—and I was carrying a set of questions for Roy. All I wanted was to get both of them delivered before I was caught.

In the meantime I had Bonnie to cover me. Her car obeyed

my hands; her purse sat on the seat beside me. Everything I wore and everything I touched was hers. I had her perfume on my neck and the inside of my wrists, I had her gel in my hair. The casual clothes that I bought for myself were made for men, and I was used to the way they fell straight, but Bonnie bought women's things and they felt all wrong for a runner like me; her jeans lay tight and curved along my thighs, and her shirt was cut so low on my chest that I kept wanting to rest my hand on my sternum to protect myself. She was slightly longer-waisted than I was, and her breasts were smaller. It was strange to think that she had walked around that way all the time, built like that, with that scent coming off and coming back to her. Every move I made reminded me that I was sleepwalking in her body, and the difference split me right in half.

As I steered down the interstate I spoke out loud, all the while listening to myself. You've never been to New York, have you? I asked Bonnie. I know we've talked about this, but I can't remember what you said. It's about two days' drive without stopping, but we should probably stop a few times to sleep. — I couldn't afford another accident just now. But we'll get there, and when we do, I'll show you how I used to live. I'll take you out; we'll go dancing; I'll take you to the lights. —Oh! Did you see that?

There was a billboard by the side of the road.

PRO 23:27: FOR A WHORE IS A DEEP DITCH:
AND A STRANGE WOMAN IS A NARROW PIT.

CHURCH OF CHRIST

What do they mean? I asked Bonnie. Why are they saying those things? But you know and I know: they're saying I'm a burrow, a snare, and I hide in the ground, and move; I'm a fraud, a fake name, an outfit of empty clothes. From my first pretending to be a good little girl, to my hollow studies in school, to my role as a wife and my job giving care, I've always done just what I was supposed to do, I made my motions and tried to believe them. Every day I'd waited for someone to come along and unmask me, but it hadn't happened: as strange as my imitations were, stranger still was succeeding at them. But now this church.

I laughed. What did they know? Beside me on the front seat I had a map charting all of America from the ocean to the ocean. The states and the cities were all there, the highways and the rivers, the mountains and the lakes. But whoever made it had no sign for me: I've disappeared, I said out loud. And no one is going to fuck me, because no one is going to find me.

Overhead there was a thick ceiling of sodden clouds. The fields came and went and the highway stayed, or it split into spurs and diversions and I followed the signs. At dinnertime, the Metroplex went by in the western distance. My friend Dallas, a vicious Oz on the edge of the Plains—mean old Dallas, with its pale warehouse buildings and apartment complexes at the edges, a middle of glittering silver foil in which every handshake was a score, and in the exact center of that a radiant red sign that showed the points piling up. I stopped in a chain restaurant about halfway to Shreveport to have dinner, sat self-consciously by myself and cautiously watched a pair of state troopers stir their coffee and scratch.

Scratch. I saw spots for a moment, my eyes went to the wall and watched as the wall came apart like papier-mâché in the rain. My senses were slumming uncontrollably; it was a lie that I'd ever had a normal thought. The waitress came by, her thick stockings rubbing audibly at her thighs, and asked me if I needed anything else. No, I said, and she put down my check and left. I don't remember paying, but I must have given them some money, because no one followed me out.

As I walked back across the blacktop I thought again of Bonnie's death. I realized that if there was someone other than me who loved her, who would have missed her and mourned for her, they would never hear. It was the most momentous event of her life and only I knew of it; it was a legend only I could relate. Right away I became jealous of her for having died young and unburdened, leaving me to worry about how to tell the story of what had happened. In my frustration I hit the roof of her car with the flat of my hand, making it sound so loudly that they must have heard it on the interstate, and while the metal was still ringing I put my head down on my folded arms and rested for a moment. I was just so tired; I'd been working like a windmill in a tornado since the beginning of the week.

A little ways along the frontage road there was a motel, a shabby place with a middle-aged woman in a housedress waiting behind the front desk, and a grimy boy watching a black-and-white television from a wooden chair by her side. As soon as I'd checked in to my room I went to the bathroom to wash up, and found a little baby something bug crawling up the side of the sink. The bed sagged as I sat on the edge, and a small invisible cloud of musty air rose up and hung about my head. The cover was scratchy underneath my legs; across the room, in the shadow above the lamp on the dresser, there was a framed print of a sailboat leaning across a dusky Alpine lake. Outside my motel window I could see the dim star of a distorted streetlight. There was a madwoman talking in a loud voice to the cars parked in the lot. The bitch can go to hell and die, she said. Bitch has the biggest face I've ever seen. Do I want to talk to her? Do I want to talk to her? No, I don't want to talk to that face. Otherwise, the air had hit one of those chords that drifts across the ground at night, with one note in the midst that was as sweet as a spoonful of sugar in a cup of coffee. Just that morning I'd been in Sugartown, in the thick of things, and now I was in a dark red room, all those small towns and crossed streams away. I took off my clothes and fell asleep, and I dreamt that Billy's shoe box was waiting for me; but it was 1890, it was 1950, 1910, 1966, and no matter how hard I sculled the air around me, I couldn't get across time to collect it.

I woke in the morning to a different world entirely. I could feel the sun shining against my curtains, and when I pulled them back I saw a bright and bustling scene outside; trucks laden with cargo were thundering by on the interstate, cars were passing on the frontage road, in the parking lot a middle-aged man in a brown-and-white-striped seersucker suit was sitting on the hood of his sedan, drinking coffee from a paper cup. You'd have thought there'd never been such a thing as darkness, nor struggle, nor a day before that wasn't part of the history of perpetual peace.

The hot water in the pink-tiled shower went on and on. Afterward I found one of Bonnie's dresses, a frock of blue posies on a white field, and I put a drop of perfume between my thighs. I stretched my pale legs thoughtlessly in the sun outside my room, yawned lazily and blinked dazedly. In a breakfast place next door to the motel I ate sugary cereal and toast with jam, and paid for it all in change. I peeked over the steering wheel as I pulled onto the highway; I had as much time as I wanted, I had something very elaborate to explain, and I started talking to Bonnie again.

When I was a little girl, I said, well . . . They'd tell you that I was a bully. All right, I had a big mouth, but I was bossy more than I was a bully, and my gang was a group of girls. We were all about eight or nine, pretty and smart; there was my best friend, Beth; Helen, whose father ran a local radio station; Eve, who lived on the block behind mine; and Kimmie, about whom I can now remember nothing except for a pair of pretty pink shoes that she wore to dancing lessons after school. We were always together, we five precious children; the world had been purchased for us, and I had been entrusted with the key. In the schoolyard, under the jump rope, my voice could be heard ringing out the rhymes above all the others; I always knew where to meet on weekend afternoons; I knew which dress looked best on which doll; and no one dared be my rival.

They were all my girls: they made up the climate I lived in. Still, there was a landscape beneath it, and an earth beneath that. I don't recall there being any boys around at the time, but there were grown men: teachers, my father's friends and my friends' fathers, clerks in stores; men on corners, in cars, in crews. They were everywhere around me, but like apes in after-school cartoons, they were too big to be anything but friendly and harmless. So I stared openly at them and smiled, I was coy and coquettish and I gave out tiny kisses, I gazed from under my brow and issued mischievous orders, I teased and danced, said Maybe when I meant Never. In response, they tied my shoes, they combed my hair, they fixed the flat tire on my bicycle while I sat cross-legged on the lawn, with my skirt hiked up my skinny legs. I was as subtle as a courtesan, when subtlety counted for everything; temptation was my ally, my companion, and my authority.

Sex began when I was ten, on a golden warm weekend evening when there were neither boys nor men around at all. Sometime that afternoon I had lost a shiny black plastic purse that I'd received for Christmas the year before; I couldn't find it; all through the neighborhood I'd wandered, trying to remember where I'd left it, and as the sun began to set I made my way home in tears. By the time I reached the front door of my house I was dizzy with grief, and I ran up the stairs and into my bedroom, slamming the door shut behind me and falling freely onto my soft, clean bed, where I began to cry so deeply that I became giddy and disabled. Cried and cried, until the room began to turn. The world outside my window was fake, the flowers of a dogwood tree were waving to me from the yard. Beneath my pillow there was a furry stuffed frog, a companion whose name I never told anyone; I pulled him free and held him between my legs as help for my suffering—and held him, and held him, until I wasn't crying anymore, at least not so as anyone would notice. I was exhausted and raw, my bed was kind and my mind was blank, I squeezed, and soon a drop of soothing heat appeared and trembled at the very tip of its source like a bead of solder—and then began to spread, rocking up my belly and down my legs. By the time the pleasure had passed all the way through me I was smiling at the unique trick I'd discovered, a fluttering dove produced from the depths of a silk hat. I kissed the frog where its fur was matted from being pressed against me; it smelled very fresh and slightly bitter, like a nut in its broken shell, that was me.

Eleven, twelve, thirteen. Girl by girl, my friends passed into puberty, and emerged from it woman by woman, having acquired a little extra gravity in each cell in their bodies, which added some mysterious but unmistakable appetite to everything they did. I lingered back in childhood, but I wasn't jealous—I thought they'd all become clumsy and rude. They couldn't run the way I could, and they wasted time in the bathroom. Still, as that year passed, and then the next, I gradually lost whatever rule I'd had over them, in a long and tortuous act of faltering: the medicine of my womanhood had betrayed me on a whim, and I didn't know what they all knew. I didn't want to show it, so I lied about having already had my great day, and spent the next year pretending to listen to demands I couldn't hear and could only guess at. I even went so far as to buy a box of tampons, which I left on top of the medicine cabinet in my bathroom, thinking at once to fool my friends and to entice my cycle into making itself manifest. In gym class I was hell-bent, hoping that the exercise would somehow shake the blood loose. I checked my underwear three, then five, then ten times a day, searching the cotton crotch for a spot. At last my period came, one day after school when I was home alone; but by then it was too late to recover the command I had once so effortlessly shown.

Instead I remade the world, better in my mind: and I began to lie, about everything, all the time. My father was working on a secret project for NASA; I wasn't allowed to say what it was. My boots came from a special store in Paris; my boyfriend was a black man from Bakersfield. A Hollywood producer had seen me walking home and wanted to put me in a movie. I went on and on, telling tales, offering elaborate details and evidence that I had drawn up from some deep and endlessly rich well of falsehood: fertile water, my imagination, which had been lying in wait, like some vast prehistoric aquifer, beneath the bottom of my common life.

I was a strange girl, with a strange confidence. I can see myself sitting in a circle of friends, narrating my vast and ridiculous untruths, my eyes by turns insistently wide, and averted so that I wouldn't give myself away. Because notoriety was what I needed instead of money, and falsehood was what I wore instead of makeup, and belief was what I took instead of other people's hearts.

Bonnie, I said. Until now I've never told anyone outright of my lying ways. Of course they must have known, but not because I confessed. God, what a stubborn girl I was. Am still.

I was on the interstate in Arkansas and there was some trouble up ahead. The traffic around me had thickened and slowed, and then thickened some more and stopped. On either side of the highway I saw bleached fields stretching to the edge of the earth, interrupted only occasionally by clumps of windbreak trees. Ahead I saw an endless, wide, unmoving line of cars, their metal shells glinting in the sunlight like so many mindless beetles marching toward some distant home. Every few minutes we would all move forward a few feet, and then stop again. What a population, the thousands, waiting patiently to pass some point of obstruction that none of us could see.

For an hour we crawled along that way. At one point I found myself pulled up next to a woman in a bright green sedan, with a young boy beside her in the front seat and two more in the back. Of the boys in the back, the fat one was slouched down in his seat until he was nearly horizontal, and he was sucking uselessly on a white plastic straw; the thin one was watching me through his window, his wide, ash-colored eyes fixed on me as I sat alone in my dirty old car and talked to myself. He was an agent for everybody who wanted to keep me in a cage and stare at me, another asshole in the making, and I wanted to yell at his mother. Instead, I reached over and pretended to play with the radio, hoping it would look like I was singing along to something, and when a gap opened up in front of me I allowed a pickup truck to pull over into my lane so the boy would have something else to stare at for a while.

But I began to feel as if I had come to a dangerous place, a purgatory of the middle classes. I was surrounded, I couldn't move. The walls of the car had become too close, so I undid my seat belt and rolled down my window, and then rolled it back up again; I didn't want anyone to be able to reach inside and grab hold of me. For a moment I thought of turning off the highway and driving out into the fields, but the last thing I wanted was to call attention to myself. And besides, where would I go? The name of the state was Don't, there wasn't a house in sight, or a river, or a forest; there was only ground. My hands were sweating, my ears began to ring. I take it back, I said. It was an accident, I'm so sorry. I didn't really mean it, I made a mistake. But no one was listening to me, because no one cared. I shut my mouth and held tightly to the steering wheel, while each moment flashed and then slipped away, like the slow frames of a slide show.

At last the cars ahead of us began to separate and come unstuck, and soon we were moving along at speed again, but I never did see anything that would have accounted for the jam. A billboard said:

750 MILES TO THE CAVERN OF DOLORES
PLAYGROUND CAMPSITE GIFT SHOP MORE

Some time later I went back to my conversation with Bonnie. In the town where I was raised, I explained to her, there were two families, the Glovers and the Galloways. Both were wealthy in that mysterious way of old families; it wasn't manufacturing money or railroad money, it wasn't this money or that money; it was something at once far vaguer and far more sure, a prosperity so indirect that it was recognized only through rumor. Each family had a half dozen or so children of various ages; May Glover was in my class, and Tommy Galloway was in the grade above, and I knew how to pick out May's younger brother and Tommy's older sister, but beyond that the siblings disappeared, so that they seemed to be at once everywhere and nowhere. From time to time one of the older ones would appear in a car that was cruising down the commercial strip, a shadowy profile appearing through the side window, with one clearly rendered arm hanging loosely out over the door panel, or else I would pass some faintly familiar girl, proceeding in a crowd of companions. But even during those periods when I went weeks without encountering any of them, I was always aware of the fact that they were around.

The two families had this difference: the one was tattered and the other was pale. That is, the Glover girls dressed in torn and mismatched clothes, and wore their hair loosely; they were careless, they were slatternly, they were disorderly. The Galloways, on the other hand, were as neat as could be, but somehow they were faded and bland; their features were sketchy, their skin was pallid, their clothes seemed to hide them as much as cover them; they were not entirely there. Frayed Glovers and faint Galloways, in an endless pattern of rivalry; for of course each family hated the other, and plotted and conspired to bring their opposite down. They were natural foes, and they followed that nature for as long as I lived there. They're probably following it today.

By fifteen I had become boy-crazy, or so everyone told me. But I was: the boys were nice to me, they were honest and I thought they were free. They had fun and then they had some more. I listened to the other girls talk volumes about flirting, it was everything to them, but it seemed much more simple than that to me. Maybe I was impatient, maybe I was spendthrift, maybe I was right: when I lied to the boys, they seemed to believe me, or more likely they just didn't care. And it was so lovely to see them, sweet and shy, with their bravado and their beautiful bodies, their careless limbs and candid gaits, intimations of a coming manhood that was unimaginable and intoxicating. Tommy Galloway, fair-skinned and full of himself, was my first in bed.

I must have had a mad crush on him, but I don't know how we met, nor how I hooked him. That's all lost in the treetops of my hometown. I remember walking back to his big house after school; he was wearing a pale blue oxford-cloth shirt over mouse grey chinos, and I was wearing blue jeans and a green-and-white sweater. Then we were in his bedroom, all but innocent. The bed was covered with an ugly off-white blanket, the sunlight on his desktop was a very definite yellow, and through the closed door I could hear one of his brothers talking on the telephone in the hallway. For some minutes Tommy and I stood and kissed, his tongue darting thinly into my mouth, his hands resting motionless on my waist while I sucked in my stomach and held my breath. Then he began to pull up on my sweater, until he had my arms entangled in the cloth and I had to help him free them. But was I graceful enough? Was I clean? *Sleek* was the word that year. Was I sleek? —Without a word and too soon for me, he stepped backward and unbuttoned his shirt. I sat down on the edge of the mattress, still wearing my bra, and immediately leaned back, not so much to welcome him as to lengthen my rounding body. He didn't notice, he just bent down and raised one leg, and then the other, simultaneously removing his pants and his briefs. Then he began to move slowly toward me. . . . So this was the minute. I glanced down and saw a single thick blue artery beating nervously through the sallow skin of his groin. I studied his expression: he was so intent that he seemed almost angry, and I thought he was taking the whole thing much too seriously; to me it was more like farm chores, dirty in a way that I didn't mind. He instructed me to spit on the head of his thing, and then he put his hands on my shoulders, laid me all the way back on the bedclothes, and began to fumble somewhere between my legs. I did my best to accommodate him, turning my hips this way and that while he felt around, but I was only making matters worse; he couldn't find what he was looking for. It was far too long to wait, his eyes were tightly closed, and I was just about to laugh when all of a sudden some membrane between us began to stretch painfully—I wondered whether we were beginning, or if he'd made some mistake—he pushed—and then the fascia snapped and we simultaneously gasped. I adored him for that abrupt breath; it was like a fantastic, distant kiss, but it was the only thing we did together all day. I don't remember how he finished— probably like the others since, with a helpless look—but when we were done, at five in the afternoon, I lied and told him it had been wonderful, and he lied and told me he loved me. I walked back home in the sore-seeming gloaming, and we never spoke again.

Good evening, I said to Tennessee. Can I have some gas for my car? Can I have some dinner for the noise in my stomach? Do you have a motel room for me tonight? The news announcer on a Memphis radio station spent two sentences summarizing the aftermath of the Sugartown riot, but he said nothing about me.

500 MILES TO THE CAVERN OF DOLORES

The highway was flanked by trees, the air was greasy from an oil spill on one of the overpasses, the exit signs were infrequent, and I drove all the way to Nashville before I found a Motel 8. There was a swimming pool out back of the place, and since the night was warm and the other rooms were all empty, I changed into a pair of cutoffs and a black T-shirt and tiptoed in, to float on my back and look into the night sky, and continue my story to the faint moon-shaped image of Bonnie's face.

This is the history of my appetite. I met Bobby in my senior year; I was in a bar a few towns from home, underage and out with a girl whom I hardly knew. Midway through the night she decided she was bored and wanted to leave. But Bobby gave me a look; he showed off with a cigarette; I thought of a song the girls used to sing when the boys weren't listening:

> *I fucked him standing*
> *I fucked him lying*
> *If we'd had wings*
> *I'd have fucked him flying.*

I dared myself to stay, and I stayed with him all night, and saw him for several months afterwards. I never could tell what he saw when he looked at me; he could have had any girl he wanted. He didn't love me, and I didn't love him, and whoever says I did is wrong. But he had hands like a thief, sensitive, mean, and strong, and wherever they went I followed: to his car, to his dingy apartment, to his thief-smelling bed. When I had him in my mouth I believed that everything he knew could be mine at will: I could feel his confidence literally collected on the tip of my tongue, while he trembled weakly and waited for me to make him play it back and pour it between my numb lips. I swallowed because I didn't know what else to do with it. I was seventeen, and not so smart.

But I did well in school; I was a better girl even when I was trying to be worse. So I read what I was assigned, I took my tests, and I went off to college the following year. I wanted to be a doctor, I wanted to be a painter, I wanted to be the Empress of Glamour.

What is the world made of? My professors taught me to ask that question. They offered their own answers, but I didn't believe a word. One said humming bits of different force. One stepped back from her blackboard and said, Soul. One said the universe was a gift box that could never be opened, and suggested we look at ourselves instead. As for me, I was already convinced that it was made of tall tales and untruths; it was not just an illusion, it was an out-and-out lie. The stars at night? The oceans? A brick of gold? I wasn't fooled, they were slanders on the idea of substance. And I, with my good grades and the roommate I got along with, was as fake as any of it, and as such in strange harmony with the will of whoever had ordered it made.

I became friends with a woman named Sandy, a tall and broad-shouldered psychology student who intimidated almost everyone with her casually revealing clothes and her complete confidence: my roommate called her Mr. Certain. I assumed that she came from some long line of American aristocrats, and when she singled me out for attention I was proud to have stolen the advantage. She met me every evening to talk to me about my day;

she listened to my make-believe without blinking, and soon she was wooing me with little collages, which she made out of melodramatic magazine quotes and photographs of pretty girls kissing. She may have been the only person I ever met who thought I was perfect, and that was the one thing we disagreed about.

On a Thursday night we went to see a movie at the student union; afterward, a drink, a walk across town, another drink. That part was very familiar. Later, she took me to her bed, but I couldn't get it to work under the sheets; her hair, my hair, my belly to her belly, my breasts to her breasts, the affinity was so real that I felt love was redundant; and everything was too round and too slippery, there wasn't anything for me to hold on to. It ended halfway through: I was sorry, she was angry, and for a while I was afraid of her, but I managed to stay friends with her for a time, and eventually she forgave me, so that we could drift apart.

The day after I graduated I moved to New York, where lying was the law, and there I floundered in the wake of my education. I found work as a receptionist in an accounting firm on Madison Avenue—a horrible, dull job, but that fall I met Roy. He was a friend of a friend of a friend, and he'd just started working in the mayor's office, it was nighttime, there were several us on a street corner, and he eyed me under the lights. It was still chilly out, and I was wearing an expensive black wool sweater and a soft grey cashmere scarf; I was all wrapped up, well fitted and warm. Maybe that's what I liked about him. He gave me a frank look and then smiled ridiculously, so I moved a little bit around toward him—and he didn't respond. A few moments later I took two or three steps away from him, and still he didn't shift an inch, but he smiled at me again. I turned away. When all the introductions and the small talk had been completed, he went one way, and I went another, with a slight voice in my head that mumbled something I couldn't quite catch; I thought it was trying to tell me that he didn't want me, but a few days later he called. When he tried to remind me of our meeting, I said, Yes, I remember, too brightly and too soon.

It was always like that in the beginning, even on the occasion of our first dinner alone, even at the useless movie afterward. He was impervious, he was immune to me; when I whispered in his ear he merely nodded amiably; when I briefly touched my hand to his thigh he just kept talking; when I lied he laughed. He called again a few days later, but I was out. I waited for a week before I returned his message, but when he answered the phone he was as sweet and solicitous as could be. We met, and he simply smiled and smiled—he had a grin like the moon. We went home and he pulled the sheets back from my bed without any piety at all. In the end I did whatever he suggested. He was the most patient man I'd ever met, and the lake was so full it just poured over the dam.

On the third day the sun shined through the clouds in places, casting bands of oyster grey light and cement grey shadow in long rhythms across the highway. The sun never fully rose. Instead, I entered a kind of limbo, a flat, unreflective light, a low room, a dull, dull day. I made about 450 miles before dark, all the way into Virginia, and I felt like I was time-traveling. The mountains around me were blue from the rain, but the brick on the buildings was shining with a rich burnt red, which stood out from the white-painted porticos and glowed with whatever sunshine there was. On a curving stretch of road I saw a coyote that some farmer had crucified on his fence, where it hung belly out as a warning to predators. In the next town I stopped and ate a bowl of salty soup, and then I sat on the still-warm hood of the car and sunned myself for a little while.

Roy in his room, before we had moved in together, sitting in a blue terry-cloth bathrobe on the bed we had unmade the night before, reading the newspaper. The pale hairs on the back of his neck glimmered in the sunlight; first thing in the morning, not ten minutes from his dreams, and already he was frowning. I was naked in the doorway, with real hips and breasts and my hair recently cut and lightened, I was as beautiful as I was ever going to be. What is it? I asked.

He made a disgusted noise, and without looking up said, the Schools Chancellor wants to cut some job training programs out of the budget. Here he is, telling everyone how much he'll save. He shook his head and turned to where the story continued on an inside page. How are we supposed to find work for all these people, when they don't know how to do anything?

Give them jobs putting makeup on municipal buildings, I replied. Organizing parades for pregnant women. Planting gardens up the mayor's ass.

He looked up and smiled briefly, but he really didn't think I was funny, my literal-minded lover; he thought I was impractical, and didn't care at all.

But do you think he would have had the wits, as I'd had, to save one man for heaven and send another to hell?

I saw a radio relay tower in the field across the street, on the struts of which a dozen black birds had alighted, posing nonchalantly against the horizon. Another one joined them, and an instant afterward three or four of them flew off.

I moved my few things into his apartment and found a new job, as an office manager for a company that made music for movies. We didn't have many friends and we had no obligations; no one else mattered. The city was a swing set with just one seat, which we rode higher and higher, becoming breathless and ecstatic, until we could see over the trees to the lights and the river.

He brought me a present almost every day, a gold chain to

hang around my neck, from which there dangled a tiny gold key that opened nothing, flowers from street-corner vendors, a book, a toy, a ridiculous tourist souvenir. At night we went for walks along the avenues, window-shopping and watching people; we went home and went to bed. His touch was nourishment to me; I fed off it until I was glossy and glowing. He was the first man who ever made me come, not from his hand or his tongue, but from the outrageous sensation he made when he moved inside me, and the contagion of his own excitement. It was the closest thing I'd ever felt, and on one of those nights I opened my mouth to tell him how happy I was, and I said, I love you, I love you, I love you.

—And there go the rest of the birds, becoming specks in the sky and then disappearing. I thought it was going to rain, so I got back into the car and started driving again.

THE CAVERN OF DOLORES →

500 YARDS

I kept going and it didn't rain, but when I stopped for gas about a half an hour later, the wind was strong enough for a storm; it blew my shirt back against my chest and wrapped my hair across my face.

His books on the bookshelf: the law, social policy, history, and a few Irish poets.

Whiskey and soda.

The sight of a small boy being slapped by his mother on a street corner made him inexplicably angry at me.

And yet, he didn't mind when I was unreasonable, he forgave me easily when I was indecisive or scatterbrained.

For hours we had been lying alone. Gently, and so slowly,

he began to reach up the back of my naked leg with his hand, and as one of his long fingers pushed its way between my pressed-together thighs, I felt myself swell and open helplessly, until my nerves dissolved and began to spill the solution down. Mine, he said, and then he lazily sucked the fluid off of his thumb.

Blue Moon

By the time it had grown dark that evening I had made my way into Maryland, and Maryland meant nothing to me. I was hurrying along a stretch of empty road toward a city in the middle distance when I saw police lights flashing in the rearview mirror; for a long second I thought about speeding up . . . but I held tightly on the wheel, took a deep breath, and pulled the car onto the shoulder. I didn't move, my car was still running and my radio was on, the trooper didn't move. Some traffic went by. He didn't move. Outside the sky was azure and the tree line was suburban, and at last his door opened and he approached me with a flashlight, a tall man with a mustache, thickly built and wearing a blue hat, a beige shirt, blue pants, a black gun. He knocked on my window and my hand shook as I lowered it. Will you turn your engine off, miss? I reached slowly for the key and killed the car. It had been running for so long that the silence afterward was overwhelming. Do you know why I stopped you?

I think so, I said. You want to beat me with your fists, I thought. Deny afterward that you did it and laugh at me in the courtroom.

Can I see your license and registration?

Was that all he was going to ask of me? I would have danced on the yellow line, I would have pulled my pants down around my ankles, if I thought it might have given me a chance to go free. Without hesitating I reached into the purse on the seat beside me and withdrew Bonnie's wallet; it took me a moment before I could find the card, but when I finally came up with it he was still standing there patiently. The registration was in the glove compartment; he took them both and disappeared.

I heard a sweeping sound coming from the side of the road while he was gone. Some birds, some bugs. In a moment he returned. You're from Sugartown, Ms. Moore? he asked.

I nodded, Yes, I said. —Although actually I'm coming from some friends in Atlanta, and I'm going up to New York to visit my family. I smiled one of my one hundred variations on the pretty smile.

He smiled back and said, O.K., and started writing. My radar said you were going seventy-five, so I'm going to have to give you a ticket. He tore it from his pad and handed it to me. You can plead guilty and pay by mail, if you want.

Thank you, I said.

And take it slow, all right?

I will, I promised. As he got into his car and drove off I felt the dread drop off me like dirty clothes. I laughed at myself, closed my car door gently, and pulled out onto the road.

For fifty more miles I drove like an old lady, and when I finally left the highway, I chose a chain motel in an industrial strip this side of Baltimore, because I couldn't imagine anyone ever being found there. The clerk was a hatchet-faced man, as ugly as a dog's ass, with long yellow earlobes and a fat gold ring on his thin ring finger. He walked me all the way to my room with a kind of insistent courtesy—well, it wasn't courtesy: he wanted to be close to me, he thought I was lewd just because I was traveling alone, and he was looking for some chance to chip off on him. I put the chain on the door and listened to his footsteps slowly retreating down the hallway, and when I couldn't hear them anymore I lay down fully clothed on the bed. *Mildred Pierce* was playing on the TV, and it was still playing when I dozed off; I went dreamless for nine hours, but I woke once to sleepwalk across the thin carpet and turn off the noise. The room was blue.

There was an evening in June when we were set to meet in a restaurant on Elizabeth Street. On my way down I had stopped to look at shoes in a store window, and I was late; by the time I got there the block was dark and the restaurant was lit. As I crossed the street I saw Roy through the front window, standing alone at the bar with a drink before him, lost in his airs. I stood on the sidewalk and watched for a minute, the minute turned into a while. He reached for his glass, held it, lifted it; I could see his eyes glitter in the bar light as he raised his gaze to look at it. He shifted on his feet and made a remark to the bartender, who smiled. Afterward he went back to his quiet and contained stance. I watched, he was waiting for me, but how could I not leave him alone and spy on him, when, one, he was charming— two, he was handsome—and three, he was mine?

We were married on a bright November afternoon; he was dressed in a dark grey suit and I wore the lightest thing I had, an off-white summer dress that came down below my knees. As a witness we had some functionary from Roy's office, another man. We kissed, my husband and I. That night he rolled me in our wedding bed, and when it was all over I couldn't tell what we had done. I loved him so much, it sometimes exhausted me. I married him, I was a wife, but I was making it all up as I went along: I wondered if he felt the same, I worried that he expected something mysterious and impossible from me. I wanted to ask him but I was afraid, and besides, he believed that our private life was so private that it would be despoiled by anyone's conversation, including our own.

I bought a fresh tank of gas the next day and took 95 north through Delaware. Once again the morning started dark with clouds, but by the early afternoon the weather had cleared and I got a good look around. I saw all the cities piled on the shelf before the Atlantic, the people spilling out of their jumbled houses, desperately trying to hold their things back from the beach over the last hill. On the radio a man was telling a tale about a soldier who had suffered, was betrayed, and died. I thought it was a story about Jesus, with his womanly bending and satisfying secrets—but no, it was a spy the government had uncovered. Philadelphia, where Roy's cousins lived, and knew nothing about him.

Then a thousand blind trucks appeared all around me and carried me up through New Jersey; I barely had to touch the accelerator. There was black music on my radio. Something had gone wrong with the car's air conditioning; it wasn't working at all, and I had to open my window to get a breeze. The weather smelled like gasoline, and my eyes began to sting. Along the road the heat proved to be too much for the trees: they were melting into a long green blur, a single degenerate species that had overtaken the ground.

I was lying on the couch, reading at night, wearing nothing but a long black T-shirt; we'd been married a year. There was a mug of hot tea on the floor below me, and an unfinished apple on my stomach. Roy was late. I heard the door open, I heard him hang up his jacket, I saw him standing on the living room threshold, but he didn't look at me; I thought that was strange. He hesitated, and then he headed for our bedroom—and as he passed me I started—and I knew in a second that he'd been fucking someone else. I didn't have to think about it, I knew at once because I was sick; it was the smell. I couldn't rise, I couldn't move, I couldn't speak. He walked into the bathroom, leaving behind the stink of citrus perfume and sweat, someone else's mocking arrow. It turned my legs numb, my chest became frost, I was lost, but at last I found the strength to get up and follow him. I found him standing naked in the middle of the floor with his back to the mirror. He didn't notice me until he turned around, and when he did I saw a pinkish red mark about two inches long on his abdomen, a welt on the body of my beloved, the body that had been mine. He covered it with one hand, and with the other he reached behind the shower curtain and turned on the water, shook his head, and in a strangely dissociated voice said, I have to do this now. The room filled with steam, it was difficult to breathe, and the boy began to disappear.

I would have been gone before the water had dried on the bathroom floor, but he asked me to stay, so I stayed. I stayed for another month, and he slept on the living room couch. Why? Why? I was there for the taking, but he didn't want me, and I missed him so much that when I went outside I could see the air dividing into translucent waves of grief. I cried anytime I wanted to, I cried on the street; I carried makeup in my purse to cover the mottles on my face when I got to work. It was midsummer and the weather was fine, so I cried some more. I stopped eating, to punish my senses with a hunger so pure that it made me high. If I'd failed at everything else I tried, if I'd gained infamy and a bad reputation, if no one ever listened to me, nothing would have hurt me more than realizing that I'd been wrong about him all along, and knowing at the same time that I'd never dream that I was quite entire again. Wrong, and lessened, and still without the solace of knowing that I was just mistaken.

A rest stop, really it was more like a tiny city built up between the two directions of traffic. Everyone was there, milling around in the parking lot. I washed my dirty face in a bathroom sink and bought a big cup of bad coffee to go.

I'm not saying everything is going to be fine, said Roy. It was the middle of the afternoon and it was far too sunny out for me to try to argue. He turned his empty glass upside down on the table, and when he moved it, a few seconds later, I noticed that it left a wet spot, a circle surrounding a tiny puddle in the shape of an undiscovered island. The telephone rang, and without getting up from the table he reached back and answered it. Yes, hello? he said, and then he stood and moved into the door frame. I'm sorry, I know, he said. A pause. I know. Wait. I couldn't see his face, but he shrank; whoever was on the other end wasn't happy. I will. . . . Wait. I will.

He hung up, but he wouldn't sit down again. Instead, he stood against the sink, his arms extended so that his hands could rest on the countertop to either side. It was very bright in there. Did I really have to ask? It was unimaginable. Was that her?

No, he said. I put my index finger in the spot that his glass had made, drawing it through the circle until it turned into a sign. Another innocent thing ruined. What do you want? he asked.

What did I want? What did I want? To be perfectly beautiful, to make milk, to hold him forever between my legs.

The sun was just beginning to set, and the highway widened and became pitted and difficult, just as the countryside ended and the suburbs began. And me, I was a mannequin at the wheel. An airplane came in surprisingly low over the road, rocking slightly, its engines burning like an industry as it crossed overhead and sank out of sight. A moment later I got a glimpse of the city and I was ravished; it made my eyes bright and I sped up until the car was bouncing dangerously over the potholes. Around we went, up, along and then suddenly down to the dark mouth of the tunnel.

A divorce, a blur. There wasn't very much to divide, but the lawyer's fees took most of my small savings, leaving too little for me to be able to move out of town. I had to save some money, I had to save some of myself, because I knew that once I started to run I'd never be able to stop. So I sublet a studio apartment in Brooklyn for the remainder of the summer, and dazedly carried on with two men whose names I can't remember. But as soon as the chilly days outnumbered the warm ones, I packed and put myself on an airplane; I started going, and three years later I landed in Sugartown, and by the time I emerged from the other end of the tunnel, coming up under the vast, rustling, starry wing of New York, it was getting dark out, everyone I had ever known was gone, and I was getting old.

I would have been afraid.

WELL, I WAS AT FIRST. I KNEW THE CITY, BUT I FELT LIKE I HAD BEEN baited with my breasts and lips, strung on a line, and lowered into a dark catch pen holding thieves and dogs and I-don't-know-what. I slid back on the car seat and grimaced through the windshield like a madwoman, clutching my wheel and clenching my jaw. When I turned onto Canal Street I saw, too late, that it was blocked all the way over to Chinatown. Jaywalkers were swarming across the road. For a half an hour I sat in the car, squeezed up against a crosswalk, while the sun went through the last routine of its setting and the lights came on, all at once. They were stage lights, weren't they? A beautiful young woman in a short black dress with grey piping walked in front of my front fender, and never glanced up to see who I was. She didn't know that we were related; she would have denied it if I'd suggested it to her. On the side of a building right in front of us I saw an enormous picture of the exact same thing: a woman in a black dress, lit with spotlights and not looking at anything. I really believed that I was never going to get out of there, not out of the car, and not out of the city if I did get out of the car. The sides of the place were sloped and oiled, so that if you tried to run up and over the edge you'd only slide helplessly back down and get tangled up in the lights again. When I looked up I saw another sign, an advertisement, it said: ALL WE MAKE IS MONEY. Aside from the Go lights, it was the only green around for miles, but there was a handful of change left in my pocket, and a pair of Bonnie's credit cards in the purse beside me. When I closed my eyes I could see her loopy blue signature written boldly on the inside of my forehead; if I kept them closed for too long, I saw the Policeman lying face up in a white bed.

At last I managed to make a left turn: I was in Little Italy, at last on Lafayette Street. Everywhere there were people streaming along the sidewalks, crossing the intersections on diagonals, dancing outside grocery stores, begging one another for money or kisses, firing handguns into the air for the sheer joy of the noise. At first I couldn't do anything but gape and shrink, and my mind started to speed through absurdities. Well, for example, what if I have to pee? I thought. Where would I go? What if my car stops running? Who would help me? But I didn't have to pee, and the car didn't stop, and soon I was O.K.: because there came the moment when I stopped feeling like an object of the city's wildness and started to feel like an aspect of it. My back hurt from sitting all day, and my feet were suffering from riding the brake, but I was confident. I pulled into a garage near Gramercy Park and parked the car.

I hid Billy's shoe box on the floor of the backseat, and by the time I'd gotten my suitcase down to the street I was in another city again: it had become a beautiful clear and calm night, there were birds among the branches of the sidewalk trees, and wherever I looked some tower was twinkling amiably down on the town below. Without a worry I wandered west, until I happened upon a big beige hotel with a dark purple awning. The doorman smiled and nodded as I passed, and I just walked in through the revolving door, crossed briskly to the front desk, and asked the clerk straight out for a room, taking Bonnie's credit card out of her purse and placing it on the counter.

How long do you plan to stay, Ms.—he read the name stamped on the card—Moore?

Oh, I don't know, I answered. A week or two. Longer? Maybe. Can you just leave the charge open?

He ran the thing through a machine, and everyone nearby—the bellhops, the maid at the elevator, the lounging guests, the piano player in the bar next door—stopped what they were doing to watch as we waited for the answer. Who would have thought electricity could travel so slowly? The yellow particles were taking their own sweet time, wandering casually out the door toward their destination and returning sullenly with their answer. Sure, the clerk said at last, and turned the registration around so that I could sign my new name with a smile. When he handed me my key I put his pen in my pocket.

Come on, I said to the floor indicator above the elevator doors as the arrow slowly wended its way around the semicircle of brass numbers. In time it came, and I stepped inside alone. Come on, old thing, take me to eleven, I said as the chamber slowly rose. Come on. The floor where it left me was light blue and brightly lit. I hurried down the corridor, and when I finally reached my room I dropped my bag onto one of the beds and pulled the curtains back to let in the lights.

Outside my window there was money, glistering and changing hands; and headlights in line for miles; and everybody, but everybody, was high. Inside there were a half dozen clean towels, and no one knew a thing about me. I put on the TV—

some local station was running *Dog Day Afternoon*—and started through the phone book for Roy's name, beginning to breathe shallowly when I reached the *H*'s, because I was afraid he could hear me approaching. When I found the Harrisons, I read the page three times, but there was no listing. Listlessly, I began to unpack my bag.

Bang! something went off on the television, and I had to stop what I was doing and turn the volume down so that I could think. But instead of reason I found myself recalling the smell of our apartment, with its mixed notes of effort, will, and exhaustion, his and mine, the clothes we had worn and worn, his shaving cream, his simple soap, a tugging train of decomposing flowers. I remembered a tree on the sidewalk outside that bloomed obscenely in the spring, pushing open its buds until they hung swollen over the pavement, and scattered the windowsill with damp green pollen; if we opened the window, the reek of senseless growth drifted in, along with the sweet smell of burning carbon from the traffic on the street, and a single biting element of dry-cleaning fluid from the shop down at the corner.

I got out of my pants to get into bed, but I found myself standing by the side of the mattress, and down went my hand, just to touch. It was warm out, and I hadn't turned on the air conditioner, so I was a little bit damp. I put my foot up on the bed, still standing, damper on the back of my thighs, and damper still along the channel they described. . . . I didn't know why I was doing it. . . . The room was too clean, but it was getting dirtier. . . . I stopped for a second, took a breath. . . . And here we go, here we go again: slowly, I reached down and drew a line upward on the inside of my thigh with an index finger, I ran the palm of my hand along the outer curve of my opposite shoulder. Who loves whom? Tell me. Who loves whom? What a long, long time it took to tell. . . . My legs grew tired and I stretched myself out on the bed, first on my back, then on my stomach, then on my back again, with my gradually numbing hand interrupting my repose. — I made myself flinch. I was a mirror on nothing, I wasn't thinking of anything at all, my hips were trembling and shaking on the mattress, I could hear the sound of myself turning somewhere beneath my daydream. . . . I was grasping at myself, trying to change, and I began to sink and soften, I took a breath and started again. . . . And in time I began to liquefy, then to transform, and then suddenly to conduct, like an ocean hit by lightning. It flashed and stopped, but the flare continued, shooting through me far below, traveling an enormous dark distance in an instant and then disappearing . . . and then a moment later it hit again, and again—at last—it struck—again, I came—and as I did I saw reflected inside me the vague face of a strange man, an image so brief and blurry that I wouldn't recognize him even if I met him. He was no one, he existed only for a moment, in a reverie, and then only to love me; but as soon as I could gain control of my hands I held them over my heart to keep it from tearing in two.

As I slept that night I dreamed that I was marrying a policeman in Reno, Nevada.

Out my window the next morning I could see a mother or a nanny walking down Irving Place with a child hanging on to her hand; it was the first week of September and they were on their way to school. In another direction I saw rooftop gardens and hidden backyards strung with washing lines and television cables, the back side of the city. At about ten-thirty I left the hotel, crossed over to Broadway, and headed downtown, dressed in a pair of Bonnie's blue jeans, a sea green shirt, and a pair of thick-soled boots. I had no idea where to begin my hunt for Roy, so I'd decided to haunt the last place I had known him to be, hoping for a little luck.

By the time I reached Park Row it was just before noon. There were high clouds scuttling far above the tops of the buildings, carrying white billows out to an ocean that no one on the ground had ever seen. I sat on a bench in the plaza outside City Hall and watched as the secretaries went beetling along the sidewalk to their lunches. A radio was broadcasting some Top Forty song, a black woman singing, Oh, my love, over and over and over. My veins were beating very hard; I imagined that you could see them throbbing in my throat if you looked at me in just the right way. My giveaway countenance, but no one was looking at all.

No Roy at all.

But there was a Royness in the air, like the essence of childhood in the air of a suburban playground, or the shade of written history in the reading room of a library: the perfume of the past, drifting down over the present. I found myself repeatedly swallowing a small thing that had become lodged in my throat. I started going through time and compressing it, first the years before I met him, and then the years we were together, and then the years since. My limbs began to tingle from sitting motionless for so long, and I got up and began to walk.

A group of pigeons had collected on the pavement, and as I hurried through them they all started up violently, big brutal things beating the air around my face and then falling again a few feet away. I believed I'd been very close to the man I married, and a million miles away. I didn't know which distance undid me more. Couldn't I just bump into him, and settle everything before nightfall? But coincidence had never been very kind to me, and she wasn't going to start by delivering him to me.

I wandered away through the narrow streets of Chinatown. Maybe he isn't anywhere, I thought as I passed through a cloud of fragrant steam outside a restaurant kitchen. Maybe the city killed him and swallowed him; maybe he melted into the air when no one was watching. At Canal Street I crossed against a light, and a rattling truck with wheezing brakes almost sent me straight to Bonnie in heaven; I played snakes and ladders through Little Italy, emerging at the top by a car wash on Houston, where I stopped in a store for a soda and watched four teenage boys as they sauntered down Lafayette. Hey, I've got a present for you, one of them said to me as he passed.

No, I said, and he walked away. After that there was no one. When a car passed its tires hummed. The bells on a Catholic church started ringing, as if they had always been ringing but could only just then be heard. A warm wind was blowing gently across Bleecker Street.

In my hotel room later that afternoon I wondered if a woman could die of loneliness, the casualty of a thousand tiny cuts to the soul, delivered one at a time. I pulled off my shirt and started raining, all alone there in my bra, engulfed in a main of my own making; my face dissolved down my chest while I gulped down mouthfuls of hot tears and shook, my breathing as wet as a Gulf wind. With a handful of bedclothes I dried my cheeks, apologized to them for being so unreasonable—and then burst upward into a fresh cataract and cried some more; I undressed, stumbled blindly into the bathroom, and turned on the shower; and still I sobbed, until I was afraid I would wash myself right down the drain, and I turned the water off again. There was nothing for it but to sit by the cold window and hide my embarrassed face. It didn't stop, it didn't stop: on and on it went—at one point I was laughing at the same time, because it was so absurd—every time I thought it was going to end, the misery swelled up and broke again, until the rhythm of my weeping made me feel like some sordid sea emptying itself onto an unwilling shore; it rose and fell; it would diminish, quickening as it thinned—and then it would turn and slide swiftly back toward another bitter flood tide. I was rocked like that until the sun went down and I grew so exhausted that I fell asleep.

When I woke that night I couldn't tell where I was, or when. The room was dark; out my window I could see one enormous glass and steel box, flushed with particular light, rising with clear and startling force several blocks away. Wide patches of it were lit up from the inside, and across the intervening streets I could clearly see a cleaning crew trying to push a large machine through a doorway into one of the offices. On the shadow table beside my bed lay a white telephone, and I picked up the receiver and dialed Eden View.

When the nurse at the front desk answered I asked for Billy. Just a minute, she said, and I heard her put the phone down on her desk and speak to someone in the hallway. He's in the activities room, she said when she returned. If you'll give me your name and number, I'll give him the message, and he can call back when he's done. But I said, That's all right, I'll try again later.

I ordered a plate of pasta from room service and ate only half, and exactly an hour later I called Eden View again: This time the nurse just put me right through to the phone on his floor. It rang a few times before he picked it up. Hello! he snapped.

Billy, it's me, I said.

Who is this? he demanded, and I pulled the receiver away from my ear. Hello, goddamnit!

A friend, I said. There was a long pause on the other end, while he forgot for a moment how to curse. Is that you, Audrey? Is that you, you bitch whore? He had gotten much older in the week since I'd been gone. His temper tore like tissue paper, and there was nothing but air behind it.

Stop it, stop it.

Who is this? he demanded.

It's me, I whispered.

Is this my friend? My friend from last week? You're dead, he announced. You died, it said so in the paper.

No, that was someone else. I came to see you after that, don't you remember?

His voice relaxed without softening. It didn't make any sense, he said.

It isn't true. That was someone else, they think is me.

There was a pause — Bonnie-the-Bottle! he said triumphantly, and then collected his reward for the thought by saying, Ha! Bonnie-the-Bell! I could hear him shuffling his feet, far below him on the other side, but whether he was dancing I didn't know, and didn't want to ask.

I just wanted to say hello.

I gave you something, he said softly. Something for the devil. Have you found him yet? Have you smelled his ugly breath? Has he laid you on his soft bed?

Stop it, I said. I'm in a hotel, I'm on my way.

Well, well, he said. Don't dally. They're all waiting for you.

Who is?

Everyone, the men . . .

I sighed. The room I was in was very cold. Whoops, he said. I have to go now. I could hear a voice behind him. He sighed. It just isn't the same with you so goddamned dead, he said, and then he hung up. I knew he was insane, but for the first time I wondered if I was going insane along with him.

You didn't know me then, you couldn't have known how crazy I was getting. Isn't that strange? I couldn't imagine living without you now. I couldn't imagine not seeing you; it would be the same as being blind. But at the time I was in a lot of trouble, and

I had no one to talk to. I couldn't see myself. All I wanted was to find Roy, so that I could discover the truth and let him go again, and for good.

I took to searching the faces I passed on the street, carefully comparing each one with an ideal template—an abstract Roy, itself becoming blurry around the edges. He was always on my mind, but his features had grown dim, his snub nose and his pale blue eyes. I kept confusing them with my senses; he had reddish hair, he had a slightly acid kiss that burned for a beat or two after he had left my lips. It was exhausting to contemplate, especially at night; I would stare for too long while I tried to bring the thing into clearer focus, and people would stare back at me, because I had forgotten how bold I was being.

Within a few days the hotel employees were treating me familiarly, nodding and smiling in the morning when I left, and watching me sympathetically when I came in every evening. I nodded and smiled in return, but I had no idea how much credit I had left on Bonnie's card, so I had no way of knowing how long it would be before they ceased being so friendly. In the meantime the weather had come to a halt for me. I remember this very clearly; it was like some gift from the airstream, to stop me from feeling that I was losing too quickly. Every day was identically sunny, slightly cool, and sweet-smelling; everyone I met was nice, and every piece of Bonnie's clothing became my favorite as soon as I wore it. And for days I didn't see a single policeman, not one, they had all been banned from the city streets.

I came home early one evening, it must have been my third or fourth day there. I had been to the public library that afternoon, where I'd leafed through a green guide to city government, hoping to find Roy's name, but there was nothing. I scanned the indices of three years' worth of daily newspapers, hoping he might have made his name in print; I looked through back issues of the alumni magazine from his university, but there was no mention of him. By the time I returned home I was tired and frustrated, my eyes were dirty and my mouth was full of dust. All the way from the subway stop to the hotel I carried on to myself: What are you doing? And whatever it is, you might as well give it up. You're a fool. I made a noise and the doorman started as I went by. Excuse me? he said, and I shook my head. I was annoyed with him for seeing me as I surveyed my disgrace; I hated him because he wore a uniform; I was afraid of the street he watched over.

Some time later I was washing a pair of jeans and Bonnie's dress in the bathroom, and as I hung them over the curtain rod, something in the sound of the water dripping down onto the bottom of the tub—I could never explain this to you—reminded me of someone I'd once known slightly, and I made a phone call.

Roy and I, we had a few friends. They all knew of our disgrace. One or two of the girls had tried to get in touch with me after he'd moved out, but I couldn't stand their voices, I turned them away, and in time they stopped calling. I would rather have scoured the city proudly than so much as mention more than once that I knew them. But there was a man, a friend of Roy's named Dennis Grady. He was an older man, maybe forty-five or fifty; he wasn't grey, there was nothing decrepit about him, but he had that sort of thoughtless patience that comes over men of an indeterminate age, sometime after they can measure their lives in a year's changes, but before they're preparing to die. He was very gentlemanly and sweet and I never had a thing to say to him; and he didn't seem to know what to do with me, either. Before Roy and I had met, the two of them had briefly worked together, and I gathered that one of them had done the other an enormous favor, though who had helped whom I could never really tell; sometimes I thought Roy bore the debt, and paid it by hanging on Grady's every word, and sometimes Grady was so solicitous of Roy's happiness that I assumed it was he who carried the relationship in the red. In any case, the friendship persisted, and so once every month or so we would have dinner; never more than the three of us, and Grady always paid.

There were several dozen Gradys in the phone book, six or seven Dennises and *D*'s. There were three uptown, where, as I vaguely remembered, he would remark that he had to return when he left us at the end of the night. It was around seven in the evening, and I called each one in turn; the first was an answering machine with a woman's voice on it, but I left a message nonetheless.

When I dialed the second a youngish-sounding man answered the phone, and when I asked for Dennis Grady he said, This is him, in a very cheerful voice. Sorry, I said hurriedly, I think it's the wrong number. Well, who—he said, and I hung up on him.

The next man picked up the phone and simply said, Yes.

Is this Dennis Grady? I asked.

It is.

Are you— And I stopped, unsure of how to fix his name. Ten seconds went by before he said, in a very gentle voice, Yes?

I'm a friend of Roy Harrison's, I said.

This time the pause was his, and then he said, Yes? for the third time.

So I have the right man?

Who is this? he asked. He wasn't angry; he was expecting to be fascinated by the answer.

My name is Bonnie Moore, I said. We've met before.

I see, he said. You're a friend of Roy's?

Well, I was married to him, I said.

There was a longer pause. I'm sorry, he said. I don't believe that's possible—and he hung up the receiver on his end so abruptly that it cut my breath off.

You go on and smile: you'll have figured this out much more quickly than I did. My face had begun to burn and I stood for a moment, holding a silent phone and feeling red and foolish. When I finally stepped over to the night table to replace the receiver I very nearly missed the base. There were only five words for me to go on and I repeated them to myself over and over, searching every half tone of Grady's inflection for some clue as to why he'd responded as he had. I don't believe that's possible. Well, why don't you, then? Believe it's possible. Because because because. I went into the bathroom to draw a bath, slowly stripped, and studied myself in the mirror for a moment. I tucked my hair behind my ear and cupped my left breast with my right hand, following the faint, pale trace of the stretch marks between my fingers. I stared dazedly at my pale, flat belly, while its elongated navel stared dumbly back at me. I was contemplating the dark color of my pubic hair when the answer I was looking for came to me; and then I had to drain the tub and dress again, because I didn't want to have to talk on the telephone while I was naked.

This time the line rang only once before Grady picked up; I could picture him waiting, puzzled, in a chair by the phone. Yes? he said.

It's me again. I'm really sorry to bother you, please don't hang up, I made a mistake. My name is Caroline—or that was my name when Roy and I were together. Anyway, I've changed it, and it took me a while to realize that you couldn't have known.

So this is Caroline? You said your name was Bonnie.

Well, I was Caroline, I am. But I've changed it. For the time being I have a different . . . Anyway, we used to have dinner, I said. Do you remember? I had been pacing in small circles on the carpeting of my hotel room; then I started off in one direction, stretching the receiver cord until it pulled the base off of the night table. The bell rang once as it hit the floor. When Roy and I were married? I continued. Hang on: I've dropped the phone, sorry. He didn't speak until I'd put the base back in its place and said, All right, go on, thanks.

Yes, I remember, he said when I'd finished. What can I do for you? He was as polite as could be.

I'm trying to find Roy. He's not working at City Hall anymore, and he's not in the phone book. I was hoping you might know where he was.

I see, said Grady, and I believed that he did see.

Do you know where I can find him? I asked.

Ummm, he replied quietly. I didn't have the courage to ask him whether that meant yes or no. I heard him take a single breath on the other end: it could have meant that the moon was plunging from the sky outside his window; it could have meant nothing at all. Perhaps we should have dinner, he said.

Dinner? The idea of eating took me entirely by surprise; it was the last thing I ever would have thought of. But I trusted in his manners, and right away I believed that dinner was how this sort of thing was settled; and I wished I had only said yes.

Why not. Are you hungry?

No, I said, because I wasn't. Another mistake: was I ever going to stop making them? —Yes, I said, because I was trying to follow him as closely as I could.

Well then, why don't we sit down somewhere? He turned away from the phone for a moment to check something in the room behind him. I'll tell you what. Why don't you come up here? I'm a little too tired to go out, but I can order in a meal, and it'll be here before you know it. Where are you staying?

Gramercy Park, I said. I don't want to interrupt you.

Not at all, he said. Please come, I haven't seen you in a very long time. Should I send a car down for you?

No, I said. I can make it up there. Just tell me where it is.

Park and Eighty-third, he said. The left side of the street. I'm on the tenth floor; the doorman will show you.

All right, I said.

Half an hour?

That should be plenty.

Good, then. I'll see you in about half an hour. I heard a crisp click when he hung up the phone.

I dug through Bonnie's clothes and found a short-sleeved dress made of navy blue crepe, with mother-of-pearl buttons running halfway down the front. I got out her black jacket, a thrift store thing that would look good enough in the shadows; I put on black panty hose and I carried her wallet and the bottle of her perfume in a small black purse. Before I left I checked myself in the mirror and tried to remove the fretful look from my features.

It was chilly out, and the wind was up. When I arrived at Grady's building the doorman came wordlessly out to the street to open the door to my cab, and I emerged from the backseat like a princess, bending gracefully at the waist and clutching my purse to my middle. Under the awning and through the brass and glass front door, the lobby was lit with fiery mirrors and smelled of metal polish, and my shoes slipped slightly on the floor. The doorman was behind me; he was the last subtle man in the world, within and without. Grady? I asked. Ten, ma'am, he answered. The elevator was waiting to carry me; I stepped inside and turned, but there were no buttons on the panel. And the doors shut, and the thing took me up, without my saying so much as thank you.

I couldn't help but believe that the kingdom was waiting for me. I stood as still as I could and felt expectation take my limbs and fill them with liquor. Inside, and inside, and inside: my dress was resting softly against the back of my thighs. I thought the feeling would last forever; then the elevator slowed and sank a little bit, dropping for a moment like a bowing courtier in deference to my entrance onto the waiting floor. It was the loving floor, and I felt an elegance emanate from my soul. It wasn't goodness or well-being, it was a charm that I felt I deserved; I was delicate and lovely, and though the sensation had passed in its most feeling form by the time the elevator opened, it lingered on like a comforting murmur in my ears. I saw only one door in the short, windowless hallway, and it lay directly across from where I stood. Grady's doorbell melted beneath my fingertip.

It took longer for him to answer than I had hoped. I looked into the small circular brass plate over his peephole and I saw a woman, very nicely dressed, looking intently into a golden glow. Then I heard him shuffling on the other side and I pulled away, afraid he would see me looking at myself, in a moment so intimate that he would know everything I had to say before I had a chance to say it. The door opened like a prop; he faced an empty audience; I was waiting in the wings. Hello? came from within the room. I was there, and he stood tall, turned sideways, and very quickly changed his expression to something more comely. Hello, he said again, this time with a well-met tone. He was bigger than I remembered him to be; he had a round, friendly face, and he was wearing black cotton trousers and the most beautiful shirt I had ever seen on a man; it was soft and tailored and as blue as Harlem. I wanted to touch him somehow, to make the contact that would prove that our positions had been right all along; we were not mistaken or deceived; but the best I could do was to shake his hand, and all I felt was a shock of his warmth and the faintly familiar smell of his citrus cologne.

Across some negotiable rooms I could see a black window shining in the space that survived three or four door frames, with the city just beginning behind it. I was turning as a woman should turn in a house she's never been in before, bright-eyed and admiring things, a polished rosewood side table in the hallway, wallpaper as thick and soft as fine cloth, imprinted with modest stripes of dark red and pale grey, a cut-glass light fixture. So beautiful, I said.

Thank you, he replied. Can I take your jacket?

I slid the thing off and handed it to him, and he hung it in a hall closet that was already full of coats. There were several doorways leading from the entranceway, and I was looking through one of them into a dark room with a chandelier when he turned around again. That's the dining room, he said. We're going this way. He turned to show me his back and started down the hall; I followed him with the strange feeling that he had forgotten I was there at all. We passed what I supposed was an office; there was a dark desk against the wall and a wooden table in the corner with a few papers arranged neatly on it: that was all I saw. We emerged out the other end into a hallway, lit from above; through a door on my right I saw another room, a lounge or a study, more private, and we kept going, past another two or three doors, until at last we came to a library; the room had that peaceful smell of dust and slowly rotting ink, and it was lined with bookshelves all around, stretching from the floor to the ceiling—real books, read, not uniformly bound in some burgundy leather; they stood on the shelves in a real order, I could tell by their attitudes against one another, but it was too much for me to read their titles. The accumulation frightened me; to think that this pleasant man before me, a man I didn't know, had been through them all. To ease my eyes, I turned to find a window. The nearest one was above a desk and faced Madison Avenue a hundred feet down; looking uptown, I could see the jeweled taillights of the leaving cars as they rose unevenly up the hill toward Ninety-sixth Street. The entire distance was alight.

Can I get you something? he said, and I turned around. I had rudely forgotten him; I'd left him at the dance, having been charmed away by luminous suitors. He was standing by a tray of drink things on a side table, and his tone was solicitous, eager, and slightly contrived, like a grown man trying to make friends with a child.

Rum? I said. Do you have orange juice?

Rum . . . he said. Orange juice in the kitchen. He started for the door.

Oh, no, never mind, I said.

Just a second, he said lightly, and he was gone, leaving me with his library. *Collected Poems.* A Paris book, another, an entire shelf of Paris books; something thick and dark that said *Piranesi* in red letters on the spine. A palace, a republic, philosophy. There was a mirror on the wall that gleamed with a prismatic sliver of rainbow where its beveled edge met the tarnished silver frame; it was one more thing to see myself in. When he returned he was carrying a tray with an ice bucket and a glass pitcher of juice on it. He set it down on the side table, turned away from me, and began fixing my drink. There should be food here soon, he said, turning halfway around and speaking over his shoulder to be polite. Please, sit down. How long have you been back?

I settled carefully on the end of a leather sofa. A little more than a week. I drove up from—

Where have you been? —I'm sorry—you were saying.

Down south, I said. In Sugartown.

Ah . . . he said. . . . Ice. When he turned around again, he was holding my drink at his side, and he was going to keep it until he asked his next question; it was a subtle gestural ransom for my answer. Did I read something in the paper? he said.

I had forgotten about it entirely, so secure was I in the man's elegant apartment. My heart remembered before I knew what I was thinking: my blood jumped: it just took a moment for me to lose control entirely. He was teasing me about what was going to happen next, telling me that they had been waiting, and now were come. He was cruel, I shrank, I didn't want to take the drink from him; I stood there trying to breathe as all of the air left the room, leaving a vacuum through which he stared at me pleasantly. The walls began to flex from the strain; the books on the shelves started to shiver and I expected the doors to burst open, the windows to shatter; any moment now, I was waiting for a concussion, a painful popping in my ears, and I squeezed my eyes shut and raised my shoulders to protect myself. *Here we go,* I heard my head say through the shouting.

Wasn't there some kind of riot? said Grady in a calm voice and from a very great distance. I didn't answer, so he said it again, this time from no more than a mile or so away. I looked up and saw the room swiftly telescope back into place at my feet, where it very plainly lay, quite as still as the original, except for a final slight trembling of the furniture. What? I said, and reached down to put my hand on the arm of the couch. Well, it was a . . . I could feel the soft leather under my fingers, I could feel an infinitesimal slick spot behind me, a small abundance, a premonition in my nostrils, a great unconscious relief. I was still alive, dripping blood beneath my dress, and I could see a living purpose to everything, however inconvenient it may have been. I stood up; he arched his eyebrows, and for a second I was afraid that he knew what had occurred, that he could tell, at the very worst that he could smell it. Can I use your bathroom for a second? I said.

Of course, he replied without hesitating. Down the hall and to your left.

I took my purse, and I walked the long way around him. Down the corridor I looked at nothing but the regular patterns of yellow light and grey shadow that his wall fixtures cast on the floor. The bathroom was perfectly still and noiseless; it seemed to me that a very soft singing had abruptly stopped. Had there been music playing in the other room? I couldn't remember. A few small flecks of blood had issued out onto the back of my underwear. I blotted them quickly with a bit of damp toilet paper, glimpsing, as I bent, a flash of my naked waist—thick—in the mirror. I thanked my dress for being dark and my purse for the tampons that were buried in its bottom depths, pulled up my panty hose, and washed my hands under a golden faucet.

When I returned to the living room Grady was waiting patiently, attentively, politely. He sat at one end of the couch and looked at me in the most unthreatening way, and I loved him for that. There were several neatly stacked cardboard containers on the table by the window, alongside a pair of dishes, a pair of cloth napkins, and some cutlery. The food's come, he said. I nodded and said, Thank you, but I didn't move any closer to it; it would have been impossible for me to eat.

He didn't ask me to sit down; I could decide for myself, and I stood. Are you all right? he asked. I nodded. Are you in some kind of trouble? I shook my head, a grand and terrible lie if ever there was one. And you are looking for Roy? I nodded again. All right, he said. I'll tell you what I can, but it won't be very much. I haven't seen him myself for over a year. —No, that's not true, I saw him very briefly in a restaurant one night; I was leaving, alone, and he was coming in. Alone. We said hello, and that was about all. I didn't know him anymore. But once I'd known him very well. He hesitated. . . .

I asked: How did you meet, anyway?

Well . . . And here he finished his drink with a flourish and got up to refill it. Will you have another? he asked; but I just gestured with my half-full glass. I don't know, he began. It's a long story, and it takes place a very long time ago. He gave a dismissive wave over his shoulder.

I had the impression that he wanted nothing more than to tell me—to tell anyone, to tell some receptive ear—all about himself and Roy, and that he'd wanted to do so for a very long time. He was facing away from me, waiting to turn around, and I became uneasy, I had to suppress the desire to slip from the room and leave him there with his story unspoken. Instead, I did as he had silently asked. Like every dutiful thing I've ever done, it turned out to be a mistake. No, please, I'd like to know, I said.

He nodded, leaned back onto the couch, and stared up at the ceiling, his hands holding his full glass in prayer to whoever lived upstairs. No more than a moment had passed, but he was already lost, he was going to be a while. . . . When I met Roy . . . Eight years ago? Nine? I was already well into my thirties and I was already very rich. I sold futures, he said, smiling quickly at a joke that was at once private and too obvious. And I was paid very well for the effort. Or rather, I wasn't paid at all, really, but when the future turned out to be as I predicted, I kept a share. At the time I was very . . . optimistic, and very good, too, at impressing my optimism upon other people—not many people, but the right number, the right people, so that my optimism would be fulfilled. What could be more simple? I thought there would be wealth, say, in January, so they thought that there would be wealth in January, so come January there was wealth, and I was given a certain part of it, just for being right. — He brought the glass down to his mouth and sipped from it absently, just to remind himself how it was done. He was ignoring me, he never looked at me. O.K. None of this was real, he continued, but it didn't matter; belief was what I traded, and there the illusion was as good as fact. At the time I was living farther downtown; when I came home from the office, I'd drop my things at the door and walk immediately into the living room, where I'd sit in a chair by the window and stare for a while at the street below. After a while I'd rise and shower, and sometimes I would swear I could see the dust of dead money falling from my skin and coiling to a kind of mint color at my feet, before it disappeared down the drain. I liked to think that some enterprising young man was waiting out there to gather it all together and reconstitute it as cash. — Here he got up again to fix himself another drink, though the glass in his hand wasn't empty yet. Are you sure you won't have another? By then my rum and orange had dwindled to bitter pulp and ice, but I shook my head. He delivered the next part of his explanation in a rising voice.

Well, you know, New York was very different then. It was much older and much more serious, and it was the most gorgeous city that man had ever built, the most glorious city, the brightest and most precocious city. I wanted, I wanted, I wanted . . . I had come here from Columbus, Ohio, where my father had owned a small clothing company, and to the boy, New York was a place of terrible intricacy and surpassing intelligence. The sun traveled all around the world just to rise upon the place; beautiful boys and girls sold sex on every corner; art was obsolete. Valentino died here, years ago; it was too much for him, he was standing on the sidewalk and his heart just burst. Did you know that? I was going to make a fortune for myself; the opportunity was there; the laws had changed, the stores were all brightly lit. When I was a boy I read, What profit hath he that hath labored for the wind? All his days also he eateth in darkness. I hadn't listened. So I went to work every day, trading shares in January's prosperity.

But what I thought was the society-to-come was only mean and dull; and what I thought was a savior economy was only vanity and a grave. At first I didn't notice; I worked hard at my office, I had splendid evenings, and at night I slept peacefully, with the shades drawn down against the city. Then one day I woke, looked out my window, and discovered that everywhere there was ruin. You can't imagine: the vulgarity, the trash, the animals. It might as well have been all my fault. If I'd had the slightest sense, I would have left immediately, but instead I kept working; I thought the problem was that I hadn't made my intentions sufficiently clear, so I worked harder. On warm nights and weekends I was in my office, finding money in a frenzy. But it was just the same, and then it was worse: whole neighborhoods went bankrupt before my eyes, the lights went out, the streets became ugly, the virus lived wherever it wanted. Then I started drinking, and of course I drank too much. In time I could no longer really work at all; I became frightened of my own power, in time too frightened to leave the house. My lover wouldn't come around anymore. I lost my job; it didn't matter; I had already taken my money and put it away. I found this place, and I haven't worked since then. . . .

Well, this is a very long story, he concluded, and I'm sorry. But you see— Why am I telling you this? —Where was I?

I hadn't forgotten for a second; I hadn't been able to follow all that he was saying, it just burned like some too-sweet incense in the room, but I remembered what I was after. Roy, I said. You were going to tell me how you two met.

Abruptly he stood and began pacing slowly around the room. Yes, that's right, he said. So there I was, I felt bad, and I was doing nothing. I had a friend who was teaching in the law school that Roy attended and I was invited out to speak to his class. I stood there, in that sort of scooped-out auditorium, and looked out at those intent faces . . . their shine, their consolation. To this day I can't recall a thing that I said, but when I was done they all applauded. Later that evening, I sat on the porch of my friend's house and spoke with the students. Roy was a very intense young man, he wanted to come here and work to fix everything I had ruined; I was impressed by his decency, his uprightness. I thought he was very handsome. He asked me for my advice, and I offered to introduce him to some people I knew in the mayor's office. We talked for a long time, and . . . Now, you must understand, I am not a fool. But Roy . . .

I was staring, not quite at him, but closely enough that I could tell he was alternately looking at me and looking at the glass-topped table in front of him. My hand was numb from clutching my cold glass, and I felt a drop of condensed water roll slowly down the edge of one finger, hang for a moment, and then disappear. Grady had stopped pacing and was wavering slightly on his feet. It had been noiseless in the room for ten, fifteen, twenty seconds. And then? I asked.

He called me when he arrived here, he replied. We had dinner a few times. I confirmed my feeling for him. A short time later he met you, and I knew that I had lost him. In any case, I did what I could for him. I did what I could for that faultless trio: the city, the money, the young man. It was the finest thing I've ever done, said Grady, and at last stood stock still.

The telephone rang, the bell bursting against his inertia. I waved permission to him, it rang again, and he got up and quickly left the room. It rang one more time. So there was nothing left but me and my mixed feelings: melancholy, for here was one more melancholy man; uneasy because the perfect symmetry of my private memories—there was Roy, saying what he said, and there was me, saying my own part—had been forced open to make room for other players; jealous because his love for Roy was still tender, and mine was not.

He came back into the room and stood respectfully at the door, like a man waiting for the dead to stop dying. Do you know where he is now? I asked.

I haven't seen him, he said. He left his job at City Hall, and I haven't called him.

Do you know where he's living?

I have an address, he said, and moved into the room. From a drawer in a small desk beneath the window he withdrew a square of white paper, on which he copied the information from memory; when he handed it to me I put it in my purse without looking at it.

Then he guided me back, through the dim passages, the anterooms and chambers, toward his front door. Not a word more. We reached the last hall. One word more. As my hand started for the doorknob, I remembered what I had to ask him. Grady? He paused on the threshold and nodded softly. I heard that he'd fallen in love with another woman after I left, I said. I heard that she tried to kill him—that she wrecked his place and ran off with their child.

There wasn't room for both of us at the end of the last hall, and for once his manners were thwarted; he didn't know whether to stand at the door so that he could open it for me when we were done, or to linger back in the half darkness, so as not to give the impression that he was trying to block me from leaving. In the end he settled for opening the door and allowing me to pass through it; I stood in the hallway while he stood on the threshold. He was awkward: I thought that was why. You heard this? he asked. From whom?

A man I met at a wedding in Sugartown. Do you know anything about it?

The elevator had arrived and it was waiting; it was going to leave again, any moment. Grady was lost; he was listening to some inner oratorio, in which it had gradually emerged through the glorious music that the heroine, she with the soaring voice, was seeking the one thing that would destroy her. His part was coming, but he was having trouble with his words. What exactly were you told? he asked.

Just what I said, I replied.

. . . Yes, said Grady. Oh . . .

Now the song had risen; the lights were as bright as they could be; the singer was down on her knees. Can you tell me?

But the pitch had become too exquisite for him; he was suffering to maintain it, he was in physical pain and he faltered, failed; the music finally broke behind his eyes, and his voice became very precise and gentle. That was the story, he said. I don't know anything more than that.

All the rest was conclusion. I felt a faint pulling in my ears; he knew much more, but he didn't want to say what it was. He was still in love with Roy, it was the one and only thing he felt, and he guarded his torment jealously; he wouldn't trade it, even for a bare-throated song, and I suddenly hated him for hiding from me. Please tell me, I said.

He shook his head. Please don't ask.

Tell me. . . . I'd never needed a few words so badly, I wanted to reach out and shake the story loose from him. He took a half step back into the doorway and shook his head again.

I don't think you should call Roy, he said gently. Best to leave it alone.

Why? Grady?

For the third time he shook his head, and this time he looked down. Good night, he said. It's been lovely to see you.

He couldn't meet my eyes, so I lost all sympathy for him. I didn't say anything, I just stared as he shut the door. There was an instant during which I found myself alone again in the empty hallway, the blazing lights were brutal. I had to say something . . . so I raised my face and screamed . . . as long and loudly as I could:

Fuck you!

What was he trying to hide?

HIS OWN BLINDNESS, MY OWN GUILT, THE OBSCURE TERRORS OF THE heart. In retrospect I did him wrong, I should have kissed his cheek and thanked him; but I didn't listen, I had to know. I stepped into the elevator, and the floor beneath my feet fell.

All the way down I wrestled with Eros: I began to kick at the base of the elevator walls, making a concussion that resounded in the room; I pounded on the brass fixtures with my fists, until the whole cube shook with a tremendous thundering noise that threatened to bring the building down from the inside; I hit the alarm button and the bell began ringing, I was banging, the room was booming, I wanted to make a racket that they'd hear all over town. When I reached the lobby the doorman was standing with his hat in his hands and his eyes wide, waiting to see what was the matter; but I brushed right past him and he didn't dare say a thing. If he had, I would have killed him and left him piled in the corner as a warning.

Outside it was cold. I realized that I'd left my jacket in Grady's closet, where it would languish forever, and I pitied it. A few blocks down Park Avenue there was one car stopped behind a light, there was one more even farther, and above them were the dark buildings. The air smelled like it had been doped for a party that no one had attended; it made me feel very big, because I was by myself. I started west toward the shivering park.

I was halfway between Madison and Fifth Avenue before I stopped to look at the address that Grady had given me. On either side, dark stoops and stone doorways led into noiseless brownstones; ahead, an expanse of humid trees rose behind a low fortress wall like the woods of a medieval fairy tale. Underneath a drapery cone of light that had formed beneath a street lamp, I took out the slip of paper and looked at what was written there:

136 West 16th Street
Apartment 2F

Stone, paper, light. Money—I put the address away and walked to a bank, where I withdrew as much cash as I could from Bonnie's checking account. Then I crossed over to Fifth Avenue and walked downtown, past the office buildings and storefronts, past the steps of the library—the lions nodded their approval as I passed—and then down the slope of the city's middle belly. It was a long way to go, in my Babylon. Bonnie was with me, and so was Billy, and the Policeman. I saw the clouds come down so low that they obscured the tops of the tallest buildings; it was getting ready to rain, I could feel the clouds dressing and bustling, and the air was so thick that it slowed my pace; the stars had gone out, and instead there was a great pale orange roof, like the dome of a planetarium with the houselights dimly on. I saw an ambulance hurry across an intersection, with its lights going but no sirens on. I stood there on the corner of Sixteenth Street—a cab came by, slowed and looked at me expectantly, and then hurried off again—and I could hardly breathe. Roy was waiting two blocks west, and I was in such an ecstasy that I wasn't sure if I was going to make it. One drop of water fell on the back of my hand, and then never again. I crossed Sixth.

This part is as obscure around the edges as a very old movie, with the weak light strobing and the figures flickering as they travel, in their herky-jerky way, down the wide sidewalk. Roy's block was lined with trees, casting foliate shadows all along the way, like puddles and pools of devil's-water. My chest was as hollow as a doll's. I couldn't make out the building numbers and by the time I found one, lit by the light from its entrance hall, I realized that I'd gone two doors past his. I thought for a second that the mistake would be enough to expose me: no one could fail to notice the woman outside their window, walking back and forth late on an overcast night. So I crossed the street with my footsteps striking loud marks on the asphalt, squatted down in the dark beside a garbage can, and lifted my eyes to his building. A woman in a light grey raincoat went by before me, with a sleek dog on a leash stretched so far behind her that it took me a moment to realize she was walking him. I waited some more, I must have waited an hour. A pair of women went by in the opposite direction: one was middle-aged and empty-handed, and one was old and carrying a glossy red shopping bag with white tissue paper peeking from the top. Time passed, I shifted from one leg to the other and back again, I watched for Roy and prayed until his doorway began to disappear.

Then a man came down the sidewalk, strolling with a familiar, lean man's gait. I felt it sooner than I saw it; he took a short ambling diagonal across the street to Roy's door, passing around a parked car with a check of his hips that made him look still thinner. By the time I'd admitted who he was he'd taken the stairs and was turning his key in the door; so I saw him only once, saw his waxen face as he turned to let the door shut, and by then I'd already started shaking. I didn't feel so nervous, but I was shaking badly and I decided, all at once, to outrun it; so I dashed down to the corner, and hid, gaspy and panting, in the darkened doorway of a closed department store. Miss, are you all right? said a passing policeman—and I took off again, running as fast as I could down Seventh Avenue, never looking back to see if he was chasing me, until I reached Fourteenth Street.

There was a bar a little ways down from the corner, and I hurried through the door. Inside, the music was loudly playing some old song for sorrow, and the bartender had his back to the room as he rang a few wet bills into the register. I took a seat and waited with my hands folded until he turned around and said, What can I get you? His voice was cancerous, but he was offering to help me; I didn't know an angel could be so old and afflicted. I asked him for a gimlet, and when it came I sipped it slowly and silently wondered, Who made this place and set it in its frame? In my change there was a dollar bill with C.D. HAS A HEART OF GLASS written on it in black ink. Now there was another song, this one fast and greasy:

> *Baby you're so beautiful*
> *You got to die someday*

> *Baby you're so beautiful*
> *You got to die someday*

> *Why don't you give me some loving*
> *Before you pass away?*

I thought it was an astonishing thing to say and I wanted to know the woman whom the singer was trying to set free.

I had four drinks and I fell in love with the bartender: he was old and fat, and he didn't want to talk. If I'd married him, I might have gone home to him every night without worrying. The worn counter in front of me was wet with rings from the bottom of my glass. My arms were tired from holding up my head, I had been looking down for a while, my head was tired from holding my eyes. A man came up to me and touched my arm, and when I jerked away from him he stepped back, but nothing was going to stop him from speaking. Now let me see if I've got this, he said. I turned and stared at him. He was wearing the ugliest pants in Creation; they were green and yellow, and they were peeling off his hips and getting ready to slink away without him, even as he stood there. He was smiling and his eyes were glassy. Well, he was drunk. Well, I was too. Numberless, murmuring, numb, mumbling. I've seen you somewhere, the man in the green and yellow pants said. He was one more person I thought I'd never have to care about. Why did he want to hurt me? I shook my head and said, I haven't seen you. You wouldn't, he answered, unless you could see through a newspaper page. Can you see through a newspaper page?

I don't know, I said.

Can they see us? He gestured to a newspaper photograph of a politician and three policemen that was taped to the mirror behind the bar.

I don't think so, I said. I certainly hope not.

Well then, there you go, he said. You wouldn't have seen me. But I really read, you see, not like some people, who just pick up the thing and turn to the funny pages. Or the sports. Not like these people in here. I go through the whole thing, every day. I'm a reader, and I remember things. He tapped his temple with his index finger: everything about him was starting to bother me. And I saw you in the paper, he went on, and it was only this morning. Hey, he said to the barman. Did you know I saw this lady in the paper this morning? When he got no response he turned to me again. Now what did you do? he asked. Don't tell me.

Nothing, I said. I've never done anything, in my whole life. Who are you, Johnny-read-the-papers?

My name is Moon, he said, and he smiled; his gums were grey. You from the South? he asked. I paid him the honor of looking at him. I can tell, he said. I read the story, I read the whole thing, and I saw your picture. I remember thinking, Hoo! Shit!

I don't know what you're talking about, I said. I really, truly don't know anything about what you're talking about at all. My name is Marie. I held out my hand and he shook it gladly. The calluses on his palms were thick and smooth, like the inside of an old shoe. I've never been outside of New York City, I said.

No? he said. If I get it right, will you buy me a drink?

I don't think so, I said.

Just a drink, a short one, if I get it right. You'll see.

Go away.

It was in the paper, it's got to be worth something to you. I'll tell you anyway, and then you can decide what it's worth. O.K.?

I sighed. Will you leave me alone then? I looked at the bartender to see if he would protect me, but he was looking at the bar.

You won't ever want me to leave you then, he said. I guarantee it.

All right, I said.

He could hardly contain himself. The cops, they're not always so dumb, he said, holding up one finger. So one, they took your friend's camera and developed the film in it. There was a picture of you in there, doing something you shouldn't have been, whatever it was. Then two—he held up a second finger— the nurse, the nurse at the door. She saw you coming into the old people's home that morning, and so later when she heard you were dead as of the night before, she knew it wasn't true. So she told the police. Now they figure that maybe you're not you after all, and they're looking for you. He held up a third finger and the tip above the top knuckle was gone.

Two and a half, I said under my breath.

The Policeman, he died, three. You didn't even know that, did you? You're a—what do they call it, a refugee? fugitive? runaway? Now isn't that worth a drink?

What paper was this? I asked. I was still convinced that it had nothing to do with me, but I was beginning to take an interest. What a heroine, what a genius and a lonesome thing.

One of the city papers, he said.

Well, that's fascinating news, I said. But it's not about me.

All right, all right, he said, to humor me. That's fascinating news, she says. All right. But is she going to buy me a drink? I nodded, and the bartender poured him a shot of rum without asking what he wanted. I watched the man drink it down, and then I left two twenty-dollar bills on the bartop and walked hastily out the door.

I stood on the corner and watched the anonymous traffic bounce by. I was beginning to believe everything that the man in the green-and-yellow pants had said; it was too terrible to be untrue. So everyone knew everything about me. Maybe I could just apologize, say that I was sincerely sorry, and they would let me go. Surely that was all they really wanted. Besides, they didn't know all the rumors about my ex-husband. Wouldn't they have understood if they had?

It didn't matter: I was down to my purse and the money in my wallet, but I was brave enough to believe that I was going to get away, whatever they decided. An entire brightly lit and alcoholic heaven had promised me that I was; besides, I was blinkered, I had Bonnie's blessing on my research. I said, Brrr, because it was cold outside, and I started walking west.

Soon I came upon a residency hotel that passing time had thought too negligible to notice. I walked up the stairs at the entrance and pulled open the broken door, and found myself in a bright fluorescent-lit lobby with dark windows at either end. Across the empty linoleum floor there was a counter, behind the counter there was a cage, and inside the cage was yet another manager. I gave him forty dollars in cash, and he turned a big book around on the counter and held out a pen. My name—what was my name? Jezebel, I wrote. He fished my key out of a blue bucket on a shelf behind him, and as he handed it to me he sneezed so violently that he forgot all about me.

At the bottom of the stairs there was a pay phone, and I

tried to call Billy on Bonnie's credit card. Four times the phone rang in Sugartown; five times, six times. On the wall by my eyes someone had drawn a clock face in blue ballpoint, but the hands were the same length, so I couldn't tell whether it was eleven o'clock or five minutes to twelve. Hello, Eden View, a nurse finally whispered in my ear.

William Mahoney, please.

It's past midnight, she said shortly. Everyone is asleep.

Billy Mahoney, I said. Can I speak with him?

Who is this? she replied.

A friend, I said. I'm sorry to call so late, but I really have to speak to him.

I couldn't have let you speak to him anyway, she said, and then her voice rose. Who am I speaking to? Do you know what time it is?

Anyway?

Yes, she said, and faltered. When she picked up her lines again she was softer and more gentle. I'm very sorry, she said, but Mr. Mahoney passed away this afternoon. Who is this? . . . Hello? she said, and I cradled the receiver with the quietest click.

The lobby was empty; there were no mourners waiting, no biographers finishing their notes, and the next I remember I was in my room on the women's floor. I shut the door silently behind me, and felt a poisonous flower of guilt in my chest; I knew it wasn't the right emotion, and felt it even more strongly. If I hadn't left, he might have survived; if I hadn't been witless, I wouldn't have had to leave. I should have said no when he sent me. But I had left and he had died, and all the way down he'd wondered where I was. So where was I?

I switched on the dim light. The room was high-ceilinged but barely big enough for the small bed and night table it contained, so that it felt like a fourth-class ship's cabin; and in fact the floor was tipping one way and then the other as we hit some waves. I fell onto the bed, and immediately I was angry. High up on the opposite wall there was a small grated window that looked out onto the black bottom of the sea, into which Billy had swum, leaving me alone—the thief, the liar, the bastard. And the light went out again.

That night I dreamed I was drowning, and when I woke in the morning my legs were entangled in some seaweed, the grey sheets that I'd kicked down to the foot of the mattress. I'd slept on my left arm, and it was dead; and I was still wearing all of my clothes from the night before, and I had nothing to wash with. I stood up and touched the wall with my hand to steady myself, smoothed down my dress as best I could, and walked slowly downstairs and out onto the bright and busy street.

There was a take-out place on the corner, and a bodega next to that; I bought a cup of coffee, some aspirin, and a newspaper in one, and a bar of soap and a toothbrush in the other. In the dark window of an abandoned shopfront I saw myself pass, hiding behind the plainest face I could muster. At a hardware store down the street I picked up a pair of scissors; from a pharmacy I bought a box of hair color. When I got back to my room I stripped down to my underwear, and in a strange fit of exhilaration that made my hands tremble and my eyes water, I began to cut my hair.

I was used to changing styles whenever I'd moved: I'd worn bangs in San Francisco, and a long cut in Charleston, and one cold winter in Chicago, I wore a ponytail under a knit watchman's cap. They had all been mild disguises of one kind or another, but what I wanted that morning was a brand-new way of being, and I cut and cut my hair until it was as short as a boy's. Then I mixed the dye and worked it in, and sat on the edge of the bed to read the paper while I waited. The mayoral election was coming up; two men were saying terrible things about each other. They were talking about crime and the police; they were talking about me. I started thinking about how they hated me, because I had killed a man, for beating I don't know who, for the second man's lawlessness, which was for a city that was failing. The Policeman was buried in the earth in Sugartown; he would still be buried there tomorrow; he would always be there, but I was still above ground.

The floor in the bathroom was slick, slippery and cold from the remains of another woman's shower; she was standing above the sink in a beautiful red bathrobe, with her hair hanging in thousand-year-old strands. She watched me in the mirror as I passed behind her. You're going to look nice like that, she said warmly as I stepped into the stall; when I stepped out a few minutes later as a dark and brooding girl, she was gone, and she'd taken the hairbrush I'd left on the bench. She could have it, I was working in a bigger time: I ran my fingers through my hair, shook it dry, and stared at myself in the mirror, a different Caroline, another one. She was frightening to see.

I used to make epithets for myself, and inscribe them on my inner face. I had a character assigned to each one, and together they made up my cast, a large ensemble that was always changing, as one or another member would quit in a huff, or show up late and be fired, or be eager and ingratiating in order to join. SWEPT-AWAY was one; BLUE-EYED was another. THE WOMAN AT WORK, FAIRGROUND, and FAR FROM HOME. That morning I found another name written obscurely on my lips. THE BRANDISHING WOMAN, it said, intelligent and impolite, with her clenched hands and scent-of-the-hunt.

With a paper-thin towel wrapped around my chest I hurried back to my room, where I dressed myself, brand-new and still blushing, in a dress that had been alive for decades, and I welcomed the cloth to hide my rawness. Then I carefully spread the contents of my wallet on the mattress: it came to $212, and I went back to sleep trying to figure out how much that was, calculating it in clothes and cheap hotel rooms, in food good or bad, all in books or all in train tickets.

I didn't leave my room again that day. I woke and slept, woke and slept again, still wearing that dress. I woke and I thought about everything: about what history I knew of the world, about a house I had once hoped to live in, about the sweet voice of my best friend and about my own features, about my ex-husband and his secrets. For hours at a time the walls of my room bent in over my bed like praying men, oh so serious; they were praying that I wouldn't be proud of myself for having broken the law, but they only partially succeeded. Kiss my ass, I said to the walls, just before I fell asleep again.

When I woke it was night, and I swung my hollow legs off the bed and walked myself downstairs. There were no clouds, and the air was peppered with cold points from the coming autumn. I wished I had worn something more practical—when was it? The night before. The night before that. It was cool; at least the trees thought so, because they shivered. I caught a glimpse of myself in a mirroring storefront and was startled by the dark-haired girl. From a bank clock on the corner I learned that it was just past ten, and Fourteenth Street was shuttered like some cow town in anticipation of a midnight shoot-out. Up the block I saw a woman ministering to a dog that was lying in a doorway; past her was a man who'd fallen asleep standing up, right in the middle of the sidewalk; his body was bent in half, his head was hanging down, he was dreaming of poppies. The signs hanging over the street swung in the wind, and the lights above just turned and turned. As for me, I went directly up Seventh Avenue to Sixteenth Street and headed down the block without thinking. It was only when I came to Roy's door that I hesitated, and then just for a moment. I felt as if the nation was seething behind me, and the preachers were crying out from their pulpits, and all the souls in Hell were asking me for help, because I, too, had thought I had a right to be weak; and I was wrong, but I hadn't been caught yet. I waited on his welcome mat for them all to catch up, so that I could bring them with me through his open door. When the storming became too much for me to bear, I rang the bell.

It was a little while before the speaker rustled loudly, then Roy. Who is it? And his voice: as soon as I heard it, I could smell it, wet with his mouth.

It's Caroline, I said, and almost added, Your ex-wife. But instead I waited. I had time enough to huddle against the cold and hate the light in his lobby.

Caroline . . . he said at last.

I'm in town and I wanted to see you.

You're downstairs?

I was staying a few blocks from here. I wanted to see you. I need to talk to you.

The buzzer rang, and the door swung open under my hands; the stairs rose up an off-white stairwell, turned at a tiny landing, and then disappeared. His apartment was on the second floor, and by the time I reached his hallway I could feel my heart beating; it put my thinking on a shaking tray. So how was I going to talk? I wondered if he knew what I had done. His door was slightly open, and there he was, standing just inside. How was I going to talk? The light was dim and he was a ghost lover, he was the shadowy keeper of some secret chamber, he was the flesh of Time, waiting to exercise its infinite dominion. . . .

I found him halfway down a narrow hallway, his back to the wall as he warily watched me enter; before I could reach him, he turned and disappeared through the far doorway. Was that him? Was it me? I followed him, and when I reached the room at the end I glanced at him once, very quickly, and saw him clearly. Right away I noticed that his features had become a little bit sharper and his hair a little less red, and he looked as if he had a few more things to carry. There are some whom passing time gathers, makes dense and fat. There are others whom it spends, drawing their skin and pinching their thoughts: that was Roy. I thought I knew about how days became wisdom, but I was wrong. I didn't realize that my love would find this difference: age, experience, my absence, the time to have made greater mistakes, each mysterious one of which was scored on his expression. It was enough to shock me. I'd expected him to be perfectly preserved through all the years we had been apart, waiting for me faithfully, if not because he loved me, then because he had no choice. But he hadn't waited. Still, I knew that if he tried to wrap his voice around me, if he gazed at me along the proper line, if he took my arm as I passed him, led me into his room, and laid me down on his bed, I would have had his dick in my gentle mouth in a moment, without really knowing why.

I couldn't bear to look at him any longer. Instead, I surveyed the room. It was lit with a simple brass floor lamp, and there were two vases above the mantelpiece, but only one of them was filled with flowers, some daisies that were drooping and about to die. I knew the couch, I had imprinted it with my own hips years before; but I didn't recognize the framed black-and-white photograph of a city street that was hanging on the wall, and the end table wasn't mine. The flowers knew how I felt: some years past, I had shed a stem, and it had grown and aged on its own. When I came back I found it had taken on some distorted form, its own life, and never thought of me.

I don't have much time, I said.

He shook his head—how simple, how possessed—and gestured toward a chair. His T-shirt was blue, with a few spots of white paint on the front. Your hair, he said. And here, what happened . . . He made an incomplete motion toward my face. His jeans were loose, and I wondered if he had lost weight; he was shoeless and sockless, and his ankles showed. . . . Are you all right? he asked.

Yes, I thought, of course you would begin by patronizing me. Would a simple hello have been too much for you to offer? I'm fine, I said. Why wouldn't I be?

I didn't expect you, he said. How far have you come?

I was living down south, I said. I left about a week ago.

He didn't say anything in reply to that, but he studied me while he tried to calculate the distance and the reason. Why are you here?

There were endless words available for my reply; they were waiting for me to divide them into expressions, and the effort was enormous. I was still standing; he sat down, very heavily, I thought, or not at all heavily, I couldn't tell. From above, his skin was very smooth and pale in the light. It was too tender for me to contemplate, so I sat. He was looking at my feet. It's been a while, he said. Why is that?

You were faithless, I wanted to say. Why was that? But I didn't want to get into it all just yet. What have you been doing? I asked.

Working, he said.

On what?

Oh, you know . . . he said. When I didn't respond, he went on reluctantly. . . . Saving the city. I smiled; he wasn't smiling, and right away I changed my mind.

Do you know the story of *Frankie and Johnny*? Swore they'd be true to each other, swore that their love wouldn't die, but Frankie found Johnny in bed one night, with a girl named Nellie Bly. The song started singing in my head and wouldn't stop. It was an old man's voice, and he would yodel whenever he ran out of words; but he never broke, the verses just kept coming, loud as a train, but in the calmest voice. She shot him right through the door. He was my man, the singer sang for that woman, and he done me wrong. Roy pulled his legs up beneath him on the couch; it wouldn't have been possible for him to get to his feet very quickly. The room was built like a black-and-white movie, and I started the examination, although if I'd known it would end so badly I never would have begun. I heard you've been drinking too much, I said.

What? He looked genuinely surprised, and his mouth fell slightly open, so that I could see the incarnadine shine on his underlip.

I heard you lost your job at City Hall.

They elected a new mayor, he said. So I quit. Where—

You weren't getting drunk all the time?

No. Once . . . I got a summons for being drunk and disorderly. It was just once, and they dropped the charges.

You weren't fired for that?

No. My boss asked me about it, and that was the end of it. They used to tease me about it. Why are you asking me?

I heard you were going to marry another woman.

I married you, he said.

I know. But there was, she was afterward.

He shook his head and dropped his hands in his lap. I really don't want to do this, he said. I've just been living here. . . .

Another woman. Roy, please, I said, simultaneously bullying him and begging him.

Where did you hear these things?

A man I met at a wedding in Sugartown. And Grady told me.

Grady? he said in a miserable tone of voice. When?

Last night.

How was he?

Brokenhearted, I replied shortly, hurting him so casually that he flinched and I felt worse. To this day I can remember a faint ugly scent that had crept into the room as I spoke; it was unlike anything I'd ever smelled before, a bitter and morbid presence. There were pale drifts of chalk yellow smoke in the air, crawling around the furniture and curling up to sting my eyes. I didn't heed. Was she beautiful? I went on. Was she smart? Did she let you come in her mouth?

Look around, he said, and he looked around for me. I'm living alone, can't you see?

I could see, but I went on. Did she leave you? Did she tear your apartment up and leave?

He shook his head again. I don't know, I don't know what you're talking about. There haven't been any women.

I heard that when she left she took your baby, I said.

He glanced at me once and then closed his eyes, and again I misunderstood, and waited for his apology. I had waited for years, I could hardly bear to wait any longer. He opened his eyes and spoke to his shoes.

What? I said.

He raised his head and looked terrified; all reason had left the world. I felt it, too, and all of a sudden I knew what he was going to say; I made a motion with my hands as if I was trying to turn a clock's hands back, but I wasn't in time. No, he said. Yes, no. Those are yours, all those stories. That was you.

I gave him five seconds to feel what I was feeling; they were going to be the last seconds we would ever share, and we divided them equally, I could see. The moment was as distinguished as the last seconds of the soul's self-conscious being before it expires. I was blind, the room was grey and yellow, and I dared not move. Then my voice, unnaturally clear and bright-toned: Oh, no, I said. You're wrong about that. That wasn't me at all.

Except that it was.

What do you mean? What are you talking about?
What do you mean, it was you?

I MEAN THIS: THE TREE WITH SEEDS HAS THE WAITING EARTH UPON which to drop them; we have the receding heat of our vulgar marriage to miss. For some time during our engagement, Roy left me, and I left him. We had made our wedding plans and we were waiting, but the waiting went on too long, so we each began to wonder. If the other wasn't perfect, then what was wedlock? And then the arguing over petty things started, and we began to harass each other helplessly.

One week we made plans to rent a car and drive out to a bed-and-breakfast in Montauk, but somehow we abandoned the idea—that was someone's fault, I don't remember whose. From the following two weeks, I stole a dozen days of peace from him, I admit it, but by the time I was ready to return them it was too late; he'd distilled liquor-of-rage in the basement, and left brimming bottles of it on the bathroom sink, for me to knock over as I was reaching for my makeup in the morning. The depth of my own hatred shocked and disturbed me. I couldn't stand to look at him, and even when I could, I wouldn't; he made it rain indoors.

There were days when, had I inherited the moon, I would have pawned it for a few days of harmony. There were days when I wished he was dead. We fought like this: one night just before dawn I woke up tossing on my side of the bed, my fists clenched underneath my pillow. I wanted to kick him awake, but I didn't; still, he heard the noise in my head and woke halfway. What is it? he said sleepily. Nothing, it's nothing, I replied. Oh.— He turned over and started to fall asleep again—turned his head up. It's snowing? he asked. It was August. It's *nothing,* I said. He slept for ten seconds more. — It's snowing? he asked again, and sat up in bed and looked to the window, where there had been no snow for six months. Why did you wake me up? he said angrily. I didn't answer because I didn't know what to say. You're not talking to me? Why can't you let me sleep?

Without a word, I got up from our bed and went to the kitchen, where I made a cup of tea. My hands were shaking. When I returned to the bedroom he was still awake, and the sun was rising on another snowless day.

He sat up, pulled the sheets up to his waist, and said to me, What have you ever done right? What? Go on, name one thing.

I looked over and saw his morning erection pressing beneath the bedclothes. — And the next moment I had him down on the mattress. My hand was on his chest; I scratched his bare skin. Shit! he hissed, and tried to turn, but I pinned him with my hips, with my hands on his wrists and my tongue in his mouth. My hair was hanging down, so I couldn't see his face, but I could smell his bed-warm morning scent, I could feel his startled tears on my cheek. He sat halfway up, I pushed him back, I reached down and took him in my hand; then I raised myself up just long enough to pull down my underwear and push him into me before I sank down again, engulfing him whole, with nothing between us, and there was nothing he could do. I would have been raping him, he was too beautiful to survive unmolested, and he fought me, but he was fighting to fuck me. It didn't matter: he thrashed around inside me, but I was the most powerful woman ever made, that morning, ecstatic and starving, I was a proud, wet, burning hole, and he was just another helpless man. It was over in a minute: his eyes closed and he came, his jerks continuing at ever-greater intervals for a minute or more while I sat solidly astride him and stared down at him. He struggled to breathe, until at last he'd recovered enough to push me sideways, and I fell onto the bed. I hadn't come myself. I didn't care.

Within a wordless half hour he'd dressed and was getting ready to leave for work, while I, still lying in bed, was preparing to call in sick. As soon as the door shut behind him I began to feel a tingling in my abdomen. I swear to you, I felt it, and I knew right away what it might mean, but I thought the idea was just my imagination teasing my flesh.

A few weeks later he shook his head angrily and said, Maybe all this is a mistake. That evening he left town to stay out in Pennsylvania with a friend whom I'd never met. For a week we spoke on the telephone, and for a week we didn't. I didn't know why I was marrying at all; the next Wednesday we spoke once, and disagreed. I was to blame, but I couldn't bring myself to crawl back to the telephone. Another day, waiting. The strain, I thought, had stopped my body, building, waiting. It didn't seem possible that my timing could be so clumsy; I thought I was just irregular; but the third month started and I was still holding back blood, and finally one Saturday afternoon, with the help of a small pale blue package from the corner pharmacy, I read a tiny, mockingly optimistic + —just the size of the soul it signified, I thought—and discovered that I was pregnant.

I didn't say a word; I didn't call on anyone. I spent Sunday under a Sunday blanket, and on Monday I went to the doctor. Wind and rain, waiting in the waiting room, green leaves stuck to the window.

On Wednesday I tried to call Roy, and left a message that he didn't return. And the fatherless thing was growing quickly: I took a look at myself in the mirror that morning and I could already see it coming, a baby to be, it was right there with me in the bathroom. I was being possessed from the inside out, like the host in a horror movie; my body was changing into some obscene and gorgeous thing, a voluptuous exaggeration of flesh and fluid;

my breasts and belly were becoming a blood-and-milk factory; I was being remade to bear this being, and every part of me was already committed, except for my mind. I thought about love and creation, the natural cunning of love, the obesity of creation. Everything I had learned through my eyes told me I was becoming sloppy and gross and out of control; everything I felt in my flesh told me I was approaching the greatest dignity I would ever know.

I became frightened and angry. How was I supposed to make all that love, so quickly and out of nothing? Besides, we'd been so furious the morning I conceived that I was afraid the baby would be born with a black heart. If I ever saw Roy again I was going to kill him, for leaving me at a time like this. Kill him, for being as weak and as selfish as I was myself. My fault was, I hadn't loved him enough, I didn't know how, every woman knew how but me. I began to bargain and argue: for three days I thought of nothing else. I said to myself, It would be worse to bring a resented child into the world than to stop a pregnancy that I hadn't intended. Because it didn't count if it was an accident, did it? —But then, it was just a child, I said to myself. Every woman who ever lived has had one. Then again, it was just an abortion: every woman has had one of those, too. — And the phrase WOMEN AND CHILDREN became lodged in my head, as I felt myself go down. Finally I said, I'm going to do it, and before I could change my mind I made an appointment at the clinic; I didn't say a word.

The room was pale beige so that it wouldn't be blue or pink, there were posters on all the walls, and a television in the corner was playing a talk show. There were four other women there, and all of us were in a brave little daze. A nurse gave me a form to fill out; they asked for my medical history, but I had no history, so I left it all blank and looked at the other women in the room. One by one our souls were dissolving, from the heat of our self-hatred; still we sat there. For a full hour, a day, I waited, until at last the nurse beckoned to me and led me into a small room. There she took some of my blood, my blood pressure, my temperature, the room was cold. When we were done she took me into another room and started to explain to me what they were going to do. She was very nice about it, but I wasn't listening. I was thinking of everyone else, all of them freely strolling down the sidewalks outside, except for me and the poor girls in the next room. We were different; we had been separated out from nature. I nodded my head whenever the nurse paused, and when she stopped and handed me a waiver, I signed without reading it. I gave them permission. That was the end.

I lay on my back in the operating room, with my legs spread. This is to numb you, the doctor said, and he turned his head to look inside me, seeing something I had never seen, the excuse for all my features, all my running around. There was no hiding. You might feel a little pinch, he said calmly. I felt a pinch. O.K.? I nodded.

Now. He began to push in a stick that would open me wider; the nurse held my hand. I could feel a kind of nudging, he was doing something up there. — And then suddenly the room turned an unbearably bright red, as the pain reached my eyes. The nurse's face was red, the doctor's, the walls were wobbling. O.K., you're doing fine, the doctor said. Just a little more. And again I felt him force a hole in me, this one even bigger: it couldn't have been what he meant to do. I thought that the procedure was going horribly wrong; the baby was fighting for every second of its privacy, its tiny form giving off an enormous hot thrashing energy. I wanted to tell them, but my tongue had been cut, and it was too late, I couldn't speak. The doctor said something I couldn't understand, as if he'd given up trying to communicate anything and had lapsed into the berserk language of his vicious technology. Another thing went in, even larger, stretching every bit of tenderness in me until it was ready to break; I became convinced that I'd come to an evil place; it wasn't just the blood they were after, it was my entire heart, because the baby's life was with mine, after all, and they weren't going to stop until they had reached it.

This went on forever.

And then the pain subsided, just enough to let me breathe, and the wand with its pitiless mouth was pressed into me, where it sucked and scraped out the remaining shreds of the double inside me. It was all over soon enough. I lay in the recovery room for an hour or two afterward, and then rose on weak legs and passed through the front doors of the clinic and into the stagy sun. On the street no one watched me, so no one saw.

But you know I was right to do what I did. Not because I hadn't carried a life—I don't care what we say when we argue, I knew what I had inside me—but because I couldn't have carried it well, and a life that is misbegotten is worse than no life at all. So I cheated a little; even heaven isn't perfect. I still remember my shame, my grief, and my anger—and my sense of release and relief, and the strange joy I felt at having made my decision and carried it through. It was over and done. Read the books: I felt just what they tell you you'll feel. But above all I remember how it had hurt, and they never tell you about that.

Roy came home two weeks later and I didn't say a word. I took him back because I didn't want to be alone, but I didn't let him touch me; I shrank from his hand, and his smell was a threat; I said nothing. I took him back, but I hated him; I was cold, his dick was obscene, and I wouldn't let him near me with it. Love wasn't love; at the end of every coupling there was going to be another waiting infant and another unready mother. I didn't tell him that; I told him I didn't trust him, and in response he became the perfect man, patient, attentive, constant. But he couldn't cure my dreams: in our speechless bed at night, during those delirious moments before sleep, I felt a tiny ghostly mouth pulling at my sore and shrinking nipples.

The nurse had told me not to have sex for two weeks, but I didn't have sex for a month and a half—though every so often, out of obligation, I would blow my boyfriend and silently spit the result on the mattress. When I finally let him inside me, he was so soft and slow about it that I wanted to pass away. It was as if he was injured as well, and soon I had convinced myself that taking care of him was the only way I could earn back everything I'd lost. Again he asked me to marry him, and we were married the following month.

We were making lazy talk after dinner one night, we were coming up on our first anniversary. He was sitting contentedly at the kitchen table and I was leaning on the counter, finishing the rice and vegetables that he had left on his plate. You don't eat enough, I said.

I know, he said. He picked up a piece of bread from the plate in the center of the table, turned it over in his fingers, and then let it drop again. But it's not the food, it's just my appetite.

I left the plate in the sink and went over to sit before him on the edge of the table, with my feet planted on either side of his seat. I took his face in my hands and examined his Irish lips. You're going to get sick, I said, kissed him briefly, and then went back to staring at his mouth.

And so it went: he had never been sick a day in his life, he explained. Never been in a hospital. And me: two or three times. Kiss. Twisted my shoulder in gymnastics class when I was in junior high school. He had a terrible fear of hospitals. He couldn't stand the thought, he said, and smiled to show that he understood that he looked foolish. Kiss. It isn't so terrible, I said. They drug you up as soon as they get to you, you pass out right away, and the next you know you're home in bed. Except when I had my abortion, I said without a thought. Then I felt everything.

What? he said.

It was pretty bad.

When was this? He spoke sympathetically and he looked concerned.

Last year, I said. I knew very well that something was going terribly wrong, but I had long since lost practice, and the lie that would have saved me occurred to me too late. We weren't talking at the time, I added.

He straightened in his seat. Wait a moment, he said, and held his hand above the table while he timed the past. It was mine? he asked.

Well, no, I answered a little bit flippantly. Really it was mine.

Why didn't you tell me?

I didn't think you would understand, I said, and I would have said anything. You couldn't have understood. I felt like I'd been poisoned, and it was so, so beautiful.

He didn't reply, he stood and turned his back to me; but I could see that he was suffering; I thought he would bleed betrayal all over the room, until his knees gave way and he fell. Instead, he went for a walk and left me there, with my mouth wide open and my womb still empty.

He never did give up the idea that the tiny thing had been

half his, and I would never stop believing that its fate had been all mine. It made no sense to me, but sense had never been our strongest bond. Still, we tried, and the conversation was endless: We discussed this, we confessed that, we misunderstood, we returned to the beginning again and again. I tried to diagnose what was wrong between us, and I changed my mind, and changed my mind, and changed my mind. It was because he was Catholic, it was because he was a man, it was because he took our marriage too seriously, or because he didn't take it seriously enough. I should have told him right away. I never should have told him at all.

One Sunday morning I threw a half-full coffee mug at him; it struck a white glass table lamp and then landed against a stereo speaker, shattering one and spilling lukewarm tan liquid all inside the other. I wouldn't let him clean it up.

Beyond that, our marriage didn't so much break as it melted. It was a book that ended unexpectedly, leaving me to a day at once more and less real—more seen and less felt—so that I wondered, in the transition and to a lesser degree forever afterward, which, after all, was the illusion, and which was the world.

In the end he came home stinking of strange perfume, and soon afterward we took a lawyer to town. My soft, hollow body, his lean and bony body: so go on, you grey judges, you bullies and you back-fence gossips; there was no counsel left for Jack Sprat and his fertile wife.

How did they hear? I asked him that night, as I stood in his living room and silently numbered with names all of his friends and all of their stories, sickening at the thought of them, and the lies they'd told about me. How did anyone hear?

He had his head resting on one hand, like a portrait of the young man disconsolate. I don't know, he said. I swear I don't. It could have been anyone; it could have been everyone. There was a sandy spot in his voice, where it had been stripped as it slipped through his rough throat. It doesn't matter now, does it?

Of course it matters, I said to myself. Everything matters. But I thought about it for a moment more—and suddenly I understood, and to my own surprise I found myself agreeing with him completely; my face had changed so utterly in the intervening years that it didn't matter. I agreed with him so readily, so entirely, with such fullness that I became lighter-than-air and my feet left the floor. No, it just doesn't matter. Not at all, I said, laughing down from my vantage point far up by the light fixture on the ceiling. I looked briefly around the room for anything I might be leaving. I saw a small plastic movie monster on the bookshelf, squatting and staring out into the room. A dictionary, a pair of black hiking boots stood next to the door to the hallway, and a small pile of newspapers sat on the floor at the end of the couch. A tennis racquet in a blue case, a pair of blue-grey sunglasses, a portable telephone. A green twenty-dollar bill lay on top of the cold radiator by the window. Honestly, I said. Not at all.

It was time to go. I waved good-bye and began floating down the hallway; he followed, I waved good-bye once more and just drifted out the door, but as I left, that old song started singing again:

> Now, this story has no moral
> This story has no end

It sang me all the way back to my dim hotel room, beside me in my narrow bed; it was still singing when I started dreaming my dreams.

I woke up an hour after I dropped off, and couldn't get to sleep again. My hands lay helplessly under my pillow. The room was as quiet as could be; I lay there, and my heart was shrunken and tightened by gravity, because I had fallen to the bottom of the world, and no one knew I was there. Then it was four in the morning and I was awake again. The heat from the city's gaze was radiating through the walls. Somewhere outside my car was still waiting, with the shoe box hidden like a hide-and-seek child in the backseat.

At five I showered in the cold light of the cold bathroom, dressed, and left the hotel. There were ghosts on Fourteenth Street, rattling the storefront grates and scattering poorhouse paper as they danced in and out of the doorways. Along the way east I saw candles burning in the windows of the buildings that passed by above, but there was no movement in any of them. I stayed close to the curb and I kept my head down, passing blindly by a fruit truck making deliveries to a grocery store, two cops in a car at a corner, one staring one way, one staring the other, and some teenagers; they were walking in their sleep. I crossed the street to avoid them. I reached the garage.

The seat of the car was still cold, the interior smelled of old perfume and plastic, but I kept the windows closed and sat lightly in my seat. I wasn't going to leave the city in that car, it was a lamp saying, Here's the one, Here's the one, as it drifted and glowed across the intersections. I just wanted to park the thing; it didn't matter where they found it, so I pulled it over to a fire hydrant and turned the ignition off, then sat back in the front seat and waited. Nothing happened, so I looked around me for anything that I might want to take with me; and there was nothing. So I took the shoe box from the backseat and stroked it a few times to reassure it and remind it of my touch. O.K., I said. Let's go then, wherever you want to go.

When I stepped out of the car, I was as light as could be, with no trappings but the small purse in my pocket and my public face; if there had been photographers all around, firing flashbulbs to get the moment of my latest debut, everyone would have known how weightless I was. I had parked near Times Square and all I had to do was walk uptown a few blocks and over to Eighth Avenue, but by the time I reached Forty-second Street I knew I was in trouble. It had been a week since I'd slept well, and the lights along the way made me feel sick. Everyone was looking at me as I passed, and every half block or so another man would step in front of me and say, Hey, miss, how you doing? I couldn't believe the gold in their smiles; I couldn't believe the cane one of them walked with; I didn't know sex had undone so many. And how was I doing? Dazy, dozy, and my mouth tasted like metal; rocking on my feet; trying not to think about the skin beneath my dress; I wanted to pass through the place like a white cat, and never trouble my lips to tell them all to go fuck themselves.

By the time I made it to the bus station the sun was all the way up, but the Port Authority was still empty and I could hear my own footsteps. All the backlit advertisements, with their sordid colors and barely disguised tone of begging, were snubbing one another like beggars will. In time I found a ticket window and paid my fare.

Out on the floor I saw a man and a woman kissing; his hands were on her hips, and her arms were around his waist. They kissed and kissed, and when they were done she went one way with a swollen mouth, and he went another with an erection that I could see pressing against the cloth of his pants. I wanted to warn her that she would be condemned to lust after him eternally, but it was too late, she left. It was just then that I decided not to breathe again until I was gone: the bus was waiting where it was supposed to be, but it wouldn't leave for another half an hour or so, and I didn't breathe at all, not once. Not when a short stocky man and two small girls got on and sat a few rows in front of me, not when the driver finally boarded and started the engine, not in the empty tunnel with its white tiles and interrogation lights, not until we came out from under the city, and I saw the first blue note of the sky reflecting off of a green lawn.

Upstate

Who were you?

Well, with my first breath I was once again Miss Bonnie Moore, a woman who'd imagined she was Caroline Harrison, who'd imagined she was notorious, until her imagination turned and she came back to herself. I was a quiet and curious traveler, wearing a look of glazed surprise and humming softly as she stared out the bus window.

After a few miles had passed I walked to the front of the bus and stood behind the driver. Through the windshield I could see the cars below us, the river to the right, and ahead the highway flanked by guardrails and green trees. The bus hit a bump in the road and I swayed slightly on my feet, but when it was over I was still standing. I had the idea that I was playing a game, it was called Safe and Not-Safe. Since I'd left Sugartown I had been losing, but I could tell that my luck was beginning to change.

I spoke to the driver and I was very polite. I said, Excuse me? Can you tell me how long it will be? Well, he said without taking his eyes from the road, where you're going is the last stop. It's kind of far upstate. We should be there by three-thirty. I went back to my seat and sat as I was supposed to, but there was some night still lingering in the back of that bus, and in time I stretched out on the noise of the motor and slept for an hour or two. In my dream, the ground beneath the grass was a machine made up of thousands of tiny engines and millions of tiny gears, which rolled and rattled under my feet as I tried to walk.

I woke to silence: the bus had stopped. Through the window I could see the man and his two girls standing outside. He was stretching and smoking a cigarette, and they were standing beside him, one staring at her feet, one rubbing her nose. Behind them I saw a general store with a beer sign in the window and another sign over the door advertising the state lottery; across the road I saw a silver reservoir; in the distance there were long steep hills covered with deep green woods. I stepped down from the door on my sleep-feeble legs and blinked in the sunlight, while a weak wind stirred the treetops. Where are we?

Outside of Albany, the man said. The radio says we just declared war. He was searching the sky for the planes.

War? I asked.

We've gone in, he replied, and with his head still raised he walked to the edge of the parking lot to throw his cigarette butt into the foliage. I could hear every footstep he took on the gravel, I could feel his eyes squinting in the sun. The driver emerged from the grocery store, shaking his head. It isn't a war, he said. They shot down a spaceship. It fell into the ocean.

Who? I said.

A spaceship? the man said.

I don't know, said the driver impatiently. A satellite. That's what it said on the little TV in there. But it isn't a war. He climbed back into the bus. So let's just keep going. He took his seat and leaned expectantly toward the door handle.

Girls, said the man to his daughters, who obediently mounted the stairs, with me obediently behind them. It was only after we'd started up again that I noticed that we'd been joined by a longhaired man in a brown leather coat. He was too old for his hair and it was too warm for his coat, and he sat all the way in the back and listened to a portable stereo with the sound turned up so loud that I could hear his headphones twittering.

The city was long gone behind, it was just some hearsay downriver. I thought of the Policeman waiting in his grave for me to make a mistake: The bitch, he said, but no one heard him. The fucking bitch. I thought of Billy; I thought of the mystery waiting for me at the end of the line. The wondering was too much for my stomach, and it began to roll over.

And then I was asleep again. I came awake for a moment, the sunshine was spilling wetly through the window onto my face, my shirt was damp. I turned over and slept, and when I woke for the last time, everyone was gone but the driver and me. We were making our way up a hill on a small state highway and the engine was straining; there weren't any houses, but there was a skinny old black dog standing sideways by the side of the road, just watching as we passed. I walked back to the bathroom, splashed some water on my face, and checked my pasty reflection in the mirror. My eyes were bloodshot, and my hair, my hair: it barely gave my ears comfort, and it framed my face, showing everything about me, but my face showed nothing. When I came out again, the bus driver looked up at me through his mirror and said, Ma'am, we're coming up on the end of the line. It was midafternoon, and all the shadows were still.

No small-town actress finding her way into Los Angeles, no welfare mother making her timid entrance into her first night-school class, no whore coming home was ever more humble. The bus pulled off the highway, traveled twenty blocks into town, turned, turned again, glided four more blocks, and then stopped in front of a tiny post office. The driver shut the engine down in stages. Do you know where you're going? he asked as I stood at the door.

Yes, thanks, I said.

They can tell you inside where it is, he replied, as if I hadn't said anything at all. He followed me down and disappeared around the corner of the building. I found my footing and set off into the center of town, and saw him one last time, without his wheel, and without his hat, making a call from a pay phone in a shattered booth.

It was a small, tidy village, set at the bottom of a bowl of green hills. There were only three or four blocks of stores, arranged in a Y down the street from the post office: greengrocer, gun shop, gas station, garden supplies. I stood on the sidewalk and stared. At the center of the intersection there was a small traffic circle, and at the center of the circle there was a statue of a middle-aged man with a walrus mustache; he was facing the sun, and he had one hand on his hip, with his arm bent at the elbow. Three teenage girls walked by without looking at me, and all three of them were happy. A breeze flew down from the hills, swooping over Main Street and circling away again. Into the gas station I went.

The office smelled of motor oil and stale coffee. Behind the counter there was a nice-looking older man, with thinning brown hair and scarred knuckles. In an ashtray on the shelf behind him a cigarette burned, all by itself. How can I help you? he asked.

I'm trying to get out to Holland Road, I said.

He nodded. You take this road right out here—

I'm sorry, I don't have a car.

Well . . . he said, and shook his head. It's a long walk. It's a *very* long walk. You can call a cab, I can call him for you, if you want.

I gave him a nice smile and said, That would be great, thanks.

No problem, he said cheerfully, and picked up the phone on his desk. I turned away and saw a woman in a brand-new blue pickup pull up to one of the pumps outside, step down from the cab, and begin filling her tank. John, the man said. It's Gary Brooks at the filling station. . . . The woman outside stood with her back to the bed of her truck, holding the handle of the pump and turning her red round face up so that she could watch me through the window. Fifteen minutes? said Green. He hung up the phone just as the woman finished with the hose, put it back in place, and started for the door. She was wearing pink sneakers. Fifteen minutes, Brooks said to me, and then he looked over my shoulder. Oh, hold on. I turned in time to see the woman step up to the door, brandishing her purse before her like a book of prayer. Afternoon, Mona, he said.

Hello, she replied in an untuned voice.

Twelve even, said Brooks, and she began searching in her wallet for the money. You're going up by Holland Road, aren't you? This young woman here needs a ride that way. I just called her a cab, but maybe you could drop her off.

She looked at me, it was one of those looks that no man has ever seen; she didn't like me, she wanted to know what was wrong with me, and I wore my most innocent face to answer her. Up Holland to the east or toward Rockville? she said to me.

East, said Brooks.

The woman hesitated and took a little time to examine me. Her mascara was so heavily applied that it was clumped up, and my stomach turned. I looked away. Yeah, O.K., she said. Where exactly? I showed her my shoe box and she tilted her head back and read the address from a distance; then she put her hand out to touch the edge, and read it again. All right, come on, she said, and I followed her out to her truck. As we were leaving, I heard Green pick up the phone again.

We drove the entire way in silence, past the town's last church, under a railroad bridge, and alongside a shallow river. The race was on, and there was no way the water was going to win. The woman picked up Billy's shoe box from the seat between us and held it above the steering wheel so that she could look at the address again; when she set it down I touched it once to establish that it was still mine, and I know she saw me, because the next time I looked over at her the set of her mouth had changed. She sighed heavily. It's got to be around here somewhere, she said. She glanced down at the shoe box again, this time without touching it—then looked up and suddenly stepped hard on the brake and pulled onto the shoulder of the road, throwing me forward and causing a cassette tape that was lying on the dashboard to skitter down to the end and fall to the floor beside my foot. Here, careful, here, she said. Out my window I could see a long driveway that disappeared up into some woods; by the entrance there was a battered tin mailbox with the number 445 painted on it. Is there some kind of school or something up there? she asked me as I was getting out. I turned to look at her again, I said nothing. Never mind, she replied, and I curtsied before I shut the door.

The car vanished. This is where I was standing: God had long ago said, This place is plenty beautiful enough for *you*, and all the people were content to believe him; anyway, they weren't going to contradict him, except for the few who were crazy, and they generally left for someplace where they were better off crazy. The rest stayed and became friendly; they had neighbors over the hill, out of sight but close enough for company on a cool evening. The land between them had human qualities, like modesty, nobility, stubbornness, and sudden fits of bad temper. A woman there was worth whatever home she could make.

I started walking. The driveway curved through some woods, rose over a rise, and vanished down the other side. When I followed it to the top of the hill I found that it had disappeared again, this time around a grey stone shelf the height of a tract house, leaving me to stare into the woods, and the woods to ignore me. Anything could have been in there, and I began to think that I might never find my way back, from the middle of my life, from the middle of those trees. I saw the Wolf of Violence, the Bear of Cowardice, the Crow of Not-Minding-One's-Own-Business. They stared back with dilated eyes, and then turned and disappeared into the brake. I kept walking, and still there was no sound but my own loud breathing. The sky above me was grey, the ground below me was cold, the road behind me was gone. Then I came to a shack on the left, black and bent, and half-obscured by overgrowth; I thought at first that it might be the place, but when I peeked inside an empty window frame I saw nothing but a room with a broken floor. So I went on, wondering if this was really what the world had been like before the city. I was wearing the wrong shoes; they were muddy, and my feet were starting to tire. Are you really going up there? Are you going? Alone?

I had been walking up that drive for about a half an hour when it suddenly went up a short slope and then down the other side, and a roof appeared above the next hill; it vanished again when the road touched bottom, then reappeared, this time attached to a white wooden frame that rose from the earth like scenery. I stopped to look; if I had been dreaming, it would have been a dream house, the kind to take care of forever. The driveway followed the edge of the lawn to a garage at the side, from which a stone path lined with waist-high bushes led to the door. There were flower beds beneath the front eaves, but there was nothing planted in them; still, the very idea of a garden was enough to hold the sky above at bay. I followed the path, trying just once and very briefly to peek through a window, but there were curtains over all of them. Two slate steps led up to the front door, and I saw a boy's baseball glove resting at the edge of the doormat; other than that, there was no sign of whoever was waiting for me inside. I readied my shoe box and rang the bell, and then turned away from the door and studied the yard. The wind was blowing leaves and twigs gently across the shadowed grass; at the far end, a row of trees was pretending not to watch me. When I turned back to the door it was still shut, so I shaded my eyes with my hand and tried to peer through one of the glass panes that framed it, but they were too thick and too green, and all I saw was a sea-dark entrance—There might be no one home, I thought, so I rang the bell again, thinking it might open for me anyway if I was insistent enough—and I rang again, almost immediately, and put my ear up against the glass so that I could listen to the inside of the house. I heard nothing, I stepped back, the handle turned from the other side, and the door swung open.

Behind the door stood a small boy; he was eight or nine years old and he was holding tightly on to the knob, preparing to shut himself inside again if there should be a monster waiting on the step. It was only me, so he stared, and I stared back, stunned by an aching in my chest so sharp that it was all I could do to keep from bursting into tears. He was the most beautiful child I'd ever seen: and more beautiful, and more beautiful than that. He had black hair that curled down over his pale forehead, and long lashes that seemed to gleam darkly, and wide brown eyes: his skin was pale and flawless, and his lips were sweet and red, they were solemn, insolent, lazy, whole: he didn't smile. He was wearing green jeans and basketball sneakers, and a yellow long-sleeved T-shirt with a picture of a cartoon hedgehog printed on it. He stood there like some fairy-tale princeling, the sovereign of his house and the woods that surrounded it, and I wondered what proud king and queen had created him, I wondered what fantastic language he spoke. I would try English. Hello, I said tentatively.

Hello, he said in a high, clear voice. He was still holding on to the doorknob with one hand, but he swung gracefully forward on his toes, just a little bit, as if he was wishing just a little that it was a ride.

Is there anyone home? I asked.

He swung back, and I almost reached out to hold him. *I'm home*, he said.

O.K., I replied. Is there anyone else? Is your father or mother home?

He closed his eyes and shook his head with just the right casual theatricality.

Will someone else be home soon? I could have gone on that way for hours, asking the same question in a different way, and getting the same reply, until it was nighttime and I had proved my patience enough to enter the house.

In a little while, he said. Who are you?

I'm a friend, I said. Is it O.K. if I come in and wait?

I don't think so, he said, and shook his head as if to say that he knew very well the answer was no. I didn't have a reply to that, so I stood for a moment and tried to imagine what magic words would make him let me in, what lyric, what immortal phrase. A moment. My head swam, my mouth opened, but not to speak: I had felt my stomach poke a pinhole in my throat—I swallowed once—and then the opening tore wide. I turned and dropped to my knees, and suddenly vomited into the base of the bushes at the side of the door—sick—still clutching Billy's shoe box to my belly as I heaved and spat, and heaved again. What a strange and appalling woman to find on the doorstep, and all I could think of to say was, I'm sorry, I'm really so sorry, coughing and clearing, a pause, and then it came up again. You poor thing, I thought. What are you going to do? I heard the door shut as I retched once more, emptily, because there was nothing left inside me, I'd cast it all onto the ground.

By the time the boy opened the door again I was sitting at

the top of the steps with my head hanging down into my lap and the sound of the filthy air whistling in my throat, still dizzy and wonderstruck at how ferociously nature exacts its honoraria of respect and care. For days I'd forgotten food and hadn't slept, I'd forfeited my place in the order of things. I'd done it to myself, I had no one else to blame, and my body had spoken by pretending to die, all at once, like some silly woman in a parlor drama who responds to an insult by fainting for attention.

Here, said the boy from the doorway; he was standing there holding a damp dark blue towel in his outstretched hand. It's mine, from my room, he said, and he gave me a grave and earnest look.

Thank you so much, I'm sorry, I said as I reached for it. I tried to laugh, but it came out a croak, and he stepped back, though without changing his expression. I'm sorry, I said again as I wiped my face. The towel smelled sweet and boyish, and the scent alone was almost enough to revive me; when I was finished with it I held it to my chest, a gesture that felt to me like supplication and looked to him like theft. He was too uncertain of me to reach for it, but I saw his eyes lower to the cloth for a moment, so I folded it neatly and handed it back to him with a nod of my head, as if to compliment him on his competence. Thank you.

Do you want to come in? he said. It wasn't an offer: he wanted to know what I thought came next.

Maybe I should, I said.

I guess you can, he said. But only into the front room, O.K.?

All right, I said, and stood, stopped; he hadn't moved yet, he was still standing in the doorway, holding the folded towel in both hands and gently staring at the ground by my feet.

O.K., he said again, and abruptly turned into the house without waiting for me.

I found him in a room to the right of the entrance hall. It was a sort of sitting room, containing a beat-up couch, two armchairs, and an end table with a folded section of the day's newspaper lying on it. On a set of coat hooks by the door there hung the boy's green winter coat and a man's black cardigan. The bare floor was dark wood, there were no pictures on the walls. The room was neat, but not clean; there would have to have been more in it for it to ever be clean; but it was warm, and when the door was shut again, the boy gave a paradoxical shiver. He gestured to the couch and said, You can sit down there. I sat, but I didn't know if the wheel was just resting or I was really home.

He stood in the middle of the floor and studied me as I put Billy's shoe box down on the table, feeling dizzy again as I moved. My name is Malcolm, the boy said.

Pleased to meet you, I replied. I'm sorry about all this. I'm Bonnie. He frowned; he didn't believe me at all but thought it might be wrong to say so. When your mother comes home, I'll tell her that it wasn't your fault.

My mother's not here, he said. He slid carelessly over the arm of a padded chair and sank down onto the cushion, ending half-sideways in his seat with one slender leg still dangling gracefully off the side. He must not have known how lovely the motion was, or he never would have done it. I wouldn't have dared be the one to tell him.

Who are we waiting for? I asked. Can I have a glass of water? He was confused, I could see at once: he didn't know which question to answer, so he said nothing. I had embarrassed him and I wanted to apologize again, but I was afraid it would just make him feel worse.

The room was filling with some kind of gas; it was like a gimmick from an old spy movie; I was going to fall unconscious, and the boy was watching to see how I was taking it. It seemed to me that the thing to do was to play along and pretend I was just fine. Do you like school? It was the most obvious thing to ask, but he seemed not to notice. His eyes flashed and he said, I don't go to school. — I must have looked puzzled. I don't have to, he explained. I work here instead.

I wanted to ask what sort of work he did, but instead I found myself asking for water again, if water was what it was called. This time he rose from his chair and disappeared through a door, returning with a full glass, which he carried with both hands and set carefully down on the end table. What's in that? he asked, with a long, unself-conscious look at Billy's shoe box.

Something from Sugartown. The show was almost over, all up.

What is it?

I don't know. This old man asked me to bring it.

What is it? he asked again, and right about then I passed out.

When I awoke there were three men in the room, standing in a line in front of the couch. They were arranged according to their height, from the tallest to the shortest; it didn't occur to me at the time that it was an accident. I just wanted to look at them.

The first man was about forty years old and he was standing with his hand on the boy's shoulder. He had chestnut hair that he'd let grow a little too long, and he was wearing black slacks, a neat blue dress shirt, and round black-rimmed eyeglasses that made him look faintly professional. He wasn't quite beautiful, but he seemed kind, and he stood by Malcolm in a way that made me suppose he was the boy's father. The second was ten or fifteen years older, but still burly and barrel-chested; his eyes were as round and hard as marbles, and there was something the matter with his expression; I stared at him a little longer than I should have, but I couldn't see clearly what it was. The third was lanky and pale, not just pale but paper-white, thin, blanched, bleached, and he was holding Billy's shoe box. The whole group looked like one quarter of a jury, and a boy, and only the boy looked like he would have found me not guilty. But I was so self-possessed, Cleopatra herself would have blushed at my presumption. I looked at the shoe box and gestured toward it. Did you get that? Good, I said. No one moved or said a word: I thought it was a bit much, but I wasn't going to argue. I'm a little bit sick, I said, and tried to smile. The man with the glasses smiled slightly in return, so I spoke to him. I haven't been eating or sleeping very well, I explained. He nodded, smiled some more, and said, I know. Why don't you sleep here? He had a nice voice; it sang me a lullaby in an accent from somewhere south. The next I knew he'd taken me firmly by the arm and was guiding me to my feet. Up, he said. But I thought he wanted me to sleep. Up. Come on.

We were in a small dusk-lit room on the second floor, empty but for a chest of drawers against the wall and a neatly made bed on a metal frame in the corner. He left me for a moment to turn down the blanket, exposing a raft of white sheets that looked so soft and clean that I almost fainted on my feet. Oh God, I thought. Please let those be for me. Please please.

Go on, the man said with a nod of his head, and I lay myself down before he could change his mind.

Will you excuse me for a moment? I said to him, just before I fell asleep again.

Malcolm came into my room as I was dreaming; Gena Rowlands and I were trying to rent an apartment, but there was a war on—we were in Rome, and that was the name of the war—and the landlord kept disappearing. The boy put a pitcher of water and a bowl of soup on the table next to the bed, taking care not to spill a drop. There was a big dog in the room; he reached his head up and lapped the soup from the bowl, and then walked slowly out the door. That was the last I ever saw of him. The man with the eyeglasses was standing down by my feet; he took the glasses off and polished them on his shirttail, examined me through startled eyes, blinked a few times, and then put them back on. Then it was dark out my window, the room was dark, and the house was noiseless.

Someone was walking quietly outside my door just as day was breaking. I turned over in bed and felt my waist with my hands, and the warmth of my own bare skin startled me for a second. When the sensation faded it left me feeling light as a feather, and I pulled the blankets over my head to keep from floating away.

It was noon: the sunlight was inside my room, and no matter how hard I tried to wish it away, it wasn't going to leave. When I sat up the covers fell to my lap, and I noticed that I'd been stripped to my underwear; my shoes were on the floor beside the bed and my wallet was on the night table, but the rest of my clothes were missing. — In an instant I panicked and blushed, all by myself; I bolted out of bed, wrapped the blanket around my shoulders and stepped to the center of the floor, breathing quickly, blood in my face. This is how they make you vulnerable, I thought: by making you naked, so everyone can see how soft you really are. From where I stood I could see out the window and into the backyard; grass grew high across the clearing, and the fruit from a crab-apple tree was rotting on the ground. Propped up against a run-down shed I saw a red-and-white bicycle—a boy's bicycle, so the boy, in any case, was real. But I had nothing to wear.

Still wrapped in the blanket, I crossed the room and opened the door; I don't know where I thought I was going—and when I stepped over the threshold I kicked over my dress, which had been washed, folded, and placed neatly on the floor just outside. Beside it were a clean towel, a washcloth, and a toothbrush still in its box and wrapper; through an open door on the other side of the hallway I saw the porcelain edge of a blue bathtub. I stood there and wondered . . . whether to go forward or back, to run to the bathroom or retreat into my room: I just remained there for a while, in the hall . . . standing . . . staring . . . while the morning-tired minute ticked on.

At last the trance broke, and I kicked my clothes into my room, fastened the towel across my chest, and hurried across. All right, I said to myself. If this is going to be my last day on earth, at least I'll be clean enough to meet whoever's waiting for me in heaven.

When I turned on the shower it made a noise like Niagara Falls, and for more than a minute I wouldn't allow myself under it; I was afraid that they were going to burst in on me as soon as they heard the sound, and I stood back beside the toilet bowl, clutching the terry cloth to my chest and waiting for the door to fly open. But no one came, and in time I shed the towel and stepped in. Glad, I was glad in an instant, for soap and water, and cheap shampoo. I could feel the sickness wash off of me in rivulets; it was someone else's problem. I was going to be new again, pink and smart again. For twenty minutes or more I stood under the water; then I stepped out and toweled off my hair, my familiar skin, my shoulders, my pale breasts and milky waist. They had never left me, they would always be mine.

When I was dry and dressed I went right downstairs. There was nowhere else to go, and I wanted to get it over with—whatever it was going to be. I didn't know what to expect, and I went down without breathing. In the kitchen I found a man washing dishes; he turned around as soon as he heard me. It was the man with the flawed face. He was wearing loose blue jeans and a faded white T-shirt that had become translucent and stuck to his chest where he'd splashed it with sink water, and I noticed at once that the blemish I had seen the day before was a trio of small black teardrops that were tattooed just below his left eye. They had no effect on his expression at all; their purpose was something other than emotion, or even a greater and more abiding attitude; I thought they had been put there by some desert angel, as a sign that he was select. —But what for? The distance between deliverance and murder seemed so small. He began to dry his hands with a dishtowel. Morning, he said with a tearstained grimace.

Good morning, I replied, just as calmly as I could. He waved his hand at a coffeemaker on the countertop and turned back to the sink; I tiptoed across to the cabinets and found a cracked grey teacup that once had been white. There was a gallon carton of milk in the fridge, buried behind huge containers of everything, a quart of ketchup, a sack of white rice, a case of beer, a pound of butter. Stacked in the door there were six dozen eggs, and I had a brief vision of the contents of the freezer—the entire rear half of a cow, a formation of frozen chickens—but I wasn't brave enough to open it.

No sooner had I sat myself down than the man with the eyeglasses started into the room from the far end; before the door shut behind him I saw a flight of descending stairs, over which a single unshaded lightbulb burned. As he had the night before, in my dream or in my room, he took off his glasses and polished them on his shirt; and again his eyes beneath were pink-rimmed and surprised, and again he blinked for a few moments before slipping them back on. He had the air of a corrupted and dishonored academic, a smart man who had lost all his colleagues some time ago. Hello, he said, and held out his empty hand. You can call me Monroe. His words were even and unhurried, and he used the firm tones of a professional. I could hear a laundry machine going in a small room out the back door of the kitchen.

Hello, I said. I'm Bonnie. . . . I hesitated for the briefest second. I guess I'm all done here, I'm ready to go.

He paused, pulled out a chair from the table, and bought me some time by gently sitting down. O.K., he said. He could have just said, No.

Right away I squandered my blood and blushed, there wasn't anything I could do to stop it. His gaze continued uninterrupted, and I had to turn my face down to the table, to burn the wooden top with the heat from my features. Still he said nothing, and in time I raised my head again; but the whole room was glass; every surface was reflective, his lenses, the windows, the shine on the table, the formica on the floor, the glint of the fixtures. Everywhere I turned my eyes, the light from my face was coming back at me. I know your name, he said, and I could barely hear him through the brilliance. I know all that. He waved his hand to indicate all that. O.K.? I know where you've been and what you did. It's all right, he told me, as I felt my face retract and compress and scald some more, like a coal from an overnight fire. These things happen, he said. But now, can you tell me if anyone saw you coming up here?

I was bewildered, still blushing, and I spoke right through a blood red wall. These things happen? I said. To who? Not to me they don't. Can you tell me what I'm doing here?

You aren't doing anything here, he replied. You're not really here at all. But I need to know who saw you coming. Could you think about it? He was very polite.

To think was to turn my memories, and it took me some time. Monroe waited patiently, with both his hands placed on the tabletop as if he was preparing to play an imaginary piano. When I couldn't think anymore, I lied. The only one was a woman who gave me a lift up here. At that he raised his eyebrows and struck a very soft chord on the wood, my sign to keep going. That's all I know.

He played another silent chord, this time with his right hand only. What did she look like? he said, as if he was just curious.

Like nothing, I said, and shook my head. Like everyone. Maybe thirty, maybe thirty-five. Not big, not little.

All right, he said slowly, as if he was trying to understand. What was she driving?

A little truck, a pickup truck.

He nodded, and there was a very long pause while he studied one hand, looked to the other, and then glanced briefly back at the first again. Color? he said at last.

Oh, I shrugged. White.

. . . He smiled briefly. Of the truck, he said.

Again I flushed. I don't know, I said. Green, blue.

He glanced up at Teardrop and sighed; then he turned back to me. Anyway, you had the sense to change your hair, he said. Again he turned to Teardrop. Would you have recognized her? he asked.

The other man shrugged. Might, he muttered.

Maybe, said Monroe.

I can go right now, I told him. I don't want to get you in trouble because of me. I was just doing a favor for Billy.

Where are you going to go? he asked.

I don't know. It doesn't really matter. I was going to go find a police station and confess.

At that he smiled, an indulgent smile that only gradually faded as he spoke. Confess? No, you don't want to do that. If . . . no. You're going to have to stay here a little while longer. Another couple, three weeks. You can have the room you're in, if you like.

I can leave, I said again. Already I felt flustered and I wanted to leave, not because I wanted to leave, but because I wanted to show that I, too, was capable of controlling where I went.

He sighed again and smiled again. Not yet, he said.

Why not? And I thought, What if I started for the door?

I looked at Teardrop, but Teardrop had turned back to the

dishes, leaving both questions to curl pointlessly up from the table. Monroe relaxed back in his chair. Didn't he know how close I was to screaming? You've put us in a bind, he said. Well, Billy did, anyway. It's just like him. God only knows what he was thinking. . . . He sent me a letter, regular post, by the way, explaining who you were and what you were coming with. Beyond that, he told us very little.

Do I want to know what it was? I said.

In the package?

. . . .

Oh, just something, he said vaguely. Just something for us. He was going to tell me only what he wanted to tell, at whatever pace he chose. Billy was an old friend of mine, from way back when. — He held his hands up on the table and glanced at the back of his spread fingers. He was an old friend of all of ours. He died.

I heard, I said. I tried to call him a few days ago.

He nodded, and there were a few seconds of requiem in the room. This is very awkward, Monroe said suddenly, and because he seemed honestly troubled, I was sympathetic. You're going to have to stay here. But then as soon as we're done, we can all go on our separate ways. Whatever way, wherever. Is that all right?

For some reason I was looking at the refrigerator, which looked like a warm thing, a warm cold thing, with its fine white front and worn hardware, and I think if I hadn't been looking at the refrigerator I might have said something else. I don't know, I said. I'm very, very tired. I'm hollow.

Hollow? he said.

Empty, I replied. . . . Hollow. It's as all right here as anywhere else.

Well, good, he said, visibly relieved that we wouldn't have to argue about it. You make yourself at home. With that he rose from the table, took a moment to tuck a loose fold of his shirt back into his pants, and crossed the kitchen to the basement door. Before he opened it he stopped and turned on an afterthought. Is there anything you need? he asked.

I don't think so, I said, and he nodded. —Except, I said, and he nodded again. Some clothes? All I have is what I was wearing.

Write down what it is, and what sizes, and someone will go into town and get them for you.

I can go, I said.

No, he replied, and gestured gently with his hands for me to stay. You can't, you see.

I did see.

A half an hour later, I found him on the couch in the sitting room with Malcolm on his lap and a baseball game on the television, and I handed him a modest list. He bent forward slightly to meet my hand with his, and the boy frowned at the disturbance without taking his eyes from the screen. I tried to hand him a few bills, but he just gave me a smile that threatened to overflow his lips like wine swelling at the edge of a full glass. That's all right, he said, and wiped the corners of his mouth with his fingers. We have money.

As the sun was starting its descent I sat on the bed in my room reading the morning's newspaper. A gentle knock came at the door. Yes? I said, and the third man entered, almost entirely obscured by an armful of shopping bags. Here you go: these are for you, he said, gesturing awkwardly with his full hands. Shall I put them here? His voice was smooth, unaccented, and calm, as if he'd came from nowhere and had no problem with it.

Sure, fine, thank you, I replied as he placed the things on the floor by my closet and quickly backed from the room, shutting the door behind him and leaving me alone again.

As soon as he was gone I fell on the bags like a child. They'd gotten me everything that I'd asked for, and more: extra under-wear, an extra bra, two more pairs of blue jeans, a few T-shirts, a blue sweater, a pair of boots and a pair of sandals, a light green skirt, which I loved, and a blue-and-red sort of snap-up shirt or jacket that I hated. Another bag held a confusion of bottles and tubes, and jars and tubs of soap and shampoo, conditioners, creams, astringents and treatments. I sat on my bed and unwrapped and unpinned everything, unfolded and unfolded the cloth with its swaths falling and its luxurious colors combin-ing, while a pile of fancy paper formed on the floor; and when I was done the stuff lay scattered like treasure around me on the mattress, and for a moment I was very happy.

But the house was silent, and I soon began to wonder. My conversation with Monroe had been so calm, so polite in its way, that I'd been reluctant to ask any questions. I'd hardly had time to wonder what they were doing, how bitter it was and what I'd brought to make it easier. It was only hours later that I began to feel as if I'd been bullied; but I couldn't say how. He hadn't insisted on anything, he hadn't threatened, but he'd told me—at least I thought he'd told me—that I wasn't going to leave the house. Still, the terms of my stay had never been explained: I might have been a guest, and I might have been a prisoner.

I knew the world was mean; I'd learned it long since. So the things they had bought for me had to be gotten with some-thing: what was it? I wouldn't sell my sex to them, I was sure of that. —Or almost sure. No, I was sure. Almost sure. —It wasn't worth that much to me just then, and I wanted very badly to live, I wanted every moment that was coming to me. —I couldn't think of what else they might have been buying. Buying, but they could have taken whatever they wanted. What else did they want? They wanted me silent, but I had nothing to say, and no one to say it to. What else? I lay on my bed and wondered what

I'd done. I didn't understand. Had I sold myself for nothing? I just didn't understand. I wanted to tell them that I'd changed my mind; I didn't want to see them; I was afraid they were going to come into my room as soon as the sun went down and suffocate me in my sleep. Downstairs, Malcolm, downstairs Monroe, Teardrop, and the third man. What do they all want? God, I repented to the ceiling, I'm so sorry. It just doesn't seem all that real to me.

I got up from the bed, crossed the floor, opened the door, and peeked around the edge. But the hallway was empty, and the last of the day's sunlight streamed through a window at the far end, revealing a curtain of luminous airborne dust that reached to the worn floor.

Carefully down the stairs I crept. The landing was a plane in twilit space, the bottom was blue. I came upon the boy all alone in the living room; he was sitting in the middle of the floor, pushing a red plastic motorcycle in a semicircle on the carpet. The thing had little flashing lights, and an engine that made a high-pitched whirring. He mimicked a siren with his slippery mouth. Rrrrrr, he sang. Rrrrrr. The sound of my soul ringing in a perfect present. Pull over, he said, in a voice that was meant to sound officious but instead was merely melodramatic. — Rrrrr. Suddenly he pushed the motorcycle violently and let it go, so that it rolled on its own for a few feet and then crashed into the wall and tipped over. He sighed and started to crawl toward it.

Excuse me, I said.

What. He had stopped and turned halfway around to see me.

What are you playing?

Motorcycle, he replied.

Do you know where everyone is?

Downstairs, he said. It was silent downstairs. We listened for a few moments.

What's going on down there? I asked.

Nothing, he said, and rolled over onto his side so that he could fix me with his big brown eyes. You'd better not go down there.

Why? What are they doing?

The boy gave an exaggerated shrug. Stuff, he said.

At that I paused to think, but I thought nothing that made any difference. I said, Do you know when they'll be back up?

He shook his head.

Thank you.

He didn't answer; instead, he turned and started for his toy again; I left him there and went to the kitchen to wait. There was a radio on the windowsill above the sink, and I found a station on it and let the music play softly. Now the sun was a fat red molten globule that sat like a senile king in the distance behind the trees. From the next room I could hear Malcolm playact an exploding car, the fire crackling, the suffering passengers screaming; soon after, I heard footsteps on the basement stairs, a line of dialogue and a line of laughter; the door opened and the three men came into the kitchen. What a sweet thing, said the third man; then he saw me and stopped.

Hello, said gracious Monroe. Did you get what you needed?

Yes, I replied. Thank you so much. Teardrop brushed past me on his way to the sink, where he began washing his hands.

We'll be eating soon, said Monroe.

Is there anything I can do?

Just sit tight, he said. Relax, enjoy.

I thought he must have been joking, but if he was he never showed it.

I watched them all very carefully at the table that night. The third man had cooked a huge pot of chili; we lined up before him, holding soup bowls, and he dished it out with a large tin ladle. As soon as we were all seated, we commenced to spooning the stuff into our mouths, and not another word was spoken for a full five minutes; in fact, the only sound was the slurping and gulping and burping of the three men and the little boy. When they were done they delivered a string of compliments to the cook, who smiled proudly and said, Thank you very much.

There was a brief respite while they caught their breath, and then a more significant, preparatory pause. At last the third man spoke. Whose turn is it? he asked, and Monroe briefly raised his hand. They turned to him expectantly; I turned to him with wonder. He leaned back in his chair and held his fist to his mouth to cover one last gentle belch, and then he smiled.

All chefs . . . he announced . . . are crazy violent.

All chefs? said the third man.

Crazy violent? said Teardrop, and then was silent again as he collected his thoughts.

After a moment the third man cleared his throat. A confident proposal, he began with a small smile. He shifted his hips in his chair, tipped his head back, and stared at the ceiling. I might say, intrepid. Bold? . . . Bold. As I say, confident, even immodest. —And also tricky. Where, after all, would any of *us* have had opportunity to meet with a counterexample? Any chef we might have encountered would have been *crazy violent,* if not in God's eyes, then necessarily in the court's. Tricky: you wouldn't have ventured so bold a claim if you weren't sure that we'd be unable to refute it quickly, by reference, say, to a kind chef, a placid chef, a sweet-tempered chef of our personal acquaintance. Then, too, your thesis has the advantage of myth, since people have always thought of the man who rules the kitchen as an ill-tempered tyrant, a devil in white linen. And again, there are certain prejudices to recommend it: only the most impartial man can contemplate the waxy skin, the sweaty brow, the grim stare of the chef—who, not incidentally, will likely be grasping a large knife in his damp hand—and not imagine that the soul of a murderer lurks behind. Well, all right. . . . He paused for a moment, but before he could pick up the glittering thread of his argument again he was interrupted.

I don't know about crazy, said Teardrop, tapping loudly on the table with his forefinger to get everyone's attention.

. . . Though it's true I met more than a few of them inside, the third man said reflectively. But still.

Well, there you go, said Monroe.

Let me say this: it gets hot as hell in a kitchen, Teardrop went on. It's hot as hell, twelve, fourteen hours a day, with the stoves, and the fucking waiters, and the customers, and if everything isn't exactly right, it's the cook's fault, right?

. . . But I don't know what each was in for, the third man concluded. It could well have been something harmless, at least to a man's body.

So, O.K., a cook's going to blow his top now and then, said Teardrop. O.K. But that's not crazy. Crazy is, a man for no reason just reaches down and kills people, right? That's a crazy man. But if a man who works all day and all night in a hot box, he loses his temper now and then? —No, not crazy. You've got to define your terms.

Clever tack, said the third man, with some amusement.

Crazy is just crazy, insisted Monroe.

And so they went, for another forty-five minutes or so. Soon enough the original topic was lost and they were talking about the best meals they'd ever had, pretty waitresses, a bout of food poisoning, fishing on Lake Ponchartrain, weather, bad weather, weather so bad you couldn't get to town. They got on to telling tales: the third man said his grandfather knew a farmer in Pennsylvania who built his house with a hull that he tarred himself. His neighbors all laughed at him, they called him Noah, but when the great Johnstown Flood came in 1889, he just dropped anchor and went for a float, and when the waters went down, he was the only one remaining.

Monroe said that reminded him of a man he'd heard of who built a house out of corn husks. The thing was, he didn't bother to take all the corn off of them. So when the first hot day came, the corn kernels started popping like mad, right there in his living room. It sounded like fireworks, and his friends all came running to see what was the matter, but by then there was blood all over the walls. The man was so full of holes that the coroner thought he'd been shotgunned. God take my balls if I'm lying, he said; then he waited for a moment, stood up from the table, pulled out the front of his pants, and peered in to see if they were still there. He shook his head and sighed with relief.

Teardrop said, Yeah, listen here. My uncle was hunting, and he got shot. He got so pumped full of buckshot once that he used to set off the metal detectors. I'm serious, serious as a stroke. When I was in Rahway they wouldn't let him visit, and at the airport, the thing would go beep beep beep. So finally he had to drive everywhere instead. But that wasn't the worst, because every time he went under a high-tension wire he'd start to glow like a lightbulb, and he'd glow for hours, until he couldn't get to sleep at night, because he couldn't turn himself off. Ha! Now what do you think about that? he said to the boy. What do you think, Chick? — And he laughed until real tears glistened among the ink drops on his cheeks, giving him the appearance of an illustration come to life.

Malcolm giggled and said, I don't know.

Do you believe me? Teardrop asked.

No! said Malcolm, and giggled again.

But Teardrop didn't laugh: his face fell into a stern expression and he rose slowly from the table and stared down the boy.

You don't? he said evenly, and without shifting his gaze from Malcolm's fallen face, he addressed Monroe. What are we going to do with this boy? To Malcolm again: Do you know what happens to boys like you, to smart-ass, skeptical boys?

No, Malcolm said very softly, looking down at his plate.

They got to help clear the table and do the dishes, said Teardrop, and with that he made a sudden feint toward the boy, who flinched and then smiled with relief. The older man started for the sink. Monroe spoke: Go on, he said to Malcolm. You heard him.

The boy rose reluctantly and started to clear his things. I was tired of sitting, so I got up to help. Not you, said Monroe in a slightly gentler tone of voice. Why don't you come in the living room?

He sat in the chair and sipped straight whiskey from a tumbler; I sat on the couch and reached my fingers up to my shoulder to find a strand of hair. There was none there, so I crossed my legs demurely at my knees and waited. The third man had disappeared. Got to have fun at dinner, said Monroe. No matter what else is happening in the house, a boy can live with anything if he has some fun at dinner. Something my father taught me. He cocked his head as if he were listening to the man, and I found myself listening along with him. Oh, well, he said after a moment. Do you have everything you need?

Yes, I'm fine, thanks, I said. But I wish—

He interrupted me by making a mocking face. But *this,* but *that,* yeah, he said, and laughed a little. I didn't know whether he'd lost his mind or if he was just carrying his good mood over from dinner, and I was terrified of the difference between the two. No, he said. Wish what? That you could take back the last two weeks of your life? Well, we all wish that. We all wonder how much we can get away with. — He began to strum an imaginary guitar, then turned his face up to the ceiling.

I fought the law and the law won.

He sang in a flat voice, and then he laughed out loud. Yeah.

And suddenly he was serious again. You make me uncomfortable, he said, and he shifted in his seat and took off his glasses. His bare face seemed more worn without them, and his eyes were slightly harder; or maybe it was just that he couldn't see. I opened my mouth to defend myself, but he spoke right over me. You don't mean any harm, I don't think, but you seem to have a way of causing trouble. We don't want any trouble here, we just want what we're doing to get done. So you should think of all this as a dream, and don't make any decisions. You just wait until it's all over.

Sure, a dream, I said to myself. I could do that: I was not lonely, I was not guilty, I was not dead.

As far as I could see at the time, Billy's shoe box contained something wanted and magical, which completed one part of whatever task was occupying them and began the next. By daybreak, all three men would be seated around the kitchen table with their breakfast. They were down in the basement most of the morning, and they would come up at around one in the afternoon to eat lunch. When the door opened, I would hear strains of song rising up from belowstairs, mostly begging and threatening country ballads. In the distance between each note I'd be able to detect a strange, bitter chemical smell—a sweet, flinty smell, an influence—that I recognized but couldn't place, and then the door would shut and the music would end. They would gather in the kitchen again and talk things over, but they lowered their voices if I drew near, and I only caught fragments of their conversation, never enough to tell. His expression is really perfect, I heard the third man say once.

. . . . Makes me come in my pants, said Teardrop on another occasion.

When lunch was finished they would return downstairs. Another two, three hours. Very often the door would open halfway through the afternoon and Malcolm would be called down to join them. An hour . . . an hour . . .

Finally the day would end, and all four of them would come up for dinner, and when dinner was done they would enact the same ritual I'd witnessed my first evening among them. The meal finished, the cutlery laid down, one or another of the men would be called upon to propose a point. Each would try to outdo the last in absurdity, or profundity, or sheer surprise. A man cannot get really clean in a bathtub, proposed the third man one night. — The skies are filled with UFOs, insisted Teardrop after the following evening's dinner. — The higher up the monkey climbs, the more of his ass he's got to show, said Monroe when it came to his turn again. After each assertion the debate would begin. Monroe always spoke evenly and sensibly; Teardrop was always short and coarse; and the third man's reasoning was always intricate, mannered, and eccentric. But argument soon gave way to anecdote, anecdote to out-and-out lie, and by the end of the hour there was nothing left but joking. I sat by with something to say, but never enough confidence to say it with.

Each day was the same. There were no weekends. Only the moon out my window changed, as it grew like some opening ivory eye, glaring down from above the treetops after midnight. The weather was becoming cold: she wanted me to know, but she didn't want to be sentimental about it.

Two weeks passed, but I wouldn't have noticed it at all had I not seen the date at the top of the newspaper that the third man brought back from town one morning; and even then the stories told below suggested that time had ended and the world had become inert. The satellite that had been shot down had eventually landed in the ocean. It wasn't ours, anyway, and aside from a stern speech from the President, the government was paying it no mind. A school bus in Illinois had gotten stuck on a railroad crossing; an incoming train hit it, and twelve children were dead. Sugartown was still cleaning itself up in the aftermath of the Labor Day riots. Several commissions, federal, state, and local, had been called to investigate. If they had asked me, I could have told them what had happened, but I myself was still missing; the pages said nothing about that, but I knew I was.

The men's activities belowstairs were a great mystery to me, the one element of my reverie that I couldn't reconcile upon falling asleep each night. Clearly they were criminals; possibly they were bad, and if they were bad, then clearly I had helped. Monroe had meant to make me forget that I cared at all, but I was curious: I couldn't help that, could I? I began to speculate about their work, though I had nothing to go on but my fantasies. I was worried. What fit in Billy's box? Almost anything, bomb things or drug things, or triggers, or contraband, or a miscellany of props. There came a point where I didn't want to wonder anymore, and I began wondering about the men instead.

At first I saw them as strangers who would never settle into figures I could compass, but as the days passed and they deepened into their roles, I began to think of them as the Three Men. It was like living with the familiar characters in some fairy tale, who walk through the pages with their personalities or their professions written on their physical selves, the banker fat, glad-handed, and grasping, the thief with his raccoon eyes, the prince too handsome for words. The souls of men are often that way, I've found. Just so, if you'd splashed water on Teardrop, his anger would have run like the colors of a cheap shirt; a match held close to the third man would have made him laugh, flare, and disappear; and Monroe just watched everything from behind his glowing eyeglasses.

They had elaborate habits and rules of conduct—for example, each ate with one arm laid out on the table before his plate, as if he was protecting his food from attack. Each exercised diligently every morning, but separately from the others, and in an odd, self-contained way, doing solitary push-ups and sit-ups in the backyard. Each wore a kind of uniform, immaculately cleaned and pressed, and unchanging from day to day, Teardrop in work boots, blue jeans, and a white T-shirt, Monroe in dress shoes, dark slacks, and a cheap printed button-down sports shirt, the third man in loafers, khaki pants, and a blue oxford-cloth dress shirt. It was as if they had all been bred in some primitive, isolated tribe and then sent down to civilization, three plain shamans, trying to pass.

As for Malcolm, he was imperious and proud, and wherever he went he left the world in his wake. Teardrop always called him Chick, a name he resented, but not as much as he resented me. He scowled at me as often as he could, to punish me for spoiling his house of grown-up men, I smiled at him as often as I could, for being brown-eyed and eight years old, and in the midst of his scowling and my smiling I fell in love with him, and I began to use everything I knew to capture him.

I'll admit it wasn't wise of me, but since when is love wisdom? And besides, what could I do? He didn't live in the same rooms I did; he lived in a paradise of boyish freedom, where he wore his face like a profane garment on a pristine soul, a mask to make him wild. And I would have been a little bit wild, too, if I woke every morning and found that face in my mirror, and didn't have to be jealous of the boy who wore it. To be so exquisite would mean more in the city than love, or money; it would mean anything he wanted, but the price would put him forever beyond anyone's real appreciation. He, too, would be a criminal one day, I knew; he'd be a thief or trade, not because he was raised to be, but because his own beauty would teach him how deeply people wanted to have something stolen from them.

In the meantime the boy was still guiltless and guileless. When he was called downstairs he would jump up from wherever he was sitting, drop whatever he might be holding, and run out of the room without so much as a good-bye to me. As soon as the basement door closed behind him a deep silence would descend; the only sound above the floorboards was the inaudible hum of my own body, resonating in the resonant house. I felt very lonely then, I missed him, and as soon as I heard the door open again my heart would begin to speed up and my face would flush.

When he reappeared he was always subdued, slightly sweaty, maybe, somehow spent, and my task would be to wake him out of whatever trance had taken hold of him down there. He would come into the front room, and if he found me reading there he'd turn quickly and slip out again, ignoring me if I called to him. The words on the page would disappear before my eyes while I waited for him to come by again—and sure enough, after a few minutes had passed he would be back to let me tease him. I think you need a haircut, I said. I think you should let me cut it for you. He shook his head no, and backed slowly away from me as my hand reached out toward his curls. No, you really need a haircut, I said. I'm going to ask Monroe if I can cut your hair. You *really* need a haircut. And he, having no rhetoric at his command, responded with the child's reliable reversal. *You* need a haircut, he said. I changed the subject. Do all the girls love you? I asked him, just to watch him blush. Do they all try to kiss you and hold your hand? —Or, Do you think you're stronger than I am? Do you want to arm-wrestle? —Or again, What do you want to be, when you grow up? A fireman? A fire?

He did his best to match me. Do you wear makeup? he said once, looking up from a drawing he was making on a sheet of construction paper that he'd placed on the floor. A little bit, sometimes, I said. *Why* do you wear makeup? he asked. I like it,

I said, and he made a disapproving noise and turned back to his work. I got down off the couch and crawled over to look at it; his hand raised from the page for a moment, but otherwise he didn't acknowledge me. In careful strokes, he'd drawn a big building, a mansion or a school, with a round two-story colonnade in front, a flagpole sticking up from its roof, and bushy trees planted on either side. It was really very good.

What's that? I asked.

It's the White House, he said impatiently. It's where the President lives, he added, and then, with a deliberate gesture of dismissal, he went back to his work.

I stood up. O.K., then, I said. I'm going now. . . . I started toward the door, he kept at his drawing. You mean, you're not going to keep an eye on me, in case I try to leave? I asked. You're not my little shadow? He didn't answer, but his ears reddened.

It's true that I loved to tease him, but I was also testing the facts: something subtle in his attitude toward me led me to believe that he was spying on me, and I assumed that the three others had told him to do it. In any case, he was usually nearby, in the next room watching terrible television, or bouncing a basketball just outside whatever window I happened to be near. It was like a comedy of manners for two forgotten characters, the fugitive woman, the boy: He spied on me, I spied on him, each of us fascinated and afraid the other would disappear.

But you didn't disappear. You stayed.

I COULD HAVE LEFT, I COULD HAVE LEFT: IN THE MIDDLE OF THE night I could have climbed down from my window and slipped down to the end of the road. I could have found a car, found a train, I could have been gone. I could have faked the boy out in the middle of the day and disappeared in the woods behind the house, walking and walking until I emerged on the outskirts of some town in Tennessee. Every day I thought to leave, but I never did. —Where would you be if I had? Still waiting patiently in some perfect preternature.

I stayed because I had no place to go, and the place I had was good enough. The rooms were warm and safe, the yard was neat, nature posed out of every window. Monroe and the third man were generally polite to me, and so long as I pretended to have no interest at all in what they did all day, even Teardrop, who disliked me, left me alone.

With nothing else to occupy me, I found myself a part to play, and I performed it as if I was born to it. I read through a rudimentary cookbook that I discovered in a kitchen cabinet, I made meals, and I dished them out. I brought the last of the year's wildflowers in from the backyard and put them in drinking glasses filled with water, which I placed around the rooms. I straightened the cushions on the couch and piled the newspapers by the back door. I opened windows to air out the rooms and closed them again to keep the rooms from getting cold. I found a column of black ants leading from the cabinet where the sugar was kept and spent an afternoon making sure there was nothing for them to return to. I cleaned constantly, and when I was done I started all over again.

I know some people say that a woman shouldn't submit to that kind of work. They say it's an insult, they say it's nothing really to do, they say it doesn't pay. All right, I felt the same, but this wasn't that. I won't argue about it: there was nothing to it: the house had to be kept, and I needed to keep something. Besides, I found it all very peaceful and purposeful; the work was mindless in a way that soothed me, and helped me to pass the hours without having to think about what might be waiting for me when all the hours were done. Call me weak, and treasonous and uninspired: you would have done the same as I did, if you'd been through my trials. I didn't care if I never had an exciting day again.

What's more, a certain infamous fantasy of mine was being fulfilled. For years I had dreamed it: the idea would steal up on me whenever I hit a dull, obsequious stretch at work, and I had a chance to look out over the coming years and realize that there was nothing much to follow but more of the same. A little house, I would say to myself. Just a little house of my own to care for, just mine, just my house, a few rooms to think about, a big kitchen and a yard out back. Sometimes I thought that was all I really wanted, and it wasn't too much. So I hadn't seen it populated with three strange men and a boy, committing crimes in the basement while I tended to things upstairs; but the point, after all, had always been to escape the law, and if the realization was more literal than my dream, there were still enough moments when I could pretend that it was harmless and I was happy.

But I worried that it was a bad house. Downstairs there was some offense; below that, in the depths of my occasional dreams, a spark of dirty revelation flickered in the distance. In time it began to develop before my eyes, like a photograph, but more slowly, its contours of shine and shade emerging by tiny degrees over the days—here a half-formed childish limb, here an expression of grim ecstasy. The entire image waited for me, I waited for it; and the longer I did, the more suspicious I became, the more scared and sickened.

I noticed, for example, how they touched the boy, they were always touching him. Sometimes they were just roughhousing; the third man would wrestle him on the living room floor after dinner, Monroe carried him over his shoulder upstairs to bed when it was time for him to sleep, all three of them tickled him until he laughed himself red and begged them to stop. But sometimes it seemed pointless to anything but their pleasure; their hands were always on him, resting on his arm, or holding him by the shoulders and swaying him slightly, or patting him gently on his backside. Each contact was a little violation; they sent him one way and then another—just for fun, of course, but it was enough to rob him of his will for a moment.

And the way they spoke. They treated the boy as they treated one another, swearing freely in front of him, and making coarse or cynical comments and then asking him to agree, which he did eagerly, because he wanted above all to belong with them, even though he didn't always understand what they'd said.

At the same time, they were strangely careful around me, the three of them. It was as if they were so unused to having a woman around that they didn't know how to behave in front of me. There was a certain mannered distance between us, a masculine formality that read as respect, but which I found eerie, like a ghost with unfinished business, a ghost that wouldn't play with me.

The boy had no friends his own age, he knew nothing of children's society, and he'd been living that way forever. He was schooled at home; there were dozens of books in his bedroom— a volume of math problems, illustrated adventure novels, an atlas, paperback baseball stories, 1001 jokes for all occasions, a child's history of the United States, a civics textbook. They lay on his floor among his toys and clothes. Each afternoon at around three, Monroe would come up from the basement to spend an hour with him, testing him on the schoolwork that had been assigned for the day and helping him as he struggled with whatever skills escaped him. He had a hard time with irregular verbs, for example: he said *throwed* for *threw* and *gived* for *gave*. And it took a while for him to understand division. How many quarters are there in a dollar? was how Monroe explained it, and then he turned his head up to where I sat and gave me a smile. Well, he was a thousand years old and still kind of goofy.

The two of them together were a sight to see. Malcolm was curious about everything, and Monroe was infinitely patient, and never tired of the boy's company or questions. I thought he explained things well, I thought he needed someone to tell him what to wear; I thought his hands as he took apart a toy car were sure and strange, at once larger than his body suggested, and very delicate. He must be harmless, I thought. So I must be wrong. —Unless I'm wrong to think he's harmless, in which case no one is right. I watched the scene before me dissolve into sex and sweat. . . . I couldn't help myself; and in the days following, I began to study the boy whenever he reemerged from the basement, looking for a sign that he had suffered some insult to the genius of his features. And then I stopped myself and shook my head to clear my risen rage to the corners, where it sat like a spider and wriggled its ugly legs.

One sunny afternoon when I was in the living room reading, Malcolm came silently upstairs, wearing the same cartoon shirt he'd had on the first time I saw him. He came into the room slowly, looking flushed and miserable, and from where I sat I caught the faint odor of childish sweat. Are you all right? I asked him.

I'm O.K., he said sullenly, and sat in a chair at the table as if it was the most tedious task he'd ever attempted.

I crossed the floor and put my palm on his forehead; he felt warm, but not feverish. Do you want a glass of orange juice?

He nodded.

As I went to the refrigerator I casually asked him, Did you have a hard day?

He shrugged and mumbled, and squirmed in his seat. Yeah.

I bet most boys couldn't work as hard as you do.

No answer. A small brown bird had landed on the outside windowsill, where it tried to distract me by pecking rapidly at some imaginary seeds.

What were you doing?

No answer.

Malcolm? What do you do down there?

He was staring at the vase of flowers at the center of the table, and when he spoke, he spoke to them. Secret stuff. Whatever they want.

What do they want you to do? What do they make you do?

Here he played sulkily with the salt shaker, tipping it on the table. I'm not supposed to tell anybody.

I put the glass on the table before him and gently touched the back of his neck with my hand, as if I could coax a confession right through his skin. Even me? You can't even tell me? What if I said I could help?

He shrugged again and I waited, but he didn't say anything. Instead, he picked up the glass with both hands and slowly tipped it to his lips, allowing the juice to run into his mouth while he gulped at it, his smooth pale throat pulsing as he swallowed.

Why can't you tell anybody?

He put the glass down again and looked up at me, his eyes so softened by his lashes that they seemed to be liquefying. Because if I do, they said, a judge will send them all to jail, and I'll have to go live with someone else.

You could live with me, I said quickly, forgetting in my agonized fantasy that I hardly had a home myself. Come on, I said to myself. Come on, come on.

He considered it, or so I thought, but before he could answer the door from the basement opened, and Teardrop came in.

Hey, Chick, you're not talking too much, are you? he said. No? But you did good down there. You did it. You did it again.

He patted Malcolm softly on his shoulder and walked past me without a glance or a word.

Soon dinner began, and after dinner, the debate: Innocence is a Vice. But the talk that night was lifeless and confused. The third man's argument broke down halfway through, leaving him with nothing but neatly turned fragments that he was helpless to reassemble. The stories they told afterward were senseless and dull, the lies were forced. From time to time the conversation just stopped while they searched for the next step: I stayed silent, but my thoughts were all a red streak. Could I talk the boy into running away with me? Could I kidnap him and tug him by the hand to Canada? Would his beauty get us stopped at the border?

I had trouble sleeping that night. A few hours after I dozed off, I found myself barely alive in bed, woken by strange dreams: Malcolm turned out to be a woman, after all, and Monroe was a pimp. They were all surprised that I didn't know. Why had I thought he was the boy's father? No one had ever said so, and I'd never actually asked. And the house was full, absolutely full, of pornographic pictures of children, their tiny genitals inflated and exposed in an obscene imitation of adulthood; they were hidden in the walls, they slid from the shelves in the closet when I opened the door, they were stacked underneath my own bed. I opened my mouth to protest, but instead sang French opera. I was awake in a damp bed, my limbs tingling and my hands in fists underneath the sheets. One more night, and what was one more night against eternity?

The next evening Teardrop, the third man, the boy, and I were watching television, while Monroe sat in the kitchen and read a book. Outside, the weather was rain and lightning; inside, the set was only getting one channel, which was playing a movie that none of us wanted to watch. By the time the second round of commercials had come, two women, best friends, had retreated to a house by a lake where they had spent their childhood days. One of the women had brought along her young daughter, and for an hour of television time the three of them laughed, swam in the sunlight, sighed, and gave each other significant looks, until it became clear that the girl's mother was dying, and that was the drama. I didn't think much of the story myself, but all evening the men had been in a particularly tense mood, and they'd been watching without speaking, until a scene where the two women and the girl were alone in their house at night, sitting on a couch in a living room, watching a television show. Teardrop toasted the screen with his glass and broke the silence. There it is, he said. One for each of us. He turned to Malcolm and put his hand gently on the back of his neck. He waited a moment and then went on, every word an argument against me. There's even a little one for you, he said. What is she, ten, twelve? A little cocksucker: you could handle that now. Yeah? Chick? — Malcolm grimaced. Oh! *please,* said Teardrop in a falsetto, and then, with an air of exaggerated femininity, he leaned over and planted a kiss in the air about six inches from the boy's cheek. The boy giggled, and Teardrop reached out and poked him in the ribs so that he jumped, giggled again, and reddened. One of these days we're going to bring a little piece home for you.

Stop it! I said, and they all turned to look, three pairs of even eyes, waiting for me to finish. Don't. Don't talk to him like that, I said. Ever again, and especially when I'm around.

The third man shrugged. It's just talk. He's used to it.

I was standing in the middle of the floor. Well, he shouldn't be. And even if he is, so what, that's worse. What does that teach him?

Teaches him what his pecker's for, said Teardrop. What's it your business?

Because, I answered, and couldn't continue. Because I adore him? Because it's bad? You're an asshole, I said to Teardrop. Immediately he got to his feet, shaking and red-faced, a fan of sinews standing out on his neck. You *are,* I said. — And with one quick movement he swung down and hit me, open-handed, on the side of my head. He hit me, it didn't hurt and I didn't fall, but my thoughts flew from my mind and I went spontaneously down on one knee, ending in a position that looked like supplication, but that wasn't what I meant. I didn't mean anything. I was embarrassed, and shocked tears began to streak down my cheeks; I looked up and he was standing over me, his enormous right arm outraised. Behind him I could see the blurred, indistinct figure of the third man, just starting to move, and to his side floated Malcolm's startled expression. — Teardrop hit me again, and instantly I got high and didn't know where I was.

All right, said the third man. —But why was he smiling? He gently reached out to Teardrop.

I'm going to bury the bitch and jerk off on her grave, Teardrop told him. But he raised his arms in surrender and allowed himself to be guided to the far side of the room.

Malcolm, go upstairs. Monroe had suddenly appeared in the doorway. Go on, and don't forget to brush your teeth. The boy hurried out of the room. With him gone, there was no reason for me to feel anything at all. I got to my feet and stood with my hand touching the side of my face, waiting. *Don't* cry. It was as if the room had been invisibly divided into two realms, the first inhabited by a woman about to be swept away, the second by three calm men. You all have some kind of argument? asked Monroe, pleasant as could be.

My mouth was anesthetized, I was silent; Teardrop laughed shortly. It was nothing, he said.

Come here, said Monroe to me, but he was the one who walked across the room. He reached for my hand. I pulled away from him. Come on, let me see. Slowly he drew my hand from my cheek and examined my face; I revealed it to him as if it was my most shameful secret. You'll be all right, he said. Are we done?

Teardrop's finishing voice. *I* am, yeah.

O.K. if I take her for a ride? The third man shrugged, sure. Come on, said Monroe to me. I looked numbly around the room for my shoes. Barefoot's better, he said. Let's go.

The car was blessedly dark, the trees the same; we could have been driving in fifty-foot circles. In the front seat, a voice and a woman. You've been hit before, said Monroe. He took his eyes off the road to look at me and I shook my head silently. No? Never, in all your life? Because you can take a punch pretty good.

I knew he was just trying to make me feel better, but I couldn't stop it from working: I felt a brief flush of irrelevant pride and I shifted in my seat. The absurdity of the moment just made me angrier. That prick, I said, but there were tears streaming down my cheeks.

He hits. I personally don't believe in it myself, but that's me. I don't see the point. Do you know why he's older than me? Because he spent a lot more time away, and that's because of his Respect-me thing. Don't-fuck-with-me. Thing. When I was away, all I wanted was to get along and get out, and I got along all right. But he cared about all that shit. I'm not going to get into it with him on your behalf. Do you understand that? I want peace, but I'm not here to protect you.

You'll let him hit me again?

I don't *let* him do anything. He does what he does. You do what you do, and I do what I do. He paused for a long moment. I'll talk to him.

Somewhere in the distance was the house again, the boy, my own prison. Monroe couldn't be embarrassed and I didn't know what else to say. Wasn't he an offender, too? Once again I had the sensation that I was someone else, watching the scene from a certain distance.

Monroe began again. He's scared of you. We're all a little scared of having you around. We don't care how it happened, we don't care what you meant, but you got yourself into some kind of serious mess—you don't always seem to remember that—and we don't want any part of it. It has nothing to do with us.

I know.

No, he said angrily. You *don't* know.

I waited a while for him to explain, but instead he fell silent, and as the minutes passed I felt the car start to pick up speed, the road out the windshield began curving around and around and around, descending toward midnight. I looked over at him. Slowly, and then faster and faster the car fell, until we were dropping headlong through the twisting stars, which flashed past my window in brilliant elongated streaks. We weren't going home, we were just going down. . . . The car began to shake violently and I held desperately on to the door handle, while beside me on the front seat Monroe sat motionless, staring grimly forward into nothing; and just as I began to wonder if this was the real punishment for my imposture, Monroe said quietly, Here we are.

Through the windshield I could see the house, standing still, steady and tall. Only the porch light was on, watching unwaveringly from above the door. Everything behind it was bad, all the favors of childhood were banished, and the rest was dirty. You go on in and get some sleep, said Monroe. Tomorrow we'll try to start over.

In the second-floor hallway I stood by Malcolm's room and pictured him lying peacefully in his bed, his legs asprawl, his lips half-open as he sighed in his slumber. I wanted to slip in with him, climb under his covers and curl around him, enfolding and enveloping him; I wanted to hold his warm, frail form against me and breathe him in like some purifying ether, until I could fall asleep and join him in his dreams. Where was he? I wondered. In what palace? I stood alone outside, listening at his door and longing for his company, until I heard Monroe at the bottom of the stairs, and then I hurried to my own bed, where I lay awake, too scared to sleep.

In the bathroom mirror the next morning I found a wide red mark on my cheek; when I touched it, the tissue below hurt, and my pride hurt more. At breakfast Malcolm couldn't look at me; afterward he went somewhere outside to play. When he was gone I studied my loneliness and looked for confidence.

The hours were pointless and uneasy and there wasn't so much as a minute for me to brace myself against. The men skipped lunch. At two, Monroe came up to fetch Malcolm and lead him by the hand downstairs. I sat barefoot in the kitchen and listened to the radio, drifting back and forth between mania and an exhaustion so complete that I could barely keep my eyes open. There wasn't a single thing out of place in the whole household; only my mind was amiss. I was in Sugartown again, standing on Bonnie's front lawn and staring at her house. I was waiting; she wasn't home. I was in New York, I was in Roy's apartment, listening to him tell me about a murderer, a mother, who was me. Back to the week, back to the car, back to the hotel room. I thought I had one chance left to redeem all those days.

— The door to the basement burst open and Malcolm ran into the room. He was shirtless, his pale and perfectly smooth chest lightly heaving; there was a shocked look in his eyes and tears glistening on his cheeks. For a long moment he stared at me; then he started to run to the door. What's wrong? I asked as he passed, putting out my hand to stop him before he could leave the room. I honestly believed I was going to save him and die, I did, I believed it would be the best thing I'd ever done.

Nothing! he said breathlessly.

Malcolm! By then I was holding him by his upper arm, my fingers meeting around the limb; he tried to twist out of my grasp, but his feet slipped and he fell halfway to the floor, suspended only by my hand as he scrambled to regain his balance and at the same time tried to kick me; the whole moment was flurrying in my face. Stop it! I said.

You stop! he shouted back, glaring at me from below as if I was the most wicked woman imaginable and he despised me. Let me go! His gorgeous mouth twisted for a second, I let him go and he landed on the floor and then quickly, awkwardly, got to his feet again. He stood and glowered in the center of the floor, his eyes bright jelly, his lips wet; his hands were raised in front of him and there were red marks on his arm in a pattern after my fingers. I swear I would have fought him right then and there, eight years old and all, or else pleaded with him and wept hot tears. But before I could do either one he reached down, squeezed his crotch, and made a humping motion with his little hips. Bitch! Suck my dick! he screamed at me in his child's high, unbroken voice, and then he lowered his head and ran out of the room.

A moment later Monroe came up the stairs and through the door frame, and started to follow the boy. It was like a silent movie chase, but he stopped at the kitchen door, shook his head, and came back into the room. He seemed about twice as big to me, and four times as heavy: God damn it! he said, and slowly sat down in a chair. What did you say to him?

My words were all wet: What did I say? What did you do to him? Where did he learn to do that? What did you do to him? Eight, eight years old. I said, I'm going to kill you. I don't care. —The third man was in the room somewhere, watching me. Monroe's face was a picture of surprise, and he pushed his chair back from the table and stood. Fuck you, I don't care, do you want to hit me, too? Come on, hit me. The third man was over there, the boy was far away upstairs, Monroe had me from behind, his hands pinning my wrists to my waist; I kicked at his legs, I kicked a chair over. Who are you? I said. You're dead, you're dead, you're dead. I spat into the air; I never saw it land.

Sit down, said Monroe, and the third man pulled a chair out from the table and placed it behind me. Sit *down*. He pulled me backward until I fell onto the seat. Still holding me, but more gently, he said, What's the matter with you?

I tried to twist my head around to face him but he had too firm a grasp, so I turned my chin up proudly. I'm going to kill you, all three of you, I announced.

His voice came from somewhere behind my shoulder blades. Why? He tugged once on my wrists, as if to goad me.

Because, I said. He's an eight-year-old boy.

He's *my* eight-year-old boy, said Monroe.

You have no right to put him through this.

Monroe stood behind me. Don't tell me how to raise my own, he warned me.

Why do you do it? So you disgusting men can make some money? Is that it? For your dicks, your dicks, is that what it is?

The third man spoke up for the first time, I had forgotten he was in the room. Make some money? he said. What do you mean, make some money?

Fuck you, I answered. I know what you're doing. I knew all along, but now I really know.

I hadn't moved in a full minute and Monroe let my wrists go. I rubbed them while he came around to face me, carefully stepping around my bare feet and lowering himself down in a crouch so that he could look at me level. He raised his eyebrows: Did Malcolm say something to you? he said slowly.

He didn't have to say anything, I boasted. I already knew.

Now Teardrop had come up from the basement, wiping his filthy hands with a rag. What? he asked.

She says she knows what we've been doing, said Monroe. He stood up slowly and backed away from me, leaving me half-free to shake in the chair. All three of them stared at me with the glazed look of men gazing on a bonfire. I don't think she does.

Proof. Taking photographs, I said. I could barely speak, and I didn't understand why they were so calm when I was so excited. Using, taking porno, making Malcolm. Making pictures, making graphic pictures, graphics, of the boy. Pornography, of the child, the kid, porn.

There was exactly one moment of bitter silence. Then the third man laughed violently and said, Uh-oh. Monroe reddened, turned, and pushed his way out of the room. A moment later he was back through the door, walking quickly toward me and stopping just out of arm's reach. The third man and Teardrop were watching like spectators at a bear fight. Monroe said nothing, but his face reflected an enormous and furious pain. Suddenly he took two steps forward, grasped me by my shoulders, and yanked me out of the chair; then he pushed me quickly across the floor to the door of the laundry room, and still holding me with one hand, he reached down with the other, pulled the door open, and pushed me inside. You stay there, he said, and slammed the door shut, locking it before he left.

Through the window in the wall, the world was wheeling. Through the window in the door, the three men were conceiving of my life to come, and I could tell by their gestures that they were disagreeing. The third man had one argument, Teardrop had another, and Monroe was undecided. They discussed the matter for a long time, while my nerves fired and stopped, fired and lay still, jumped once when they startled me by simultaneously laughing, and then settled into a swift, even stroke. At the end, Monroe had his head down, and the third man put an arm around his shoulders and shook him to loosen him up. He shrugged just like Malcolm did, and I could see him say, All right. Then he raised his face and looked across the room at me—his eyes met mine, and he broke right into my chest, falling in between my ribs and organs and taking up there as if he had dominion. I wasn't scared of anything. I began to wonder who he was; I wasn't scared of that.

The third man came over and unlocked the door. O.K. Why don't you come out of there, he said in a low but firm voice. He gestured with a vast elegance and I had to pass very close by them all as I padded into the kitchen. Monroe pointed to a chair and I sat down; he stood against a countertop, with Teardrop on one side of him, his fat thumbs hooked through his belt loops, and the third man on the other side, his thin arms folded across his chest. We were all right there, we were right there in the kitchen, with Malcolm still hiding in his sweet room upstairs. I wanted proof that he had nothing to hide from. They must have known I felt that way.

On the one hand, said Monroe at once, Billy was very fond of you. He had plans for you. He made me promise to take care of you, and I promised him that I would. And you did us a favor bringing that package from him. He put his hands flat on the counter to his side and tapped his fingertips silently on the surface. I think he wanted to play some elaborate joke on us all before he died, he went on. He could have just sent the fucking things by registered mail. Christ almighty. He was a difficult man. He turned to his two friends: We all loved him, we all owe him a lot, but I can say that, can't I? He was a goddamn difficult man. What did he want to see happen?

They were all waiting for an answer, not from me, but from Billy, who was dead and wouldn't reply, or from some man-in-the-moon, who was alive but waiting, huge and still, for an answer from them. So I spoke myself. If you want me to shut up, I said, you're going to have to show me what you've got downstairs.

Monroe said, We'll show you, but not because you won't shut up. Go put on some shoes.

The third man followed me upstairs to my room and waited while I slipped on a pair of sandals. As soon as we returned to the kitchen, Monroe stood and started for the door to the basement stairs; I followed, with the other two behind me, crowding me slightly. We went down under the light of a bare bulb; the stairs turned once, and then we passed through another door, this one much heavier; beyond it was black. Wait here, said Monroe, and he was gone. I could hear Teardrop breathing in my ear; ahead of me there was nothing; it was too blank to be dark, and the blankness was without meaning; there was no evil waiting, no depravity, no violence, just the world before God was born and light was made. Then Monroe suddenly found the switch and turned on the light, and I saw everything, all at once.

I suppose I'd imagined some dark and sordid cave, filled with criminal litter; instead, I saw a single bright and immaculate room that ran the entire length and breadth of the house, interrupted only by eight iron pillars. The ceiling and the walls were covered with a thick grey quilted padding, and there was grey carpeting on the floor. Scattered about the place I saw three or four dully shining machines; in the air there was the faint odor of oil. In one corner there were stacks of paper covered with a

clear plastic tarpaulin; in another I saw a few white plastic buckets, one of which wore pale green drips down its front. Against
the far wall I saw a large glass table that held white computer
equipment, from the midst of which a darkened monitor rose.
Teardrop crossed the floor and sat at the desk; Monroe beckoned
me to his side and I went. We looked for a long time to find the
right place, he said; when he spoke there was no echo, and his
words died against the walls. We found it here a few months ago.
There was a note of pride and satisfaction in his voice, and it
occurred to me for the first time that he, too, was just a boy; he
wanted to show me what he'd done, and explain it all, so that I
could praise him for his efforts.

Teardrop touched something on the desk in front of him
and at once the screen flashed, the image expanding suddenly,
like matter at the first moment of time, and then gradually settling into a full picture of the front of a twenty-dollar bill, an
enlarged and phosphorescent version of a real bill, which, I
noticed, was fixed to the wall before him with a thumbtack in
each corner. The image on the screen glowed a fair green; it was
beautiful, with its web of fine decorative lines, its banners and
numbers, its seals and scrolls, and in the midst of it all, a white-
haired Andrew Jackson wearing a stern expression, as if the look
in his eyes was all there was to keep men honest forever after he
was dead.

We had to buy everything separately—at auction—in cash,
said Monroe. An offset press, a platemaker, a letterpress, the cutting boards, the whole show. We went down to Florida, out to Illinois, up to Maine, we went everywhere. — He looked around the
room. We brought it all here in pieces and put it together, he continued. That was just the beginning. Then there's the paper: only
one company makes it, they sell only to the government, and
nobody steals it. So we had to buy small lots of bond-paper stock
and dye it. He gestured toward the third man: He's been working

on getting it right since I don't know when. I won't even explain to you about the inks. They're magnetized, they shift colors.

Teardrop moved his hand, and the picture changed to a close-up of the edge of the portrait, around which the words *United States of America* were written repeatedly in tiny letters. The camera couldn't pick those up, said Monroe, so we had to put them in ourselves. These lines here, he went on, pointing with his pinky to an intricate geometric lattice around the edge of the portrait, they become blurred; it took us three weeks to get them right. Details. There are tiny polyester strips that you can only see when you hold the thing up to the light, and tiny red and blue silk threads, and a watermark. We had to print all that right onto the paper.

He paused and remembered. But the bills we made weren't good enough. They looked all right, great, but they didn't feel right. Have you ever gotten a series of new bills, maybe out of a bank machine? You know how they feel a little sandpapery, they stick together? That comes from the imprint of the press. We tried to offset them. Different kind of technique, you know? Much easier, but then the bills didn't have that feel. The three men meditated for a moment on their frustrations.

Billy thought we were being candy-asses, Monroe went on. He told me so, and he was right. He said, If you're going to do this, do it properly. For years he'd been working on engraving a set of plates himself. We didn't think he could do it, but his eyes, his hands. . . . He could have cut the Constitution into the edge of a nickel. And he had a lot of time, and no one bothered him. What he wound up making was perfect. So we went and got ourselves an intaglio press, and waited for you to bring them to us. He paused.

Still, he said, that meant we had to begin again from the beginning, and intaglio is a bitch. There are about a dozen steps to go through before the bill is done—printing, waiting, matching, printing again—and there are a hundred ways for it to go wrong. The machine is always breaking down, and . . . We had Malcolm come down because his hands are small and he can reach the little parts. Otherwise we'd have had to dismantle the whole thing every time something fucked up. So it's frustrating. But when the last step is done, and you're looking at that bill . . .

I felt something stirring far below, or if not below then behind, a beast building from the back of my mind, from my memories; it was moving, whatever it was, not just forward— although it was coming closer, too—but from side to side, as if it wanted to touch every story I've told you so far. I didn't know what it was, but I was willing to wait.

It's very easy to counterfeit cash, Monroe said, but it's hard to do it well. Any fucking secretary, any copy-shop clerk can run something off on a color copier, pass it off in a dark bar, and be gone by the time anyone discovers. But the banks find that sort of thing very quickly and they burn it: a little labor, a little scam, and then it's gone. We're sort of old-fashioned, I suppose. This here, this printing, is very old-fashioned, quaint. Nowadays you've got all this electronic money riding the wires, credit here and charge there, there's always some way to tap into that, if that's what you want. But we're just printing in the basement. Because we want to make bills that last forever, and never get told from the real thing. We want them to pass from one hand to another until they disintegrate. We want them to buy groceries and clothes, to buy lovers' flowers and widows' coffins, and keep buying them. The profit will be ours, but the money will be everyone's.

And if our bills are perfect, then who gets hurt? he asked. A painting perfectly forged should be art enough for anyone. An actress who acts like a star, is a star. I read a book once that said, There can't *be* a difference that doesn't *make* a difference. That's what I mean.

You see, he went on, money is just a medium, like the ship to a sailor, or God's word to God. It's a rendering of confidence: confidence won by the ink—here he gestured to Teardrop—and the paper—here he gestured to the third man—and the man who hands you the bill—and he took a deep bow. The confidence of the world, he concluded, is held prisoner in the hands of men who haven't earned it. All we're doing is setting some free.

Now the gathering something in my mind was growing. It was a big swift thing and when it finally came it was going to knock me down. My belly began to tremble in anticipation; my chest swelled; my tongue began to twitch in my mouth.

Here, Monroe said, and he walked across the room to a grey tarp cast over a pallet on the floor. Lifting back one edge, he removed a brick-sized stack from a short pile and threw it to me. I managed to catch it, but I didn't dare look at it. It felt heavy in my hand, and it seemed to give off a faint odor of heat, like a bar of radioactive metal. It's money, Monroe concluded. We made it.

So it was: so they did. I removed the band that held it together and fanned the stack out in my hand, but that just multiplied the miracle beyond comprehension. They were all green, and numbered on and on and on. They were perfect, still slightly stiff, twenty twenty twenty twenty. . . . It was money if they said so; I had never experienced anything more real in my life than those three men with their printing press, and my position in the middle. It was the world that had gone phony: all its names and its histories were ruses: all those people: my lies were better, and Monroe's were even better than mine.

¡Rise!

he said suddenly; his voice was jubilant and he was wearing an enormous, unexpected smile. As the exclamation mark faded there was a moment of clear silence, through which I could see

all the way from my first lie to my last conversation with Roy—
and I began to laugh. Teardrop whooped, whooped again, and
started to dance a jig, his elbows out at his sides like a chicken's
wings as he bent his knees and wagged one leg back and forth;
the third man clapped his hands loudly, and Monroe took me by
the arm and pointed his chin at the ceiling, and as I laughed he
took me out onto the carpet and began to reel me around the
floor, still holding all that laughable money in my hand as the
room spun beneath the fluorescent lights. Teardrop began to
wave an imaginary hillbilly hat in the air and the third man
clapped some more, nodding along so violently that his combed-
back hair fell forward over his eyes. Yah! he cried, and stamped
his foot, dancing and dancing for joy, all by himself across the
floor of the basement.

As Monroe and I rounded the pallet and started for the center of the room again I noticed Malcolm standing at the door,
lured down from his bedroom by the sound. The child wasn't
laughing; he looked lost and bewildered, and bothered by my
presence in among his men. I tapped Monroe on the shoulder
and he dropped my hand and turned. I'm sorry, I'm sorry, I said
to the boy, and reached out a trembling hand to his face. But I
was still smiling; he flinched, turned away from me, and stumbled back up the stairs. Gradually the noise in the basement died
down, leaving the four of us standing there, sheepishly panting
and sighing. All right, said Monroe at last, with a satisfied tone.
Let's go back up and work this all out. Come on. He took me
firmly by the arm and guided me toward the door. As we were
mounting the stairs again, Teardrop gave out one last short laugh
and said, Jesus fuck.

Monroe went up to tuck the boy back into bed; while he was gone,
Teardrop fixed himself a drink. You're a piece of work, he said as

he stirred the ice with his index finger. You're a good dancer. He laughed to himself and then cracked his knuckles loudly. You come in here, though, and nobody knows who the fuck you are. You play with the kid. Then all of a sudden you're all over the place. He wiped his finger on his shirt and then tapped his temple with it: And you have a sick mind. Who are you?

I sighed out one breath and drew in another. Oh, no one, I said. At all. Just no one.

Monroe returned, and the three of them sat down at the kitchen table, all three on one side, while I sat on the other. Between us there was nothing, and all the noise had died to quiet. There was an air of exhaustion in the room, a near vacuum that prevented our laughter from burning any longer. The silence took me by surprise. All right, said Monroe. We're done with our secrets. There isn't going to be any more waiting. So what are we going to do?

I studied my hands and smiled. I knew I'd be much better off if I apologized, but I couldn't bring myself to do it. There were so many of them, and only one of me. Besides, I was pleased with the way everything had come out, I couldn't pretend otherwise, and I was enjoying a little ecstasy of comfort and relief. Then came the reversals.

Monroe spoke up again, and suddenly he was very serious. —Was that a scar he had at the base of his neck? I'd never noticed it before. We've been thinking of just handing you a sum of money, he said, sending you on your way, and taking our chances.

It took me a moment to see what he was suggesting, and then just like that my smile fell. —What? I thought. But I don't want to go, now. I don't have to go now. Now I can stay. I don't want any money, I said quietly. That's O.K., keep your money.

He nodded, but it didn't matter just then what I said. In any case, it wouldn't have been enough, he went on. If you leave, you'll eventually be caught. And if you're caught, you'll have only one thing to bargain with, and that is us. So you'll bargain, and we'll go to jail. We can't go to jail, so you can't bargain, so you can't get caught, so you can't leave. Am I right?

I really didn't know if he was right or not, but I said, Yes, you're right.

But soon enough we'll be giving up the house and we'll all be leaving, he went on. And then you won't be able to stay.

It hadn't occurred to me that anyone would ever be going, and the thought of the empty house wounded me. You're going to leave me?

We have to go, he said. Look at the town—the economy is no good; there isn't even any *real* money here. How would it look if we suddenly started passing thousands of dollars? It would take about a minute before someone noticed.

When will you be finished? I asked.

He shrugged. A week or two.

Where will you go?

Can't say. He was giving me nothing at all.

What happens to Malcolm?

What do you mean? He comes with me, said Monroe, and shook his head to stop me from asking any more questions. Anyway . . . The two men on either side of him didn't move. . . . This is our dilemma. Do you have anything to add?

I get it, I thought. I'm not so stupid: I've read the books and I've seen the pictures, I can imagine a life much worse than the life I know. Teardrop's tattoos seemed very real to me then, and ominous; it wasn't he who was weeping for the world, it was the world that was weeping for itself, and he just happened to be wearing it. It was as if we had each been wondering all along when we were going to die; but the question was particularly urgent for me. I hoped it didn't sound like a silly thing to ask, and I asked it quickly, so that I could have an answer before my face fell apart. Are you going to kill me?

They didn't think it was silly at all; not one of them so much as smiled. Monroe hesitated and then said, No. It was only then that I became nervous; I stared, and my hands began to shake so badly that I couldn't take them off the table.

I have a question for you, too, said Teardrop. He was angry at the way things had gone, but I wasn't listening to him; I was listening to my nerves talking to themselves. I have a question, too, he said again.

All right, I said.

What do you want?

I could never have told him what I wanted, I didn't know the words, so I lied. Nothing, I said, and shook my head slowly. What I'll do is, I'll just wait here until you're done, and then I'll go on my way.

How do we know that? he insisted.

I looked at him with no expression at all, and said nothing. I had nothing to trade for his trust, and if I'd had something, I would have kept it for myself.

Well, if I were her, here's what I'd do, said Monroe to the other two. I'd say, I promise, on my honor.

I promise, I said quickly.

. . . On my honor, said Monroe again.

On my honor, I repeated. None of them asked me what honor I was referring to, but Teardrop laughed for a second.

She promises? he said. What the fuck is that worth? He didn't even look at me; he laughed again, and I knew I was going to have to fight him every day that remained. I was tired.

Tell you what, I said, and I was going to stand up, but I changed my mind. You can tie me to my bed if you want. Take away my shoes. Do what they do in movies, I don't know what it is, I don't care. All I want is to get through it to the other side, where it's all over and I'm O.K., I'm still alive.

There was a break; I felt as if I'd said everything I would ever have to say. At length Monroe spoke up. You'll get through, he said. I think we can guarantee you that. Fellows?

The third man nodded slightly; Teardrop neither spoke nor moved.

Late that night I sat up by my window and looked out on the moonlit backyard. I didn't care what I had promised: I wondered how far I could run into the woods, with a pocketful of counterfeit money, before someone found me or something ended my life. Hush. I went across the room and opened my door, hush, it was dark in the hall. Softly down the stairs I went, wearing only my underwear and a thin T-shirt. In the living room I sat on the couch and watched out the window, as outside every tiny piece of my past fell softly, like snow, and collected on the ground. What if I left? Before morning it would all have melted, and taken my footprints with it, along with whatever virtue I still possessed. What if I stayed? The debt on my peace, already too large for me to repay, would grow with every day. What if I left? I would have no servitude, but I'd have no sleep, either. What if I stayed?

Malcolm, beautiful little Malcolm, was standing in his plaid pajamas in the shadows at the foot of the stairs, with one hand resting on the post of the banister. I can't sleep, he complained softly.

Me neither, I said. Do you want to sit with me?

He nodded, came across the floor, and sat in the armchair, leaving his leg dangling over the side, just as he had the first time we'd met. I watched him test me from a few feet away, with his pretty mouth and long eyelashes, with his perfection, with his anger and his lack of age. Just him and me, and the whole history of mankind watching to see if I was good enough. If I'd had every sacred poem ever written at my command, I couldn't have begun to describe how it felt, to be sitting there with him.

Who sent you? I said. I wanted to show him that I wasn't so stupid; I knew he was put on earth to be my trial, but the question surprised him. He furrowed his brow and began swinging his leg back and forth. He was barefoot, as befitted the boy who saved my life.

I couldn't sleep, he said again. I had a nightmare.

What happened in it?

There was a man with a horse and a gun, he said. And then I was in a car, and the car went into the river. And then I don't remember, I woke up.

O.K., I said. You know it's all right now?

Yeah, he said slowly. Did you have a nightmare, too?

No, I said. I was just thinking.

What were you thinking about?

Your father.

His foot stopped swinging. My father says I should be proud. He says I should try to remember, because when I have a little boy of my own I'm going to want to tell him what it was like.

Remember what?

Living here, he said. Outside, the wind was trying to get in; it jostled a windowpane and then hurried around the back of the house, but the house wasn't fooled and held it off easily.

Do you think you will?

He shrugged his narrow shoulders and frowned. I don't know what to remember, he said. I'm bored.

I know. It'll be over soon. He nodded. I wanted to ask him something, it was important to me. I was all right when I started the sentence, but my heart was hammering by the last word. Where is your mom? I said.

He looked at me wide-eyed. He was going to surprise himself by revealing the biggest secret he held, and then dissolve before my eyes. I don't have one, he said.

None at all? You never had a mother?

He shook his head, and I believed him, not because no woman could have been beautiful enough to bear him, but because no sex could have been innocent enough to persuade whatever hides such things from the world to have brought him forth. I never brought the question up again, either with him or with Monroe.

One day passed, another day. Wasn't I going to live forever? But I knew that I'd never again be able to use my own name, or Bonnie's; I would have to keep my hair cut short and dyed, change the way I dressed, change my handwriting; I could keep my memories, but never speak them out loud; I couldn't ever ask for help.

You know, I need to become another woman, I said to Monroe after dinner.

He nodded and smiled. You were always that, he said.

No, I said. This is serious. I want you to make a new name for me. You have everything you need already here. I want you to turn me into another woman.

He turned and walked away from me, and I followed. From behind he seemed bigger, world-clearing. In the living room he sat down heavily on the couch. You want to be someone else? he asked.

I nodded.

But I don't even know who you've been. He patted the seat beside him. Why don't you sit down and tell me?

I waved the idea away. You don't want to know.

Sure I do. I already know some; sit down and tell me the rest.

I sat down, but I didn't start. I wanted him to ask one more time, just so that I could be sure he meant to listen. He leaned back and extended his arms along the backrest, until one of his hands almost touched my shoulder. Go on, then, he said—and I began to tell him everything, just as I've told you.

I was self-conscious; I started by saying, Once upon a time, and then I stopped, and started again. In the beginning I tried to render myself as an exemplary figure, honest and good: I suppressed my bad decisions and lack of faith, toned down my temper and hid my lies. But as I turned forward and then turned back, I discovered that it didn't matter; what I wanted was to make him laugh, and he laughed whenever I did something destructive. I was no one's heroine, there was no such thing. He didn't care: it was the tallest of tall tales and he enjoyed it enormously. I told him about my car crash, about Billy and Bonnie, the wedding, the baseball bat and the Policeman, I explained the shoe box; I described Grady and the history of Roy, the man in the bar and the bus driver. I could hear my own voice rising and falling, as if it was me but not-me that I was telling about, falling down through the branches. At first he just lowered his eyes, shook his head once or twice, and chuckled to himself, and I would smile behind him and try to keep going. But as one horror led to another his laughter got louder, and in time I began to laugh along with him, to laugh at him laughing at me. Helpless, shameless, little by little I lost the ability to be embarrassed: that was my reward, my reputation, I owned it, it was mine. I told him everything I could remember, we hooed and hawed like the audience at a slapstick show, and when I had finished he clapped his hands slowly in an imitation of applause.

Now that's a classic, he said with a smile. That's a ride through hell, with a station for every sin and vice. — Here he laughed again. Just one fuckup after another. You can't teach someone how to do that, they've just got to know.

So then how does it end? I asked. I really wanted him to tell me.

He stopped and searched the room behind his eyes, but I couldn't tell whether he was summoning something he had once seen or remembering something he'd read. At length he spoke. The way I recall it, he said, with the stars.

So the three of them set to work in their spare time, creating another woman from a new birth certificate, a Social Security card, a driver's license, a passport, and little things for distraction: a frequent flyer card, a bank receipt, gym membership. They started the next morning and it took about a week, with Teardrop mixing his inks, and the third man dipping into a locked metal briefcase that he used to hold his most precious paper samples. Fake, fake, fake. They had done it a dozen times before; it was nothing to them. They didn't tell me just what my new incarnation would be, so all week long I waited with women's names murmuring in my head: Beverly, Kimberly, Katherine, Rose; Valerie, Sara, Patricia, Christine. I imagined what it would be like to be each of them, in turn, to be pouty, shy, smart, man-eating, mature. Hello, I said to myself.

One evening when a fire was burning in the grating and Monroe was teaching Malcolm about square roots, I came downstairs with everything I owned that had a name on it: it wasn't much, after all. Bonnie's identification, her credit cards, and a silver ring that, I had realized, was inscribed on the inside *From Roy to Caroline with Love 2/14*. As they watched I cast them all onto the fireplace, and stared at the flames until my eyes burned and teared. I heard Malcolm ask his father something, but his father didn't answer. Except for the crackling of the fire, there was silence, until everything I had been was gone, and I ran from the room.

A few minutes later, while I was satisfying myself with a few tears in my bedroom, I heard a knock on the door. It was Monroe, and as soon as I saw him standing there I turned and started sobbing; I apologized for sobbing, but I didn't stop either one, crying or saying I was sorry. He turned and then changed his mind, came across the threshold, and stood a few steps away from me. Shhh, he said. He held his hands up. It's all right. I kept on, not sparing him a drop. Shhh, he said again, and I wondered what he thought he was doing. Leave me alone, I said. This is my room—will you go away? He started to back toward the door and then stopped to stare intently at me. Another man who didn't know how to act or what to say. Was the answer really so obscure? Get out! Go away! I said. He took a step toward me. Leave me alone. Just leave. But the more I told him to go, the closer he came; it was as if he could only believe me if he thought I was lying. I was lying, and at last he was close enough to put his hands on me and take me into his soft shirtfront.

Late the next morning we got into the station wagon and rode to the county capital so that I could have my picture taken for my new passport. It was the first time I'd been out of the house in weeks, and the countryside was very erratic; the day was cloudy and self-conscious, the trees by the side of the road were in very sharp focus, and the highway signs were written in some foreign language that I only half-spoke. I knew they were words, the world. All the people in the passing cars were looking at me, but none of them could see.

We stopped in a photo shop in a strip mall on the edge of the city. The girl behind the counter was very young and white, and she wore candy purple clothes. She bit her lower lip as she fiddled with the big box camera, then came out from behind it to peer at the buttons on the side of the lens with a pained expression. She stepped back again and without any warning pressed the shutter button: when the flash went off I felt the light go right through me, meeting no resistance on its way. I was still trying to catch my breath as Monroe paid the woman with a twenty-dollar bill; when she handed him back his change he put it in a different pocket.

The clouds had lifted and the parking lot floated weightlessly in the sun. He didn't unlock the car doors; instead, he leaned in against the driver's side, rested his hands on the door frame, and spoke to me across the roof. It's as easy as that, he said, and lifted his hands for a moment. Just a gesture, a small exchange, a paper impostor in the register, a little tuneless noise in the huge symphony of banking. It's beautiful, isn't it? And when I nodded, because it was, he said, That's why I do it.

His hair was blowing straight back, and behind his glasses his eyes were squinting against the sun. I thought you do it to get rich, I said.

Of course I do it to get rich, he replied. But there are a million ways of making money, and most of them are easier than . . . making money.

So, then?

It's the only one of them that I'm good at.

I knew that wasn't it, and I said so.

He paused, he didn't speak, and I was afraid I'd offended him. The trees on the far side of the highway bent in a gust of wind. Shhh, I said to myself. Everything else was Sunday glass.

Monroe put his hands in his pockets, and finally smiled. O.K., you're right, he admitted. The truth is, since I was young, all I've ever wanted was to make a revolution so subtle that no one ever noticed it.

At that my mouth fell open: it was the sweetest thing I'd ever heard, and as soon as his meaning broke over me, I felt a sensation of almost overwhelming, sentimental happiness and good fortune. Yes, of course he was right—and not just right, but pretty. He was pretty and patient; pretty, patient, and he knew everything; I knew, too, I had known all along, I just hadn't realized it, and I couldn't keep from smiling, all the way home.

It would be an overstatement to say that from that moment forward I was accepted and trusted and loved. I still occupied a place outside the real tenor and purpose of the house; and all four of them still treated me with careful suspicion. I don't remember them having a single conversation about their counterfeiting while I was in the room, and they never told me what they were going to do when they were finished. But I didn't feel quite so captive. We all knew that to try one another now would be pointless; the end was coming. Even Teardrop let up on his anger a little. Only Malcolm was an outright trouble. I began to sit next to Monroe at dinner, and it must have seemed to the boy that the table had tipped like a seesaw, so that he didn't know which way to lean as he ate. He had sensed that something had changed; I could feel his eyes on my elbow when his father touched me there for a second. I was a wicked being to him, however seduced he had been by my soft voice and soft manner; he didn't know what creature lay underneath my clothes, he only knew that his father had come over to my side; he didn't know why. He scowled, but I didn't mind if he hated me with all his heart, because his rage only made him more beautiful.

Still, some terrible brat inside him escaped and took over. Gone was his sweet sullenness and lazy grace; in its place was one long, devilish tantrum, which he mounted with all the contrariness at his command. He deliberately left his things all over the house, and when I picked up after him he complained that he hadn't been finished, he had just left whatever it was for a second, and now he couldn't find anything, and anyway it was ruined. He couldn't read if I was in the same room, and if I didn't leave, he did, stamping his feet all the way up the stairs. One morning when I was showering I was startled by a pounding on the door. I immediately shut off the water, and with my hair still full of shampoo I put my head out of the curtains and said, What is it?

I need to get in there, Malcolm shouted from the other side of the door.

What's the matter? I said.

Open up, he said, and thumped on the door again. I need to get in there right now.

Quickly I found a towel, wrapped it around myself, and opened the door to him; he was standing impatiently on the threshold, wearing just his underwear and a sleeveless T-shirt. What a skinny, pale chest for a demon to have. I suppose I was staring, but he just slipped past me, and then, having wrested possession of the room, he stamped his foot and said, You have to leave. I was genuinely worried that something was wrong, so I left; he slammed the door behind me, and I went into my room and sat and shivered, while my hair turned to straw and my skin raised goose bumps. A moment later I heard the shower start up again. Ten minutes after that the bathroom door opened, and he emerged, wet-haired but wearing the same underpants and T-shirt. Are you all right? I asked him. I'm O.K., he said shortly, and disappeared into his room, again slamming the door behind him as soon as he was inside.

At dinner that night he refused to eat the chicken and rice I had cooked; he touched it with his fork and then dropped the thing with a clatter and pushed his plate away. Monroe paused for a moment and looked at him darkly. What's the matter? he said.

It's all mushy, the boy replied.

It's supposed to be.

I don't want it. He shook his head at his plate.

Well, that's all there is, so if you don't eat it, you aren't eating, Monroe said calmly.

Malcolm thought about that for a moment, and then said, Can I go upstairs? Monroe nodded and the boy left the table. But later that night, after everyone else was asleep, I heard his bedroom door slip open and his feet on the stairs; and I noticed the next morning that he'd found the sweet potato pie that I'd left prominently positioned on the refrigerator shelf.

In the meantime the money was still being made, every day. The house felt purposeful, I felt purposeful, I had something to do anytime I wanted, and when I was done I saw a point in stopping. It was all very fine, that accumulation of days. It came to two weeks, I think, but it might have been a month, and it might have been a thousand years. I had never experienced time out of time that way, its medium weight and medium surface. It was a little bit like heaven, because I knew that as long as I stayed there I would never grow old.

Occasionally I would stop down in the basement to watch them labor. When I opened the bottom door I would invariably flinch: the space was stuffy and sweltering, it stank like a men's locker room, and the noise of the press was so constant and repetitive that it quickly grew trying. I would stand on the threshold for a moment, and as soon as he saw me, Monroe would come to me, wiping his face with his shirtsleeve; and he stayed near me until I left again, but I didn't know if it was because he needed to touch me or because he wanted to watch me. I would help pull the sheets of paper from the press, or take a few minutes at the cutting board, or just turn the chair at the desk and sit and watch them.

It was difficult work. The press was violent, the paper was reluctant, and the ink was ornery. Each print had to be passed through the press a number of times, with time for each run to dry before the next stage; first the greenback, and then the face of the bill went through, then went through again to imprint the mint-colored seal and the serial number. Everything was delicate, nothing could be rushed, and the men approached each minute with the idea that it was the finest amount of time the mind could discriminate, and perfectly precious for that. When a sheet was done it was carefully cut and set to one side.

Despite the attention they paid, bad prints appeared in sufficient quantity to buy freedom for a hundred women. Monroe went through each one, squinting as he scanned them; he would remove any bill that was less than perfect and then stack the rest in carefully counted and labeled piles, each two thousand dollars high. The stacks were then encircled with a fat rubber band and placed in growing rows on a small pallet in the far corner of the basement; and the rows grew. We burned the flawed notes in the fireplace at night, feeling the heat on our faces and watching as they disappeared up the flue as grey-green smoke, to pour out of the chimney and into the sky, as evidence to the stars, the only living witnesses to our extravagance.

Still, the money in the basement was accumulating quickly, in thousands and more, riches for a lifetime, printed in a month or so. To me it was like a magic ring granted in a folk tale, which turned leaves into banknotes and left them on the ground. How much? I asked Monroe one day.

A lot, he said. Pick a number. —O.K.? Now double it. O.K. Now forget that number, it doesn't mean a thing.

But I didn't really care. I loved the paper and I loved the colors, but the money meant nothing to me. So what was it about the crime that made me so happy? It wasn't a fight for freedom from bondage and it wasn't some hiding game for girls. It wasn't a walk through fire, or a burst of laughter during a funeral oration. I could never claim that I'd been hurt enough by anyone to want revenge on everyone. I knew I was wrong, I would say at once that I was. But what's a wrong woman to do except join with a wrong man and his wrong child, and help them make wrong money so perfectly that it's right?

Is that life's path, then? Down so far it becomes up?

THAT WAS MINE, YES. I HOPE YOURS IS DIFFERENT.

Rising: up. —Very suddenly they were done, and for a moment we all hung there, feet off the floor, turning gently and looking around us, at once puzzled and exhilarated. It was a chilly late morning toward the end of October and I was fixing some soup in the kitchen, with the door open to the basement. In went the chicken, in went the carrots and the beans, in went the spices, when suddenly I heard the silence of a stopped press. I stood over the simmering water and listened for a minute, and then went back to my cooking. In an hour the soup was ready, and still no sound from below. I called down, and Monroe came up just long enough to explain that their work was finished, and then he made up a tray of food and disappeared downstairs again.

All afternoon I was uneasy. Malcolm and I ate lunch in silence, and afterward I went up to my room and sat in the sun by the window. There was another change coming and I wanted to be prepared. Myself in a moment of contemplation, myself at the end of the century. The trees outside stood like teachers at a graduation: You're done, they said stiffly. It's time to go.

The three of them had finished dividing the money just before dinner, and as the sun was setting I wandered downstairs and found them sitting silently in the living room. They had brought the bills up in three large suitcases that I'd never seen before, and had left them, like luggage for a very long life, next to the front door. For the remainder of that evening there was quiet all through the house, it was as if they were chagrined by the completion of their work; Monroe couldn't decide where to put his hands, the third man was breathing heavily, as if he'd just finished a thousand-mile run, and Teardrop spent at least an hour restlessly guarding the back door from no one. There was nothing else for him to do.

The next morning they dismantled the equipment and carried the pieces out back, to bury them in a square mile of woods and then carefully arrange the floor of leaves back over the graves of their beloved machines. There was no ceremony, and there was no show of sentiment. I thought there should have been, but I wasn't going to bring it up.

The third man was the first to return from the burial party; he came in to the house through the back door and stopped at the kitchen sink to wash up. Tell me something, I said.

Yes? he replied, still scrubbing his hands under the water.

What are you going to do with all that money?

He said, Oh . . . the money. He reached for a towel. Well, first I'll have to pass it.

Yes, I said. And then?

After that. He turned around and leaned against the countertop. . . . Ten percent goes to the Church of Latter-day Saints, and fifty percent goes to my children, and I suppose I'll just live on the rest.

Children? I said, and was immediately sorry that I'd shown such surprise.

He just opened his mouth and laughed. Honey, he said, I've got children, yeah.

Your children?

Mine, he said. Ten of them, ages three years to twenty-one. I've been married twice, in my time. Together with the first, I had eight children; with the other, I had but two. His eyes were twinkling with the sparks of benevolent paternity, bits of jubilation that floated across his gaze. Every one of them has to be clothed, and fed, and sent to school, he said. He smiled and held both his hands up with the fingers spread. Ten children, he said. Ha! And with that he left the room, bouncing slightly on his toes and chuckling at the very thought of his issue.

Teardrop was the next to arrive back to the house. Once inside the door he wiped his hands on his shirt, which he then stripped off and tossed into the washing machine. With his barrel chest unclothed he sat at the kitchen table, sipping from a perspiring glass of iced tea and wiping the condensation from his brow.

Excuse me, I said.

He waited a second. Yeah? he replied without looking at me.

I was wondering how you learned about all this. Ink, and . . .

He leaned back in his chair and put his hands behind his head, with his fingers laced together. Why do you want to know?

I turned my eyes down and shrugged. I don't know. I . . . don't know.

He waited some more.

I was just hoping you'd tell me.

He paused and studied the tabletop with a sidelong look. He still hated me, but the job was done and he felt like talking. Well, ink, he said at last. Printing. He cocked his head and watched me. When I was a kid, he said, my father ran a print shop in a small town, over in Texarkana. He made up flyers, wedding invitations, that kind of thing, and I helped him after school. Every day, after school. I took to it, I was good, and sometimes, at night, you know, I'd sneak in and make little things for me and my friends, fake IDs so we could go up drinking in Pine Bluff, and so on. New papers for a stolen car. Like that. — Now he was in deeper, and his voice became warm. So I was fifteen, I had a girl, I wanted some money, so I started making things for some of the bootleggers come in from the hills. This was around about 1958, and they still did that shit, just like on TV. Hillbillies. Just like the fucking . . . on TV. I started out making labels, and I made the labels, and I made the tax stamp. I forged the tax stamp, but the revenue man came around and I got caught. I got a year's probation, right? — He was staring at the floor from the corner of his eye, remembering just how it went. But then I got caught again, passing bad checks downstate. So they put me in juvi. My father said, Don't you waste your fucking time in there. So I started learning for real about paper and things, printing and things, in juvi. But the kick is, the funny thing is, I didn't even know that the old man had beat me to it. I didn't know. I really didn't know. But then he went in just as I was coming out, ten years for making five-dollar bills. So it was obvious what I should do. You know . . .

He stopped there and sighed, and something in the sound of his breath seemed familiar. It took me a few seconds to place it, and once I had I was afraid to ask.

He saw me. Go on . . . he said.

Billy?

He gave me a smile of black logic and said nothing.

Was he your father?

He nodded. Not just mine. Billy was all our daddies, he said sensibly. Don't you know? He was everyone's daddy. We're all out of Billy's house.

He had been folding a paper napkin on the table in front of him, performing a kind of backcountry origami; he took it up in his fingers and tossed it out onto the tabletop, and then stood up from the table. Is that all right? he said. Thank you, I replied, and he nodded and left the room. When he was gone I picked up the paper he had been playing with and turned it around and around, trying to discover what he had made. It was nothing but an assortment of planes leading nowhere and edges bent to no purpose. I unfolded it, but when I was done all I was left with was a blank napkin, a paper nothing that nonetheless made me laugh to myself.

Monroe arrived home last; by then it was late in the afternoon and the wind was up. I saw him standing in the backyard, having just emerged from the thick of the woods; he was looking up at the rear wall of the house with an odd frown on his face, his hands dropped at his sides, his glasses opaque. I watched him through the window and wondered what he was thinking, just a few feet from home. When he came in the door I asked him, and he considered for a moment, and then said, What I was thinking was, how much I love my son, anything that tried to hurt him, I would stab right to death.

With that he grinned and walked past me, certain and crooked-smelling; and as he was leaving the room I suddenly happened on the thing that would solve all my problems—not just the petty problem of life in prison without parole, but the solitude of my sleep and the hole in my head. I had known it all along, but I hadn't known; I'd been living in a comedy as old as mother-may-I? and there was only one right way for it to end.

There remained Malcolm's rage, and how to placate it. The next day at noon the three men went into town to settle the lease on the house and have the car tuned. I stayed home and made the boy lunch, and tried to think of what to say. I wanted to tell him that it all was just a game and he didn't have to worry: this house, these men, this circumstance, and I was no more a succubus than I was the Queen of Sheba. Instead I gave him his hamburger and sat across the table from him. He put his napkin in his lap and started into the food.

Your father and I . . . The boy stopped eating, but he said nothing. I tried again. You're a very special boy, I said.

He turned his eyes on me. Why did you come here? he asked.

I didn't mean to, I said. I didn't even know what was here, but someone . . . Did you ever hear of an old man named Billy?

At that he nodded, and his eyes lightened a little bit.

He was a good friend of mine; at one time, he was the only friend I had. He asked me to bring a package here, so I brought it. I was in a lot of trouble. Do you remember the day we met? He nodded again. When I showed up on your doorstep I had a soul so small, and it was growing tinier and tinier each day, until it was just about ready to disappear. Just like that— I snapped my fingers and he blinked.

What did you do? he asked.

Oh . . .

Did you tell a lie?

Not to you, no, never. But I told lies to everyone else.

Did you break the law?

I hesitated. . . . Yeah, I said. I did. He looked down at his plate to hide his face, but still I noticed a slight upturn at the corners of his mouth; and as soon as he picked up his fork his smile took over and there was no use; he turned his perfect face up to mine, and his eyes were glittering over his enormous grin. Tell me! he whispered hotly. Tell me what you did!

But the moon has a side no one can see: who wouldn't hide behind such an alluring light? So a thousand sordid hours are slaughtered for a single moment of true glamour. Never let anyone know what it was really like. That, I said to Malcolm, is for another time.

When evening fell we began to pack. I put my things in a pair of plastic bags, and then I went from room to room, both to see that we weren't leaving anything behind and because I wanted to say good-bye to the house. In the living room cold ashes had spilled out onto the tiling before the fireplace; I bent down with a hand broom and began to sweep them back. In other rooms upstairs, I could hear the men cleaning out their closets. I heard Monroe call, Malcolm! Is your room clean? There was no answer for several moments. Malcolm? I heard something stir behind me and turned to catch the boy standing in the doorway, watching me with an expression of mingled curiosity and awe, like a petty thief who's discovered a diamond the size of his fist. I smiled brightly and said, Hello; he said, Hello, giggled, and ran out of the room. So I had wanted his trust and affection; I had wanted his confidence. But it was his childish apprehension of me as lawless and bold that won me his esteem; and that's how he'll remember me, if he remembers me at all.

At noon the next day we said good-bye to the house and rolled slowly down the long driveway; soon we were traveling together toward Chicago, singing cowboy songs and whooping out the window. In the backseat of the station wagon there was a pile of suitcases; underneath them all were three that contained three fortunes. Malcolm sat beside his father in the front seat, bouncing up and down and chattering endlessly. We're going west. West young man. Go west young man. What does that mean? Are we going to California? I want to live on a ranch. Can I have a horse? At every tollbooth he demanded to be allowed to throw the coins into the basket. The third man got his attention for long enough to teach him an obscene poem about a sailor on shore leave; Teardrop looked blankly out the window the whole while. There was nothing by the road but cold fields and empty rest stops; there was nothing on the radio; the wind blew so heavily that the car was buffeted from one side of the road to the other. We would travel together for the remainder of that afternoon; the two men would leave the next morning, and I myself would be gone the following day.

There was a knock on the door of my motel room that evening. I opened it and found the third man standing on the walk outside, filling the doorway, with a halo around his head and shoulders from the light outside. From the horizon behind him I could hear the faint, low sweeping sound of traffic on the interstate. That was the nation, some distance away. For a long time I had thought it was so late in my life; only then did I realize how early it was. Come on, he said. It's time.

The three of them had made a ceremony of it, a ritual on the rough blanket of Monroe's bed. This is why I love this country, the third man said, between sips from a cup of coffee. You can be anyone you wish, provided you know how. Doctor. Senator, celebrity. Or someone no one has ever heard of, or no one at all. Or.

What becomes born again, into the light? asked Monroe. He was gazing emptily out the motel room window into the still parking lot beyond. The caterpillar in its cocoon, the prophet in the desert. And Americans who've made mistakes.

Let's get started, said Teardrop.

I sat in the armchair and they stood on the other side of the coffee table, and one by one laid out the documents they had fashioned, every one perfect, more perfect than me. The paper was heavy and stiff, the print was immaculate, and they had even dog-eared one or two of the cards and folded my passport almost in half, so it would look as if my life had been lived in. I waited until each document, card, and booklet had been placed lovingly down, and then I took them up in order, to discover who I had become. My name was Linda Roberts, I was twenty-six years old, five foot six, with brown hair and blue eyes, an only child born in a county hospital near Sacramento to a single mother. I had been to France some years past, I had good-enough credit, I had two convictions for speeding. Don't try to use the passport, Monroe said. You'll never get past customs with it.

I said, That's all right. In my imagination I was looking down from the oculus of the sky at a vast floor strewn with hillocks, farmhouses, towns, and tiny lights, which were twinkling as they were refracted up through the atmosphere. So many ideas, so many folks hurrying here and there, so many second chances. It was exhausting to try to think of them; all I could do was watch the whole display as it went through its constant dissolves and redesigns. But I knew, because I'd been told, that one light here had gone out, and another one there had been lit: and I knew that both of them were me, persisting through the night.

The next morning we drove the third man to the bus station in Buffalo. He was gracious to the end; he hugged me tightly, his arms hardly thicker around than my own, but much stronger. When we had separated I stepped back, and he raised his eyebrows, smiled, and nodded as if he knew what I was going to do that night and gave me his blessing. He shook hands with Monroe and Teardrop, and Malcolm he lifted off the ground, whispering some secret in his ear before setting him down again. You come see me when you're grown-up, he said, and then he was gone.

That afternoon we dropped Teardrop off at a small county airport. He hauled his suitcase grimly out of the back of the car, clapped Monroe on the shoulder, and patted the boy on the head. I stayed in the car and stared out the window in the opposite direction, turning to look at him just once as we were pulling away. He was hunched over in a plastic chair in the waiting room, his bag at his feet, an unlit cigarette in his mouth.

Linda Roberts, Monroe said softly, as his hands reached for the buttons on my shirt that night; he was trying the name, whispering in my mouth. It's been a long, long time since . . . I shushed him. The motel was dingy and the bed was too soft. Malcolm was dreaming in the room next door; we had gone in together to say good night an hour before and had found him sleeping above his sheets, with the television turned on and the heat lamp in the bathroom running down on its timer. We tucked him in and kissed his unconscious brow, and backed out of the room. The time was exactly right; two weeks had passed, there were two weeks to go, I was waiting, my whole body hovering in a ripe balance.

On the balcony outside my room I had faced the man, I stared at him until he realized I was there; an instant later he understood, and we kissed, softly at first, and then not so softly. The light in the passageway was fluttering from the shadows of a hundred moths; the breeze was warm and cool. We kissed again. We kissed again. We kissed again. I led him inside. He was hard before the door was closed.

Linda? he asked. He didn't mean anything by it. I felt his hot mouth on my nipple and I knew that I was naked. I don't know how he did it; I never felt my clothes come off. Underneath there was another dress, my bridal body, with its fit and its cloth, its seams and pleats, its folds and buttons; beneath that, my blood shivered. The room was gone, in its place was a bed, on the bed was a man who couldn't speak. He took his glasses off and he, too, was naked: I'd never seen anyone more so. I thought he was smart, I didn't know what he would be like without clothes. I didn't know he would smell like some gorgeous mushroom; I put my mouth at his navel and took a deep breath. His belly was pale; at his abdomen a channel of fine black hair began, spreading into a delta and forming refined circles on his chest. The declivity of his throat was warm and fragrant. I sucked at the scar on his neck, and he jerked and made a noise. Too late: I had my mouth on his mouth, he could tell it to me another time.

I had been dry for so long that my skin was dusty, like the skin of a plum. When he stroked me I swelled; he pushed my legs back, more forcefully than I would have expected, and wrapped his hard calf around my soft thigh. Mouth. He slipped the tip of his finger inside me and lifted gently, parting me—and I burst, spattering the sheets with pulp and seeds. I could feel the stuff between my fingers; I left some on everything I touched, on his face and his lips; it got into my mouth, where it remained, slowly dissolving on my tongue, long after the fruit had been forgotten. I wanted to swallow him whole, but he kept escaping, taking my heart with him until it was stretched taut like elastic: I thought I was going to scream, ecstatic, I kept drawing him in, I wouldn't be satisfied until I was carrying him. It went on and on, turned into agony, turned into roughhousing, rudeness, took a turn again for tenderness, a long moment of sore stillness, then a sudden clambering, again, climbing, until there was neither reason nor pleasure. But I couldn't possibly stop. I was famous, I loved him just enough, and he had my answer.

He groaned afterward as he lay on his back in bed, his belly throbbing and the smell of his spent breath rising into the room. It sounded like his voice was coming from inside me; it often felt like that, later. In a little while he was asleep, a man I loved, dreaming alongside every other man in the world. I stayed awake with my hands resting on my belly, reflecting and smiling. I had gotten what I wanted from him: I had stolen you out of nonexistence, I don't think he ever knew.

They dropped me off in the parking lot of a Detroit train station the next day. At first Malcolm wouldn't get out of the car; he just sat in the backseat with an exhausted electronic game on his lap, staring forward through the windshield while his father and I said a few words. When we were done Monroe opened the back, took out Billy's shoe box, and put it in my hands. What's this? I said, but I had already guessed what it was.

It's twenty thousand, he said. What you do is, you take it to Tahoe. Now listen, because this is where you get caught, if you aren't careful. All you have to do is walk into a casino and cash in a few thousand, not too much. Even less than a few thousand, maybe five or six hundred. Don't play anything, or you may start losing it all. Play the dollar slots. Wait a few hours, have dinner or something. Then go to another window and cash out again. Wear a hat or a scarf on your head. Do that in a dozen places, until all the money's changed over; then take the first bus out.

Tahoe, though, or one of the Indian reservation casinos. We're going to be covering the other towns, O.K.?

He kissed me quickly. Then bending down, he spoke through the side window of the car. Do you want to come out and say good-bye? No, Malcolm shook his head. Yes, he changed his mind. When he stepped out onto the blacktop he was once again gorgeous; the shoelaces on both of his tennis sneakers were untied and he was shielding his eyes from the sunlight with his forearm, though if the sun had had any sense it would have shielded itself from him. The moon, too, was riding the after-noon horizon over his shoulder. Sun and moon. The boy hesi-tated as he tried to figure out how to approach me; I crouched down on my knees as he started toward me, and he walked right into my arms. I hadn't realized just how small he was until I held him against me, his soft cheek against mine, his sweet scent brushing me. When he backed away I said to him, I'm going to go now. He nodded. His eyes were dry, but his features were tense and his mouth was set in a frown. I was searching for some-thing to say, while the floor of the planet turned over to set me free. When you're a man, you'll be a man, I said. Until then, be good. Good-bye.

So I left, floating away forever on Monroe's false money, into the country again.

And me?

You were born just nine months later, with his brown eyes and my blond hair, the skin of my skin. By then we were living in a small house in the Denver suburbs, wide green streets, high white heavens, broad blue mountains, and your mommy working in two different restaurants. You won't remember that house, you were just a baby girl, my little Bonnie, even more beautiful than her half brother; but I remember that you were a tiny pale sugary thing who never cried and never slept, and whose tiny translucent pink fingers grasped at whatever was within their reach.

My illegitimate daughter, the newspapers say. That's irony to them.

You were born in Denver. But later we moved, and moved again . . . fifteen times in eighteen years, and so . . . Fifteen houses. We had a high old time, didn't we? Just you and me.

. . . They've been putting something in my food that makes it hard for me to think sometimes. . . . My food is forty-five-year ashes, which is justice.

You wanted to know, and now you know, who I was before I was your mother. I was the girl they were looking for, and you were the girl that I found. You wanted to know what kind of work I did back then. I was a ballerina, I was on the hit parade, I put the red in the sunset.

I came to you.

THAT'S RIGHT. YOU WERE MY CONFIDANTE, MY HELPMEET, MY ride-along, my liquor, my lullaby, my partner in crime, my prayer, my diary, my station, my garden, the report of the starter's pistol . . . the spout of the whale, the diving whale, the scent of gasoline, the beat blooding in my heart, the perfume in my bath, the port, the landing strip, the lit house, the high laughter, the needful glance, the kind ear. Everything, my book, my estate, my confidence.

You wanted to know why those police cars came to our home that afternoon, those policemen trampled the flowers in the front yard, broke down our door, and rushed inside, why they pointed and pushed me down, why they overturned our furniture and tore through all of our things, with their yelling and their guns waving. They found me, they took me away, they put me in this prison, and they want to judge me.

Lights out.

They can't judge me. . . .

Do I have to go?

YES, IN A MINUTE.
There's some savings, some bonds and things in the bank. There's some jewelry in a lacquered mahogany box in my top

drawer; keep what you want and sell the rest. Ignore the neighbors' black gossip. Don't marry a weak man, or a dull man, or a sour man. Pray for righteousness and vision.

Judge me? They can't judge me.

Someday you'll see what a fiction this world is, but the way I love you is a fact. You'll want to know why, and that is why, when the trial begins I'll be smiling at you from the witness stand, why I'll smile when they announce the verdict, and why I'll still be smiling, in the darkness under my hood, when they hang me for everything I've ever done.